SHE BELONGED TO HIM

"Honey?" Turning in his arms, Amber ran her hands over his body, her finger touched the exposed skin of his neck, his lean hollow cheeks in an anxious caress. "Are you hurt, sweetheart?"

A grunt was his response as he fought to catch his breath.

"Ray! Talk to me? Should I call a doctor?" Amber was frantically raining quick kisses on his lean cheeks and neck.

"I'm fine," he managed tightly.

She wiggled against him, trying to get up. "Ray?" she questioned when his arms tightened around her.

"Be still for a second. Let me catch my breath."

"I knew it, you're hurt!"

"Shush," he whispered, his mouth close to her ear, his breath warmed her cheek, her throat. The pain was leaving, but in its place was a rush of exquisite yearning.

The softness of her breasts on his chest, the slender length of her thigh between his, sent flames of uncensored desire throughout his system. The need to possess and claim dominated his senses.

Ray slackened his hold on her but did not free her. Instead he clasped her by the waist and slid her up so that he could reach the delectable temptation of her beautiful mouth. Suddenly his need for her was all that seemed to matter. He had to taste her fully or die from the longing.

When she welcomed him, her lips opening under his, Ray took what he had denied himself for so long. There was no hesitation on his part. He ground his mouth against her soft full lips. He ravished her, savoring the sweetness that was hers alone. No other woman had ever tasted so good as Amber or felt so right in his arms. She belonged to him.

ALL THE LOVE

Bette Ford

Pinnacle Books
Kensington Publishing Corp.

http://www.pinnaclebooks.com

PINNACLE BOOKS are published by

Kensington Publishing Corp.
850 Third Avenue
New York, NY 10022

Pinnacle, the P logo, and Arabesque are Reg. U.S. Pat. & TM
Off.

First Printing: January, 1997
10 9 8 7 6 5 4 3 2 1

Printed in the United States of America

To Sisterhood!

To my editor, Monica Harris
A very talented lady. Words cannot express my gratitude for
your help and faith. From the very first, you believed.

To my agent, Rob Cohen
You are the best. Thank you for sharing your wealth of
knowledge and for your support on this roller coaster ride.
It has been fun.

To new friends: Crystal Hammonds and Brenda Jackson
To longtime friends: Barbara Drain, Jeanette Jefferson, and
Jackie Szczepaniak

Chapter One

Ray Coleman winced as the cab went over a rough patch in the road. It was a painful reminder of the reluctant stitches the doctor had removed only that morning. His heavy African features quirked in self-mockery. It seemed as if his luck had finally deserted him. While in Beirut he'd been caught in the cross fire between rival factions. That mistake had nearly cost him his life. He was fortunate to have gotten out of Lebanon with only a couple of bullet holes in his gut.

An exchange of gunfire wasn't uncommon, especially in that part of the world in spite of the strained peace accord. A award-winning photojournalist, Ray's work had taken him all over the world and had been seen in leading news magazines, newspapers, and been featured in numerous documentaries.

It had taken him six months to compile the photos and documentation he needed for his latest project, a book analyzing the political and human situation in the Middle East. Whether true peace and acceptance could ever come to that part of the world was an issue that Ray felt deserved investigation.

He focused on the towering evergreens and bare-branched maples as the taxi sped along US 7. His window was open despite of the frigid March air coming from Lake Champlain.

He was on his way home. Home didn't represent a place to Ray. Home was synonymous with Amber. It had been so long since he'd seen her, even longer since he'd allowed himself the pleasure of being near her.

He groaned aloud, pressing a hand to his aching side.

"Say something, son?" The elderly cabdriver peered over his bony shoulder.

A rare smile tugged the corners of Ray's wide mouth beneath the fall of his thick mustache. He'd been in some tight situations and was beginning to suspect from the way the elderly man sped down the highway that this might not be the exception.

"Cold for March," Ray remarked, more for something to say than a real complaint.

The driver flicked the cigar that seemed to be a permanent fixture in his mouth. "Well, that depends. Why, I remember back in thirty-nine when . . ."

Ray had spent nearly two weeks in a hospital. The rolling snow-covered countryside was a welcome change from the hospital routine he'd been forced to endure—not that he'd been awake much of the first week.

Although it had been only a few hours since his release from the hospital in Virginia that morning, it felt more like a month. He was beat and felt every one of his thirty-nine-years. Instead of heading for his town house in Georgetown, he had boarded a plane destined for Burlington, Vermont.

Resting his dark close-cut natural against the back of the seat, Ray wondered for the umpteenth time that day if he had made the right decision in coming to Amber. He had taken such care over the years to protect her from the danger that was so much a part of his life. She had built a wonderfully secure new life for herself—a life without painful reminders of the family she had left buried in Massachusetts. A life that excluded Ray.

He'd stay only until he was back on his feet. A week at the most. Hell—he shouldn't have come. If he had any sense, he would tell the driver to turn around right this second and take him back to the airport. He would get on the next plane going anywhere . . . away from Amber . . . away from temptation.

Dear God, he needed to see her, needed to spend time with her. "Only a little while, I promise, angel," he whispered to himself.

When Amber Spencer, an African-American beauty with dark brown hair and honey-colored skin, entered the nursery school's business office, she pointedly ignored the frantic waves and gestures her secretary, Lynn Baldwin, was making with the telephone. She closed the door to her private office with a decided thump. Making herself comfortable behind the large oak desk, littered with paperwork that needed her immediate attention, she promised herself that she'd tackle the mess on the weekend. That was one advantage to owning her own business—no hours. At the moment it was the only advantage.

"So sorry to bother you, Ms. Spencer, but this can't wait." By merely looking at Lynn, one would not guess that the attractive, tall, coffee-colored, African-American woman with the stylishly cut natural was the mother of three sons, two of whom were in college.

Amber did not feel the least bit guilty when she said, "Go away."

Lynn had been with her since they opened, and Amber had come to depend on her efficiency, sound advice, and her keen sense of the ridiculous. It had not taken long for their working relationship to blossom into friendship.

"Billy Henderson smacked Cindy McDonald in the mouth just for the sheer hell of it. Right in front of me, no less. Then he had the nerve to deny it."

"I gather substitute teaching isn't all it's cracked up to be," Lynn said dryly. "Gee, I was thinking of taking up the job myself."

Amber smiled in spite of herself. "You can joke, but if this flu bug does not ease up, you may very well be teaching next week! You don't know how hard I'm praying that Jennifer Green has recovered by Monday and can take back her kindergarten class."

"Should I call the paramedics? Do you feel warm?" Lynn said with wide-eyed innocence.

"I'm serious!"

"Amber Spencer, the way you live and breathe this place, I am truly shocked to hear you, of all people, complain about the children."

"Did you come in here for a reason, or just to get on my last nerve?"

"Bad news. Harris called. Seems the poor dear has an upset stomach, thinks it's the flu."

Amber moaned, dropping her head into her hands. "Well, I guess I should be glad that he took time from his busy schedule to actually call rather than just not show up like he did last week. Lynn, dear—"

"Amber, I'm sorry. I've been cook and secretary the last four days and haven't made it home before eight. Besides, Alex said if I missed another faculty cocktail party, he would divorce me. Amber, I can't help myself—I do so love that man. I must go. Honey . . ."

"Don't worry about it. I appreciate all the extra work you've done. Frankly, I could not have made it these past two weeks without you. I suppose I should start thinking about getting more help."

Amber didn't dare admit that she admired the close relationship Lynn shared with her husband. In the last few months she had been forced to put up with Lynn and Ginger Adams's matchmaking attempts without the least bit of encouragement on her part. It had something to do with her turning twenty-nine on her last birthday.

"Praise the Lord!" Lynn clasped her hands. "I've been telling you as much for months."

"I know. I just so wanted for us to remain small, close knit."

"Amber, I understand your concerns, but we are being pressured to expand. And with the university and community growing, we have no choice but to keep pace."

The nursery school was situated on the outskirts of a small black university town.

"Yes, I know you're right. For goodness sake, nothing has to be settled today. You run along and enjoy your weekend. Tell that sexy husband of yours hello and try and get some rest. If we're lucky, no one will call in sick, and I can really get to some of this mess on my desk. Just think, five days of uninterrupted work."

"Yeah. Then you'll only be three weeks behind instead of five, right?"

Amber and Lynn laughed.

"Date with Elliott this weekend?"

"No . . . too much to do."

"Amber, will you forget about this place for a while? Come out with Alex and me. You know most of the people at these things. Besides, Elliott is bound to be there."

"Thank you, but no."

"Why not?"

"Did you ever think that Alex might not want to share his wife?"

"Alex doesn't mind and you know it." After a pause, Lynn said, "Don't tell me you've broken off with Elliott? You have, haven't you?"

"Lynn, there isn't much point in continuing to see so much of him."

"Amber, you could have tried."

"He deserves someone who can love him."

She did not so much as glance at the photograph on her desk. She didn't need to. She knew it was there, just as Ray Coleman was in her heart.

"But—"

"Good night, Lynn. Have a great weekend. Give Alex my love."

"I can take a hint. I'm out of here!"

They turned off the main highway onto a narrow rutted secondary road. After ten minutes of being bounced against the door, Ray was beginning to think that he survived countless bombings in the Gulf, a trek through the Central American jungle, and a flight across Turkey on foot, only to perish on a back road in the wilds of Vermont.

"How much farther?" he mouthed through gritted teeth.

"Not far, not far a' tall, sonny."

Some fifteen minutes later they eased to a stop in front of a large renovated nineteenth-century farmhouse. Like most of the buildings in the area, care had been taken to preserve the early New England flavor. The huge sign embedded in the front yard, THE THREE BEARS NURSERY SCHOOL, brought an immediate light to his dark brown eyes.

"This is it," the driver said, shutting off his meter.

A bright blue bus, with fanciful bear characters stenciled on the side, stood in the curved drive. Two women, surrounded by what looked to be an army of little people, came tumbling out of the wide front door. It was the taller of the two that caught and held his interest.

Amber's face was wonderfully animated as she, along with the other woman, ushered their tiny charges toward the bus. Ray waited, eager for a glimpse of her ready smile. He was not disappointed.

Ray sat watching her easy movements much as he had done six months earlier. She had not seen him then, either, since he had taken particular pains to make sure that she did not.

Some men were addicted to nicotine or drugs. Ray's obsession was for Amber's smiles. Every so often he had to see her, expose himself to the radiance of her warmth.

Unfortunately he could not recall a time when he was more in need of all that was uniquely Amber.

"Greg, please—stop that. You would not want Dana to pull your hair, now would you?" Turning to her co-worker and friend, Amber Spencer said, "This day seems endless. All I can think of is a long hot soak in the tub and bed."

Ginger Adams, a petite blonde, like Amber was fastening the youngsters into their respective seats. It was a shame she did not have a free finger to shake at her friend, so she scolded with flashing blue eyes. "You can't take the entire world on single-handedly. We need two more full-time teachers. How much longer do you think you can continue to be substitute teacher, administrator, driver, cleaning lady, and goodness knows what else when someone doesn't show up for work? Even you, my dear, have limits."

Amber sighed. "I'm just tired. And annoyed with Harris. This is the third or fourth Friday in a row he's missed work. I'm going to have to do something about him and soon."

Neither woman noticed the tall man who cautiously eased himself from the taxicab.

Ginger was strapped into her seat when two-year-old Brenda wailed, with her mitten-covered thumb still in her mouth, that Pooh Bear had been left behind.

Amber gave the little girl a hug. "I'll get him. Don't want him to get lonely tonight, now do we?"

Amber had just reached the wide porch when Ray rounded the hood. A sixth sense warned her that she was the object of observation. She glanced back over her shoulder.

Amber felt so many sudden emotions that she was not sure what was what. She did not stop to sort them through. She flew back down the wet steps onto the pathway and flung herself into his arms.

"Ray!" she cried. "When did you get back? Why didn't you call me, tell me you were coming?"

Ray buried his deep copper-toned face in her sweet-smelling shoulder-length curls. His six-two, muscular frame towered over her slender, five-seven softly curved body.

"You've always been full of questions, angel," he mumbled near her ear, his long fingers tangled in her curls. He struggled to ignore the soft pressure of her breasts against his chest. He did not dare think of how fully he loved and desired this woman. Circumstances being what they were had forced him to accept there never would be a right time for them. He could not give her the home and security she craved.

"And you were always unpredictable. There is no point in my questioning you. Oh, Ray, I am so relieved that you're here and safe." Amber whispered the last, not daring to indulge her senses in the whipcord strength of the man she had loved for too many years.

Ray barely managed not to wince in pain as Amber gave him yet another hard squeeze. "I assume that means you've got an extra bed for a couple of nights?"

She stepped back, far enough so that when she lifted sparkling golden brown eyes, she could meet his dark brown gaze. Ray's heartbeat accelerated and his body tightened. She was so beautiful.

She smiled up at him. He was not a handsome man. One might say he was homely, with that large nose and full wide mouth partly screened by a thick black mustache and piercing dark eyes. To Amber he was masculine perfection with beautiful deep copper skin tone.

"For you, my dearest friend, anything. Oh!" she said, whirling around and realizing they were the center of attention for no less than twenty-five curious preschoolers. "I forgot the children! What a tale they will have to relay to their parents over dinner tonight." She laughed, then said, "Come inside, Ray. You can get settled while I deliver that precious cargo."

"You wrote that you had found a driver, so where is

he?" Ray retrieved his travel-battered leather bag, strapped the heavy camera and computer case over one broad shoulder while keeping an arm around Amber. They mounted the stairs together.

"Harris has been so reliable until just recently. For some reason, he's been skipping Fridays and disappearing for hours on end." Amber saw his frown and added quickly, "Nothing to worry about."

They entered a wide foyer that opened on both sides. The large rooms had been cleverly converted into classrooms. She gave him a quick peek into the art, music, large muscle and play rooms, complete with a Wendy House. Amber led the way through the roomy kitchen at the rear of the house.

She fished a key from her pocket. "That door leads to the back hallway. My apartment is at the top of the stairs. Let yourself in with this. I won't be gone long—then we can talk and talk and talk." She beamed at him. "I'm so glad you've finally come for a visit. Oh, Ray . . ." Amber gave him a quick kiss on a lean hollow cheek. "The guest room is the first on the left, rust and brown spread. Make yourself at home."

"I'll find it."

They exchanged a lingering smile. With a quick wave, Amber was gone.

Chapter Two

"Well?" Ginger, having waited until the very last child had been delivered into his mother's waiting arms before she ran back on the van, demanded an explanation. "Who is he?"

"Ray Coleman," Amber supplied with an indulgent smile before pulling back onto the road.

"Oh!" Ginger gasped, as if air had been forced from her lungs like a bursting balloon. "So that's the famous man I've heard about for so long."

"Sorry I didn't get a chance to introduce the two of you. I promise I will rectify that. *If* he's here past the weekend," she forced herself to add. Her hands tightened on the steering wheel.

"I'm sure he will be," Ginger said, aware of Amber's skepticism.

"With Ray one can never tell."

"Don't jump to any conclusions. He just got here, for heaven's sake! Look, honey, I know how much he means to you. I've always suspected that he's the reason you won't allow yourself to care for any other man. Until today I was secretly convinced that Ray Coleman was an icon. You have to admit he has a romantic image, being such a famous photojournalist and traveling constantly.''

Ginger had been teaching at the nursery school since its inception. Amber, Lynn, and Ginger worked well together and had become fast friends. Lately, Ginger had frequently arranged nice little dinner parties, excuses to introduce Amber to yet another one of her husband's colleagues. Like Lynn, Ginger wanted Amber to be as happily married as they were.

"I'm as surprised as you are to find him on the doorstep. But then Ray lives by his own rules. I never know when he will call or send me a ticket to meet him in New York or Boston or Houston. Over the years, it has not mattered that he's a modern-day gypsy. He's family . . . brother . . . uncle, for more years than I care to count. If I need him, he's only a phone call away. That's all that has ever really mattered.''

She no longer focused on the bleak years when they had been estranged. Luckily, that unhappy time was far behind them.

Amber was determined to ignore Ginger's comment on her feelings for Ray. She didn't dare examine them. She'd learned years ago that the depths of her feelings for him was one area she could not afford to explore too closely.

"For your sake, I'm glad he came. Maybe the two of you can have dinner with us on Saturday. I'm sure Wayne would love to meet Ray," Ginger suggested as Amber eased to a stop in the drive of the old Tudor house the childless couple had shared for many years.

"Thanks, Ginger, but I can't speak for Ray. I don't know his immediate plans. I've learned to take him a day at a time." Amber looked impatiently at her friend. She was in a dreadful rush to get back to Ray, but she did not want to appear so.

"We'll talk more later. Have a nice visit with Ray." Ginger squeezed Amber's hand, holding back her own concerns. She wanted her friend happy and wasn't sure Ray Coleman was the man for her.

"Good night."

"Start thinking about finding another driver," Ginger called.

"And then be stuck with having to drive for another six months or more until I do? No thanks." Amber waved, shifting gears.

She had chosen the area and the old farmhouse with care. It was a bit isolated, on the country lane beside the lake, and so lovely with wooded lands on two sides and wide meadow on the other. It was perfect for her and the children. Because of the isolation she had bought the bus and had it specially equipped with safety seats for the children. Each year her love for the area and the people grew even more. The hamlet of Shelly felt like home.

Pasta! Amber's eyes sparkled. Ray loved the stuff. She decided to stop at the small market in the center of town for the ingredients necessary to make a special home-cooked meal. She felt such an inner excitement at the prospect of finally being able to cook for him. She'd never gotten the chance to show off her culinary skills.

When she and Ray were together, they usually stayed in a hotel and took their meals in various restaurants in the area. There was always the security of a crowd to provide a buffer against the attraction that prevailed between them. They'd made a pact long ago: to love yet never become lovers ever again.

It had been more than a year since she'd seen him. Oh, he called from time to time. Yet it was not the same as gazing into his coppery brown rugged face or his dark eyes. Only then, when she saw him, could she assure herself that he was really safe and well.

"Looks like the makings for a romantic dinner, eh?" Mildred Moore said, with a broad wink at Amber as she totaled her purchases. The sometimes overly friendly middle-aged black woman, along with her husband, owned and operated the small store. There wasn't much that got by her.

"Very special," Amber confessed as she wrote out a

check. She'd grown comfortable with the small-town charm of the area.

"Wouldn't be Danny Echols, would it? Big-time lawyer working in the capitol? Make a great husband for nice single gal like yourself," she quizzed.

"For someone else. Yes, I'm planning a nice dinner for an old friend of the family, visiting from out of town," Amber said, picking up her purchases.

"How's Marie? Still crying every day? I tell my daughter-in-law she needs to give up that dress shop and take care of the little ones. She has been blessed with beautiful twin girls. Can't figure that gal out. Those babies need their mama! But no, my George had to marry a modern woman. Needs to fulfil herself! Ha! I didn't leave him with strangers. I stayed home until all my children started school."

Amber bit her cheek to hold back her humor. "Marie is doing wonderfully. I know how proud you are of both of the twins. Margie drew a beautiful watercolor only yesterday. I know I shouldn't tell you this because I think Margie plans to surprise you with it, but—" A broad smile spread across the woman's face. "Promise, you won't tell on me?"

"I promise. Those girls are smart like their daddy."

"Bye!" Amber called. She chuckled all the way out to the bus. Turning on her headlights, she reversed out of the parking space.

Young working mothers like Christina Moore were only one of the reasons Amber had decided to open her school in the sleepy New England town. Many of the women would have been forced to abandon promising careers without an available nursery school. Several were divorced, others were single parents raising their children alone. Most of the children's parents worked for the college or owned many of the small shops in town.

Ginger was right—Amber didn't discuss Ray's work with her friends mainly because she didn't know all the horrible details herself. He routinely risked his life for the story. She had learned long ago not to burden him with questions that would serve no purpose other than leaving her frightened and worried.

Amber's shiver had nothing to do with the sharp March winds vibrating against the bus. She had spent more nights than she cared to remember, lying awake, wondering where he was and if he were safe. She hated to think of him alone in some foreign country with no one to care if he lived or died. Over the years she had gotten quite good at keeping her fears hidden. Ray had enough to contend with, without worrying about her.

Tonight was special. Ray was waiting at home for her, and that was all that really mattered. She would not let herself think about the fact that he had not really kissed her. They both knew why he did not . . . why he could not.

Ray quietly appreciated the beauty and comfort she had created by using her natural flair for color and texture. Amber had converted the upper level into a spacious three-bedroom apartment, complete with a fully equipped kitchen and laundry room.

The stucco walls and velvet drapes were honey beige. A stone fireplace dominated the large living room, and twin terracotta-colored velvet sofas were placed before it. Two sand-colored easy chairs were in front of wide curved bay windows.

Everywhere he looked, he saw a reflection of the sparkle and warmth that was so much a part of Amber. Despite the nagging pain in his midsection, he crossed to the fireplace to study the Spencer family portrait above the mantel. Brad had been about seventeen, Amber seven, when the portrait had been painted.

Ray recalled how nervous he had been that first time he had met the Spencers. Ray had been a loner, while his college roommate, Brad Spencer, had been outgoing and well liked. Even though they were both enrolled in Columbia's School of Journalism, those first few months of rooming together had been a major adjustment for both of them. Brad's high spirits and open warmth had gradually penetrated the wall of reserve Ray had erected around himself. He found that he not only liked the other man but trusted him. Brad's friendship had come to mean more to Ray than he had ever been able to express.

In spite of their closeness, it had taken Brad a while to convince Ray to come home with him. Ray was uncomfortable with the idea of spending the Christmas holidays with one of Boston's most influential African-American families. The Spencer name was long on tradition and money. In spite of Ray's misgivings, the visit had been successful and the beginning of many to follow.

The portrait had once hung in the Spencers' plush home and was one of the few items Amber had not sold five years earlier, after her folks died in a plane crash. She had disposed of the huge estate, with its lovely antiques and priceless paintings—too painful a reminder of the past. Her mantel was crowded with antique framed family pictures. Every last one of them was gone now, except for Amber.

Ray saw his own image in several frames. There was one of the three of them: Brad's arms were draped over Ray and Amber's shoulders. They'd spent that day sailing. The picture was a tender reminder of a carefree summer day that had been fated never to be repeated. It had been their last day home before Ray and Brad were off to cover the civil war in Ethiopia.

Brad and Ray shared more than friendship. After graduation they become partners. Brad focused on writing the story, Ray concentrated on the photographs. They traveled the globe together, fearless in their efforts to get that all-important story. They not only were successful but made a name for themselves in the industry.

Less than six months after that ideal summer day when the picture was taken, Brad returned home in a pine box. Ray's hand was trembling as he carefully replaced the frame. The years since had served to help him accept the loss, but nothing could have cushioned the horror of seeing his best friend killed and being unable to stop it.

Ray had no trouble finding the guest bedroom. He set his bags down on the beige carpet. Although the room was attractive, done in shades of burnt orange and cinnamon, it held no fascination for him. He continued down the hallway to the single door at the end of the corridor.

Ignoring the fierce pounding of his heart, he entered Amber's bedroom. He had no right to be in here. But damn it, for years he had denied himself even the simple pleasure of being in her home or having her visit his. At long last he was were he yearned to be, surrounded by her things. He indulged himself by drinking in the sight of where she slept and performed the most personal tasks.

Perhaps he had come too close to death this time. Maybe that explained why he felt so compelled to come. His dark eyes slowly moved over the brass queen-sized bed covered with an apricot comforter and lace-edged pillow shams. He walked over and studied the white wrought-iron vanity—littered with her creams and perfumes—in much of the same manner in which he would have paid close attention to each detail of an assignment. He inhaled deeply, submerging his male senses in her feminine domain.

"You've got it bad, Coleman," he spoke his thoughts aloud. He'd been in love with Amber since she was a teenager. Only once in all the years they'd been close had he lost control. That stupid mistake had nearly cost him what he treasured most, his place in her life.

Lacy pink satin scuffs had been left at the base of the chaise longue, the oak bookcase on the far side of the bed was filled with volumes on art, music, and knitting. Every object held a significance for him because it belonged to Amber. An ethnic historical romance novel lay facedown on the nightstand. The oak rocker directly in front of the window was cushioned in a cream and apricot floral pattern as were the drapes and chaise longue. On the side table beside the rocker was a basket of yarn and knitting needles.

He bent to retrieve the pink lace-edged nightgown that

lay at the foot of the bed. He lifted the tiny bit of fluff to his face, rubbing the satin cloth over his stubbled cheek and across his lips.

"Amber . . ." he groaned her name aloud. It held the scent of her softly rounded body. His own body hardened in spite of his weakened condition.

"Hell, what am I doin'?" Ray unconsciously crushed the garment in one large long-fingered hand. "Why torment myself this way?"

There was no logical answer, just an overwhelming hunger to lose himself within her and know the sweet warmth that was such an intricate part of her personality. His heart was racing as he placed the gown back on the bed and almost ran from the room.

In the guest room he stood in front of the window, staring out at the lake. A stupid mistake! Why hadn't he made that one stop after he'd left the hospital, before going to the airport. An hour with a woman would have eased the ache in his groin, although he found the thought of coming to Amber with the smell and feel of another woman on his body distasteful.

He laughed with self-mockery. His body was making demands that were impossible to fulfill. No doubt about it, he definitely was not dead yet. The plain truth of the matter was, he had not desired another woman in an extremely long time.

He fortified himself with small doses of Amber. He had not quite managed to convince himself it was enough. It had to be, for it was the only option open to him. With his mouth turned down in a grim countenance, he accepted the truth. That was why he was here. He needed another fix . . . of her smile . . . her laughter . . . her sweetness.

It was not much, but it would keep him sane. Nothing could be as bad as the seven years they'd been apart. He learned long ago not to ask for more than she could comfortably give. He knew how lucky he was that she'd forgiven him for that one painful mistake.

Enough! Self-indulgence was a weakness he could ill afford. If he had been using his head instead of his emotions, he would never have come here in the first place. It was a stupid move on his part, especially in his present condition. The time in the hospital had left him feeling alone and empty inside. This was not his first brush with death, but it was the most alarming.

After Brad's death, he'd focused on developing the journalistic aspects of the work. He was determined to work alone. He did not want to care that deeply ever again. In his view closeness brought pain. While the photography had come naturally to him, the writing did not. Yet as he worked at it, he discovered a talent. His writing over the years had grown in intensity and depth. His articles were right on target, and his photographs illustrated the human sufferings in war-torn areas that words could not possibly convey. He had a rare gift that continued to send him all over the globe. His first book on South Africa had created a sensation and had been the basis of an award-winning documentary.

His long-awaited book on the Middle East would, he hoped, make a difference—help shed some light on the complexities that were being ignored.

But he was tired ... so tired. Ray finally gave in and dropped wearily onto the bed. The pain he had refused to give in to could no longer be ignored. He sneered at his weakness, resting his head against the sweet-smelling pillow.

He needed a few weeks to recover, then he would complete the job he'd left unfinished. The political situation was changing every day. Although he'd spent a fortune on his town house, he never felt at home there. It was a place to hang his hat when he was not on the road, which had been more often than not in the last half dozen years. It was as if he had to keep moving, keep working—never allowing himself time to dwell on those bittersweet longings and poignant needs that could never be met.

Amber had made a new world for herself here in Vermont. God knows she had suffered enough in her short life, having lost everyone she held dear. Now this! He must have been out of his mind to come to her like this. What had he been thinking? That was the trouble—he had not been using his head.

He could not let her know that he had been badly hurt—he couldn't. Ray shook two pills from the bottle of pain medication he had been carrying around in his pocket all day and popped them into his mouth. As his heavy lids slid to a close, he acknowledged that Amber would be disappointed when she learned he was not staying after all.

All was quiet when Amber let herself inside. She left the groceries on the kitchen counter. The guest bedroom door was open.

"Ray?"

He was sprawled across the center of the bed. His broad shoulders and deep chest were covered by a cream cape-knit sweater. She smiled, recalling each loving stitch she had painstakingly knit into it. Black cords hugged the long lines of his muscular legs, trim middle, and lean hips.

Amber smiled indulgently when she noticed his long narrow feet were still inside low-heeled black leather boots. Crossing quietly to the bed, she carefully tugged first one and then the other boot free, all without waking him.

He looked older and so tired, she decided with a frown. She covered him with the large wool throw from the arm-chair. Only for a brief few seconds did she allow herself the pleasure of really touching him. Very gently she smoothed a tender finger over his thick mustache. She blushed, recalling how often she had wondered how it would feel against her bare flesh, before she chased the thought away. She caught her breath when his lashes fluttered, but he did not awaken. She tiptoed out, easing the door closed behind her.

"Dinner or me?" She had to laugh at her own vanity as

she headed for her bedroom. She intended to be more appealing than a plate of pasta. She shed the gray wool slacks and red sweater she had hastily pulled on that morning.

Money had never been a problem for Amber, nor had it been important to her. She had been born into it. What mattered was family and goals. Ray was her only family. And after years of hard work, she had reached her crowning achievement. She was an early childhood educator, and she owned her own school. The Three Bears was one of the best child-care centers in New England, and it served the community well.

She did not even glance at the large tub in the center of the L-shaped room. She went straight to the shower stall and turned on the water full force. At the end of a long day, she loved to indulge herself by soaking in the sunken tub. She would lie back and enjoy the jetting action of the whirlpool while gazing up at the star-studded sky, which could be seen through the skylight overhead. The tiles were a rich peach and cream marble, and the features were cream, situated between the two bedrooms. But tonight Amber did not linger.

Amber caught sight of herself in the full-length bedroom mirror. Although she was tired, her eyes sparkled and her mouth turned upward at the corners. Her spirit seemed to soar. She felt as if she were on top of the world. There was only one explanation for her mood . . . Ray Coleman.

She hummed to herself as she creamed her skin with scented body lotion and pulled on a cream lace-edged teddy. The bronze-colored velvet caftan she had chosen was shot with gold thread that shimmered when she moved. Gold combs held thick waves of sable hair away from her face. A spray of perfume, a swipe of mascara, and a touch of deep coral lipstick and she was ready.

Was it last April or June when they'd last seen each other? They had met in New York. He had missed the holidays and their birthdays: his in January, hers in February. They ended up exchanging gifts and toasting the new year. The actual date on the calendar held little meaning to either one of them. Forgotten was the lonely Christmas past or the empty holidays ahead. She and Ray were together, and that was what they celebrated.

Now after so many years, Ray had come to Vermont. It was an unexpected treat to have him here in her home, asleep just down the hall. She wiped impatiently at a tear. No, she must not spoil it by crying. He was here. Soon they would sit down to a meal that she had prepared for them.

As she rinsed fresh vegetables, she accepted that regardless of the questions that raced through her mind, she would never ask any of them. She didn't need to know the exact danger he faced. For now he wasn't in Bosnia or Iraq. She laughed at herself when she thought of how weepy she had been feeling. She was thrilled to have him here. It was so like him to show up unannounced, with no advance warning. So like him.

"Mmmm, something smells good," Ray said, one shoulder resting against the doorjamb.

Chapter Three

Amber swung around from the stove, happiness reflected in her eyes. A smile of welcome lit her delicate-boned, light brown face, and a spoon tinted with her special sauce rested in her hand.

"Homemade spaghetti, garlic bread, and crisp salad greens. Interested?" She laughed with delight at the boyish grin that split the hard lines of his masculine face.

"Really? You wouldn't kid me about this, would you, angel? This is one man who takes his food seriously," he said, eyes twinkling with amusement. Amber's warm laughter bubbled forth, sending shivers of pleasure down his spine. Dear God, he'd missed her.

"Want to taste?" she asked, dipping the wooden spoon back into the rich fragrant sauce simmering on the stove.

"Mmmm," he moaned, "heaven!" Ray planted a loud playful kiss on her cheek. "When do we eat?"

"As soon as you set the table. We have no freeloaders around here!"

His grin spread even wider. "Just point the way."

Sometime later Ray said, leaning comfortably back in his chair, "Amber, I can't recall enjoying a meal more. I haven't had home-cooked spaghetti since—'' Ray stopped, suddenly aware of what he had inadvertently let slip.

"Since Mrs. Katz made it for dinner the night the folks and I celebrated your safe return from Sudan." Amber didn't look away from his inquiring gaze. "It doesn't hurt any more to think about Brad or my folks. Time really does have a way of easing the pain." Her smile was brilliant. "Have I told you how happy I am to have you here, in my home? Finally, I have a chance to show off my cooking." She reached over and squeezed the strong lean-fingered hand resting near his plate. "Would you like another helping?"

She ignored the simmering excitement she received from touching his warm brown skin. Her breath quickened despite her best efforts to overlook her ever present underlying attraction to him. Now was not the time to remember how his caressing hands felt on her skin or how the brush of his lips on her cheek had only made her long for the feel of his tongue deep inside her mouth.

"I wish I had the room. And it's good to be here. I can't get over the fact that you can cook."

Ray also felt the attraction, his flesh hot with awareness that must be ignored. He reached for his wineglass, casually disengaging himself while refusing to recall how perfectly she fit against his long hard length.

Amber laughed. "It took me a while, but I eventually talked Mrs. Katz into teaching me." Her amber-colored eyes were reflective when she said, "Mother was against it, naturally. I was such a disappointment to her, and she never let me forget it. My interests were too traditional for her liking: cooking, knitting, needlepoint, and then the final insult, insisting on a career in education rather than corporate law. She never quite figured out how such a liberated female as herself managed to produce a painfully old-fashioned daughter."

"Grace was never disappointed in you, angel. She was very proud of the woman you became."

"Perhaps . . ." Although she shrugged indifferently, Ray

saw the doubt in her eyes. "I'm not saying she didn't love me, for I always felt loved, despite the demands of her and Daddy's careers. It was just that she set such firm goals for me."

"Goals that didn't interest you."

"Yes. Thank goodness, Daddy was different. He never tried to change me the way she did. He accepted me. She never understood that I didn't want the same things from life that she did. Or why I had no interest in corporate law or any kind of law. They approved of Brad's and your interest in journalism. That's another reason why my parents liked you so much. You were so good for Brad. And besides that, you shared their fascination with the world. I couldn't share it."

"You didn't have to. Amber, you're special just the way you are. Don't ever change." His eyes glowed with a dark intensity that she found impossible to look away from. Ray was feeling such a wealth of emotion for her that he in turn had to force his mind into sober, safer channels. He refilled their wineglasses, praying she didn't detect the tremor in his movements. He mopped the sweat beading his forehead.

"How's the book coming?" She could not hold back the unwelcome question, even though she knew he did not like talking to her about his work. She rarely knew where he was half the time. She more often than not found out the full danger he faced after the fact.

He grunted. "Slowly."

"That's it?"

He stared at his plate, refusing to give any more details.

Amber sighed, knowing him well enough to not press the issue. She was so sick and tired of him treating her like she was made of spun glass. "Dessert?" she offered, busying herself with collecting their empty plates, rather than wrapping her arms around him and hanging on for dear life. She could only imagine the dangers he had faced since she had last seen him. No, she would not dwell on that. He was here with her now, and that was all that mattered . . . now.

Both of them knew there was no earthly way to reach beyond the barrier between them. Years ago they had accepted their separateness as a necessary part of their relationship. Yet Ray was the only man she was capable of loving, and Amber was the one woman he could not have. They each silently warned themselves to take care. Nothing could interfere with the joy of being together again, not even dark thoughts of what could not be.

"What have you made? Banana cream puddin'?" he asked wishfully.

"Ice cream, straight from the Häagen-Dazs freezer to mine." Amber laughed with spontaneous delight. "Vanilla swiss almond."

Ray joined in the merriment. "Naughty! I think I'll pass. Go put your feet up. I'll do the dishes. You've worked hard enough for one day," he said, following her into the bright sun-yellow kitchen, a platter in one hand, salad bowl in the other.

"Oh, no. Tonight I'm planning to spoil you with tender loving care. Tomorrow it's every man for himself."

"But—"

"If you insist on being useful, you can set a match to the kindling in the fireplace while I bring in the coffee."

"Deal." He smiled indulgently.

Huge snowflakes hit against the window pane. It was a beautiful winter night. With a flick of his wrist, Ray had the fire going. His thoughts were far from peaceful. He told himself how pleased he was to find her so happy here. Nevertheless, his heart ached with loneliness as he faced the very real threat that she had a new man in her life. A man who was able to love her without shadows from the past getting in the way.

"See, that didn't take long," Amber said, carrying in the tray.

"Let me take that," he said, turning from where he had been staring into the fire. "Where would you like it?"

"The coffee table, please." Amber sat on one of the twin high-backed sofas flanking the fireplace. She surprised him when she held up a slender wrist, setting the tiny golden charms on a fine gold chain into motion. "Thank you, it's so lovely."

He grinned. "I'm glad you like it." He had sent it for her brithday. "Do you still love peaches as much as you did as a kid?"

Amber made a face at him. "No! What made you think of that?"

He shrugged.

Amber laughed. "Cream, no sugar." She handed him his cup while trying not to be hurt that he had taken a seat across from her rather than the cushion beside her.

"I like your place, Amber. You've made a real home for yourself."

"Thank you. That means a lot coming from you."

"You're happy here, aren't you? You've found what you've been searching for."

Light brown eyes stared into dark brown ones. "I think so, but then there is always something to look forward to."

"The future. You've worked very hard to forget the past, haven't you, angel? From what I could see, only the portrait and the photographs remain."

"A few sentimental things. Yes, it's all gone. I sold the property, the furnishings. I had to," she said, fighting tears. If only the pain could have been left behind.

Ray came to stand behind where she sat on the sofa. His large hands cupped her shoulders, giving them a gentle squeeze. "Sorry. That was tactless."

"No need to apologize," she said, lifting one of his hands to her cheek to rub the palm against the golden softness. "No one loves or understands me more than you. You're my best friend . . . my family."

"And you are mine." Ray cleared his throat in hopes of disguising the huskiness in his voice. "Now tell me about this school. From what I can see, you've made a real winner of it." Resuming his seat, he leaned back against the cushion in hopes of easing the ache in his gut. He casually lifted one leg to rest across a knee, refusing to give in to his body's demand for rest.

"I've been very lucky." Her face was radiant with happiness.

"Ha—from the looks of it, you've worked darn hard—and you're still not letting up, I'd guess."

"Hard work never killed anyone. The truth of the matter is we're growing and much too quickly. I've been fighting a losing battle to keep the school small and family oriented."

"Wasn't the idea to be successful . . . profitable?"

"Not this successful. You know I don't need the money. And I certainly can live without the headaches. I have my hands full keeping up with the administrative end of the business. Lately I've spent more time filling in for absent employees than doing my own job." She shrugged. "A complaint I'm sure most small entrepreneurs share."

"How many people does it take to run the school?"

"Let's see—we have a cook, a combined driver and maintenance man, a cleaner, five instructors and their assistants, and a secretary. Fourteen in all not counting myself or my secretary's son, Jason, who works after school shoveling snow, raking leaves and such. The problem is we have a two-year waiting list."

"Sounds like there is a definite need for your services. Have you considered opening another facility?"

"Never! I know each one of my employees, all the children and their families. And they know me. We're small. I'm able to keep abreast of each child's developmental needs. It's an ideal situation. I can see that my educational goals for the children are being met."

"But?" he prompted.

"I'm getting so much pressure from the community to enlarge, I'm beginning to wonder if I'm being selfish."

Ray shook his head. "Stubborn, opinionated, hot tempered maybe, but selfish . . . never. Stand up to them. You, better than anyone, know what it takes to make the school work." Ray was impressed by her talent and devotion to her work, but not surprised. He expected nothing less than her best. She was a Spencer after all.

"Thanks," she said warmed by the understanding in his eyes. His opinion of her mattered. She so enjoyed sharing her work with him. She also acknowledged to herself that she resented that he would not do the same. His work was as much a part of him as hers was an extension of herself.

Ray was a very wealthy man in his own right. His photographs of the children of the world were overwhelming. His one-man showings in New York and Washington had been highly successful. Amber also knew about his profitable investments. He could afford to indulge himself. He donated a considerable amount from his showings to children's charities around the world. The starving children, especially in Sudan and Ethiopia, had left an everlasting impression on him.

Money was not his driving force, and it certainly was not why he risked his life. Each new assignment, whether it was for an upcoming book or a magazine assignment, was what kept him going, what challenged him.

"I know I need to hire more employees, but I really don't want to, especially if I'm not assured of obtaining reliable help." She paused. "I don't know why I'm telling you all this. I probably wrote you about it in one of my letters."

"Tell me again. You may have left something out," he teased, determined not to let his gaze linger on the soft fullness of her beautiful mouth. She had small delicate African features like the women of the Sudan.

Her skin was such an exquisite shade of golden brown, creamy smooth . . . flawless. She was like that all over. Her breasts were high and full, her large nipples were dark, the color of semisweet chocolate. Hell, what was he thinking? In another instant he would be remembering how thick and soft were the rich brown curls that shielded her femininity. Enough! He had to stop this and now. He was all ready semi-erect.

"Ray?"

"I'm listening."

"I hated it last fall when Mr. Westmore, our cook's husband, couldn't drive the van any longer and was forced to take an early retirement. For the first time, I had to use an employment agency in Burlington. Unfortunately, Harris may have to be replaced."

"That's the new driver, right?"

"Yes, Foster Harris. He has been so dependable. Yet suddenly in the past few weeks he's been like a different person. He's been late for work twice in the last week. Once I thought I smelled liquor on his breath and had to refuse to let him drive. I suspect some of my discomfort is because I don't feel as if I really know him. He's too private. He doesn't talk about himself, nor is he close to any of the staff. He's so cold, almost distant." Amber had no idea she was scowling.

"Can I help? I might be able to find out more about him."

"No, but I appreciate the offer. I'm probably overreacting. I've already checked his references. There is no real reason to worry." She put down her cup. "Why am I burdening you with all this?" She didn't wait for an answer. "Tell me about you. How long are you staying?" She tried not to reveal how important his answer was to her. She longed for him to stay.

"I'm taking a flight out in the morning."

Over the years he'd made a point of keeping Amber as innocent as possible of the dangers inherent in his work. He never told her more than where he was located, making sure to leave her a telephone number in case she needed to reach him. She did not know what he was actually doing until it was over, then he sent her a copy of whatever he'd been working on. She'd lived through enough hell.

Ray sighed, realizing there was no way he could stay on without her discovering he had been shot. He didn't want to go, but he had no choice. It had taken all his strength to keep up appearances this evening. He was hurting, and he needed to take another pain pill. Damn it, he had to

be realistic. He could not afford a bout of jungle fever due
to his weakened condition, especially not here with Amber.
He could not bear for her to see him like that. How much
longer could he afford to continue ignoring the dictates
of his body? He had to get some rest or take a chance on
suffering the unpleasant consequences.

Amber looked at him with those beautiful golden eyes.
The hurt he saw in them caused his heart to ache with
grief. "You've only just arrived. We have not had a chance
to really talk. Stay the weekend, Ray. You have not had a
chance to look over the school or meet my friends. Please,
can't you stay until Monday? Even I can see you're worn
out. You work too hard. You don't take proper care of
yourself. Stay . . . you could use the rest. If you must work,
I'm sure your precious laptop is in your bag. Please, I
promise not to—"

"Don't, angel." Damn it, he was hurting her yet again.
He should not have come. "Don't make this harder on
either one of us."

"But, Ray, we've had so little time together." Amber
fought the tears rising in her throat, aware of the tremor
in her voice despite her best efforts.

They had been together long enough for him to realize
how much he still wanted her. Like a stupid fool, he had
given in to his weakness, his need to see her, to be with
her. If it were not for this blasted pain, which had obviously
destroyed his common sense, he would not have taken
such a huge risk by coming here in the first place. He
would have waited until he was stronger, completed his
business in the Middle East. Then he would have sent her
a ticket so that she could meet him in London, Detroit—
anywhere but in her home or his. He had to get out, had
to leave before he did or said something to destroy the
precious balance that was their relationship.

"I've enjoyed our time together. Dinner was a real treat.
We'll get together again . . . soon. I promise."

"Stop it! Don't humor me. I've known you too long.
Soon in your vocabulary means in maybe six months . . .

a year—that is, if everything goes well on your next assignment. Why do you pretend what you do isn't dangerous? Ray, I'm not a child anymore. I know what's happening in the world. It isn't just a book you are working on. You're risking your life every time you leave on one of these assignments."

"I won't have you worrying about me!"

"Just how are you gonna stop me, huh? I love you! You're the only family I have left." Although she turned her face away, he caught a glimpse of the moisture shimmering in her eyes.

She could have found no better way to convince him that he was doing the right thing by leaving. She was too precious to him. He'd be damned if he'd have her worry herself sick over his injuries, and that was what would happen if she knew. No way!

"Amber . . ." he began, although not knowing what he should say.

"Don't say anything. I'm sorry. I didn't mean to make you feel guilty. I know you're doing what you must. Your last book on the changing political situation in South Africa was brilliant. This new one will be even better. Please, just overlook me. I was being emotional. I just wish sometimes that you'd stayed on at the university. You were so good with the students. They need a professor who knows what he's talking about."

She was referring to the few months he'd taken off to teach a course in photojournalism at Columbia. She was right—he had enjoyed it. But he had done it only as a favor to one of his old professors, who had been recovering from surgery. He looked at her, his dark eyes hooded. "Amber—"

"More coffee?" she interrupted, knowing darn well she had said too much. Photojournalism was his passion, the rest was just gravy.

"No, I think I'll turn in."

She began to rise. He shook his head. "Stay, relax, enjoy

the fire. I will see you in the morning. We'll have breakfast together, okay?"

She nodded, forcing a smile. "Pecan pancakes, just the way you like them."

He chuckled. "Only if you let me help. I know my way around the kitchen." He got up carefully, approached her slowly, determined not to let his discomfort show. Cautiously bending at the waist, he placed a kiss on her cheek while battling a wave of dizziness and light-headedness. Perspiration glistened on his coppery skin as he said, "Night, angel."

"Night," she whispered, her arms tightly folded beneath her breasts. She held herself so she would not reach out to him. She wanted the impossible, the warmth and comfort of his strong arms.

She didn't dare say more or she would end up begging him not to leave in the morning. She so hoped he would stay at least for the weekend. Their partings were never easy, but this one was going to be another disappointment in a long line of separations. Five long years of partings since their reconciliation.

Alone and unaware of the trickle of tears that slid down her cheek, Amber knew he had made his choice long ago. She did not like it. In fact, she hated it! When he left in the morning, she would paste a smile on her face and pretend her heart was not crumbling.

After refilling her cup with coffee she really didn't want, she tucked her legs under her and sipped, her thoughts moving backward to the first time he had come home with her brother Brad for the holidays.

He had been so big, threatening to the nine-year-old Amber. Later she had come to recognize how nervous he had been on that first visit. In spite of the fact he had inadvertently broken one of her mother's crystal vases and trampled her father's prize roses, her parents had liked Ray.

They both knew the struggle it took for an African American to succeed on his own without family support. They admired his determination to make something of his life. They especially thought he was a good, stabilizing influence on their carefree, somewhat reckless son. Brad never had to struggle for anything including his parents' loving support.

Amber was the only one who resented Ray's appearance in their lives. She was jealous of his closeness to her beloved Brad and was prepared to hate him for life. Yet Ray had been so gentle with her, so kind and patient. He never complained when she tagged along with them.

As their college years passed, Brad and Ray's friendship remained steadfast. Ray spent almost every vacation at the Spencer estate. He and Brad worked well together. Not only were they good, but they were not afraid of taking risks. The story was all that mattered. Amber's feelings for Ray changed as she changed from a girl into a young lady. The bond between him and all the Spencers had grown until he was a part of their family. As she looked back on the past, she knew she had been in love with Ray Coleman since she was a teenager.

Stop this! She had wasted enough time focusing on the past. Ray was here in her home this very second, and she was grateful. He had taken time to come to her. The rest should not be important. She wouldn't let it be. She'd made a success of the nursery school by looking forward. No backward steps for her.

Concentrating on positive thoughts, Amber performed the nightly chores of locking up, putting out the fire, and rinsing the few remaining dishes.

The light shone beneath Ray's door when she passed. After changing into her nightgown, Amber was in bed when she remembered she had not set the timer on the percolator. There was nothing so pleasant as waking to smell of fresh-brewed coffee on a cold winter morning. Saturdays were especially pleasant because she indulged herself by sleeping late. One disadvantage to working at home was she more often than not put in a few extra hours at her desk, even on the weekends.

Ray's light was still on when she returned from the kitchen. Pressing an ear to the door, she smiled when she heard the sound of his snoring. He was exhausted, she thought, as she carefully turned the doorknob. Her bare feet made no noise as she crossed the plush carpet, intending to switch off the bedside lamp.

Amber's gasp of alarm caused Ray's lashes to fly open. Instead of the tension leaving his system, it spiraled as he studied the horror stamped on her features. It was not necessary for him to follow the line of her vision to his bare chest, where the bedclothes stopped at his bandaged midsection.

Chapter Four

"I only came in to turn off the light," she mumbled.

"I'm all right, angel," he said groggily.

Amber, having momentarily lost the use of her limbs, used the back of the armchair for support. Upon regaining control of her voice and her legs, she brushed tears impatiently from her cheeks. "If you were not already hurt, I'd punch you in the nose for this, Ray Coleman!" She stroked his damp forehead tenderly. "How dare you hide something this serious from me? Don't tell me those bandages are decorative!"

"Calm down, baby. It's not as bad as it looks." He gingerly eased himself up into a sitting position, clenching his teeth to hold back a groan.

"Don't lie to me, damn it! You've been shot, haven't you?" Her eyes were wide with grief and fear.

"Yes."

"How did it happen?"

"I ran into a little trouble in Beirut. Ran into some folks that didn't care which way their bullets went." He tried to joke. "Amber—"

"When did it happen?" She did not have to ask why she wasn't notified. She knew why, damn him!

"Ten days ago," he responded without hesitation, his mind clouded with pain.

"How have you managed to keep this out of the press? You're too well known not to be featured on the evening news."

He smiled. "Friends. Pulled a few strings. Amber, I'm fine, honest."

"You're not fine," she snapped, resting her cool palm against his overheated cheek. "You're burning up with fever. And you're as weak as a kitten."

"It's just a bout of the jungle fever I picked up in South America a few years back. Nothing serious. Don't worry. I've had it before." Then he moaned—"Angel . . . please. Can I have . . . some water. I'm so . . . hot"—before flopping back down on the bed. He kicked free of the blankets, mindless that his hard muscled body was bare except for a pair of low-riding black briefs and the bandage wrapped around his midsection.

"Don't do that. You need to stay covered." Amber quickly covered him. Hurrying into the bathroom for the water, she was back in a flash. She was shocked at how weak he was as she held the glass to his lips. He had to have been in pain this evening. But he had not said one word. He probably would have left in the morning without her even knowing if she had not come into his room. The fool!

"I'm calling the doctor." She reached for the bedside phone.

"No!" He caught her hand with surprising strength. "I've got enough antibiotics and pain medication with me. Just give me one of each. I'll be fine by morning. It's my own fault—did too much today. First day out of the hospital."

She was ready to shake some sense into him. "You left the hospital today? Oh, Ray! Please let me call my doctor. Something could be seriously wrong."

"No," he said, holding on to her hand. "I don't want a doctor. All I need is sleep. Promise . . ."

As far as she was concerned, he was in no condition to expect her to keep such a promise. "Honey," she begged, pressing the cool damp cloth over his lean cheeks and forehead. "We've got to bring down your temperature."

"Seen too many doctors . . ."

"Well, at least let me go so I can get the thermometer and a basin of cool water. You are too warm."

"Promise me, no more doctors," he persisted, although his voice was fading and she had to lean forward to hear him. His large hand still held hers.

"Okay, if it's what you want."

Although Amber was frantic with worry, she was willing to agree to anything just to be allowed to help him.

She began the slow process of sponging him off and coaxing him to drink liquids.

"Of all the stupid—" she fussed in frustration when she soaked the bandage covering his midsection. "Well, I don't have time to change it now. It will have to wait until I get your temperature down."

"Hot . . . so hot," he mumbled, constantly kicking off the comforter.

"I know, sweetheart," she soothed, pressing the cool cloth over his forehead and lean cheeks. His coppery skin had taken on an almost gray tint.

Although he could not seem to understand her, she talked to him anyway. Her soft voice remained soothing, comforting as he tossed restlessly on the bed. She told him over and over again how important it was for him to get well. The sun had lit the sky when he finally slipped into a natural but exhausted sleep, his body no longer racked with fever.

Even though her entire body ached with fatigue, and her head pounded relentlessly, Amber changed his bandages. She worked calmly, forcing herself not to react to the sight of his extensive injuries. At last, she curled beneath a blanket in the armchair she'd moved close to the bed.

She closed her eyes, trying not to give in to her fears whenever she thought of the vicious scar that ran from his navel across the right side of his midsection. It was a brutal reminder of how close she had come to losing him. She brushed impatiently at the few stubborn tears that trailed down her cheek.

They both slept through the morning. She woke first, groggy and with cramped muscles. She threw back her covers when she heard a masculine groan.

"What is it?" She leaned over him, placing a hand against his lean stubbled cheek.

"Amber," he whispered. His eyes were bloodshot but lucid. "I'm sorry—"

"Shush." She smiled, pressing a finger against his lips. Thankful when she found his body cool to the touch, she teased, "Were you expecting someone else? How do you feel—you had a bad night, I'm afraid."

Ray did not respond. He was asleep, his breathing deep and even.

Amber took a hot shower and changed into jeans and a pale pink sweater.

"Good, you're awake," she said as she carried in the breakfast tray with a bowl of hot creamed cereal and milk-laced coffee.

"Thanks," he mumbled as she helped him to sit up and propped pillows behind him. He was in a great deal of pain and docilely took the medication she gave him.

He was so weak that she had to help him into the bath-room, but he insisted on seeing to his own needs. As she waited nervously listening to the shower, she worried that he might fall. She did not relax until she had him back in the freshly made bed. Soon after that the chills began. No matter how many blankets she piled on top of him, or how high she turned up the temperature in the apartment, his body was tormented with shivers.

Amber could not bear his suffering. She raged against the promise she had given that she would not call the doctor. She was close to tears when in desperation she stripped off her own clothes and climbed into bed with him. Holding him close, she wrapped her legs and arms around him, praying he would absorb her body heat.

"Amber ..." he mumbled groggily.

"Shush, sweetheart ... I'm here," she whispered into his ear. He seemed to understand. With his arms tight around her waist, he rested his head on her shoulder and dropped off again into much needed sleep. Soon after that the shivering stopped. When Amber tried to get up, Ray held on to her. Too tired to fight with him, Amber gave up and they both slept most of the afternoon.

Late that evening the fever returned, and Saturday night became a repeat of Friday. It was after midnight when Amber and Ray were finally able to rest. One day flowed into the next. Sunday night was his most restless.

Ray awoke slowly, aware of a pleasant warmth along his left side. As he opened heavy lids, he realized the softness against his thigh was Amber's sexy bottom. Wedged against him, she slept on peacefully with his arm over her shoulder and extended down between the soft lush swells of her full breasts. His palm cupped her bare stomach, his fingertips scant inches from the mound of thick brown curls between her satin smooth thighs. Although she wore a white lace-trimmed gown, it had twisted itself above her small waist.

For the first time since Friday evening, his head was clear and his senses were alert. His response to Amber was intensely male, his shaft had thickened and lengthened in readiness. He was cognizant of her softness in every cell of his large frame despite the heavy weight of his limbs and the nagging pain in his gut.

He burned all right, but with a different kind of fever. He wanted her ... wanted to bury himself inside her tight, hot sheath. Instead, he forced himself to lie very still, filling his lungs with her wonderfully feminine scent. Although her gown was made of brushed cotton, meant to be soft, it couldn't begin to compare to the texture of her creamy golden skin. He did not need to touch her to remember what she felt like. He knew that Amber Spencer was soft and warm all over. He swallowed the groan rising in his chest.

How many times had he dreamed of having her back in his bed? Too many for his own good. Yet even in his wildest wide-awake fantasies, he had never considered the possibility that he might be too blasted weak and sore to do anything other than hold her. Ray grinned. The injustices of life.

Ray did not shift a muscle to alter their closeness. He closed his eyes, and for a short time only, he warned himself, he would allow himself to savor the utter sweetness of the moment.

The telephone on the nightstand rang, shattering the stillness. Amber rolled over onto his chest. She snuggled against him, her small opened hand scant inches from his nipple. If that was not bad enough, her soft thigh had slipped between his suddenly ultrasensitive hair-roughened thighs. Ray ground his teeth against this new exquisitely sweet torment. His heart was pounding wildly in his chest, and his erection pulsated with such urgency that he began to have serious doubts about the iron grip of control he had long prided himself on maintaining.

She sighed in her sleep, but she did not open her eyes. He picked up the telephone, intent on putting an end to the noise.

"Spencer residence."

The deep husky tremor of his voice close to her ear caused Amber to slowly surface from the most wonderful dream.

"Who was it?" Amber mumbled as Ray set down the phone.

"Your secretary. She was worried when you didn't come down for work this morning. Told her you opted to sleep in. How are you feeling?" he asked as if it were the most natural thing in the world for them to wake in the same bed.

Amber blushed furiously. She was fully alert and furious with herself for being caught half naked in his arms. What must he think? She was quick to disengage herself and yanked her gown down over her legs, all while trying to appear calm.

"How are you? Fever all gone?" she asked as she ran the back of her hand along his forehead, smoothing over his close-cut natural.

"Weak but clearheaded, thanks to you. You took care of me, didn't you, angel?" He didn't need an answer. Her warmth had touched even the hellhole he'd slipped down inside of. "How long was I out?"

"It's Monday, Ray." Her eyes were filled with heartfelt relief and love. "You gave me a scare." Sitting up on the edge of the bed, she nervously smoothed the blankets separating them. She could not quite meet his eyes as she explained why he had awakened to find her in bed with him. Her concern for him outweighed her embarrassment. Her voice was soft when she said, "I was so worried, and you made me promise not to call the doctor."

"I'm sorry, Amber. I never meant for you to see me like this. I should not have come," he grumbled with impatience.

"Don't say that!" she snapped, losing her temper. She jumped up, breathing rapidly, yet hoping to bury the hurt his blunt statement had caused deep inside.

There would be plenty of time to explore it later, when she was alone . . . when he was once again gone. For now he was so much better, his chills and fever were gone. That was all that mattered.

"Angel—" He caught her wrist before she could move away.

"No, Ray. We'll discuss your mulish tendencies at another time. Right now I need to shower and get ready for work."

"Listen to me. I never—"

"Don't you dare say it again! I know how you feel, and I'm not up to discussing it this morning. Look, we both could use some space. Just tell me one thing though. Will you be here when I come back this afternoon?''

Ray's eyes were like dark flames as he stared into her eyes. ''I'm staying. I owe you that much.'' He did not add the obvious. She had already witnessed the worst. There was no point in his leaving so soon. Even if he had the strength to go, which he did not, he could not leave. Truth was, he needed her . . . needed to spend time with her.

''You don't owe me anything.'' She turned her face away so he could not see the sudden rush of tears flooding her gaze. But his large hand encircled her wrist. His fingers gently caressed the silky flesh.

She knew she should leave it there, but she couldn't hold back the words burning the back of her throat. ''How could you? How could you keep something like this from me? Damn you, Ray, you were shot! From the looks of that wound, you are darn lucky to be alive.''

''See why I didn't tell you,'' he said, brushing at the tears that ran down her cheeks. ''I didn't want to see you like this. You're upset and you're frightened. I'm not worth it.'' She had suffered enough. She didn't need more pain.

''I could smack you for that bit of wisdom,'' she said, yanking away from him.

''Amber, please. Don't be angry—''

''How long were you in the hospital?''

''What possible—''

''How long, Ray?''

''Nearly two weeks. Are you happy now?''

''Hardly. This happened over a week ago, and I didn't even know you were hospitalized. Did you tell your secretary not to call me?'' She glared at him.

''You've been through enough. It's time you had some happiness.''

''That was supposed to be your reason for not calling? It stinks! We're family. You had no right to keep this from me. You would have had a fit if I'd gone into the hospital without telling you.''

''Yeah, that's true,'' he trailed off. He had been protecting her for so long now, he no longer questioned it. Besides that, he knew the limits of his own strength. He could manage carefully measured tiny doses of Amber. Any more would unleash the ruthless hunger that was always just beneath the surface.

"I want an answer, Ray Coleman. We adopted each other a long time ago. Has something changed that I don't know about?"

"Even as a kid you were pushy," he said impatiently. "Stop looking at me as if I cheated you. I was protecting you." Perhaps he was really protecting himself.

"I had a right to know."

"I know that." He swore softly. "There was some damage. It meant a lot of surgery. It took a while for me to remember my own name. There was some doubt as to if I was going to make it. I was not prepared to watch you suffer another loss, angel."

"In case you haven't noticed, I'm all grown up, Ray Coleman. It happened a long time ago. It's about time you accepted that."

They glared at each other—Ray stubbornly clinging to his need to shield her, and Amber thoroughly annoyed with him as well as terrified of the risks he took, day after day, as a matter of course.

Finally, it was Amber who broke the silence when she said, "I need to get dressed." Her spine was stiff with anger as she left him staring after her.

Chapter Five

Amber had not gotten around to the interview with Foster Harris until early afternoon. Now as he sat silently staring at his hands clasped between wide-spaced knees, she wished she had canceled it entirely. She was fast losing her patience with him.

"Frankly, Harris, I still don't understand. Your behavior borders on irresponsibility. According to my records, you have been late for work several times in the past few weeks. You don't even bother to show up on Fridays. Your thoughtlessness has inconvenienced our children's families, not to mention diminished the reputation of this school."

Amber sat with her back to a window, behind the large oak desk in her corner office. She had a view of both the lake and the woods. Floor-to-ceiling bookshelves covered two walls, the taupe and cream geometrically patterned velvet sofa and oak coffee table were positioned beneath the picture window against the far wall.

Harris sat in one of the two caramel leather armchairs directly in front of Amber's desk, annoyed with himself when he found no matter how hard he tried he could not meet his employer's eyes. It wasn't her reprimand that intimidated him or her cool professionalism. It was her beauty.

Beautiful women had always affected him. Harris remembered how his mother looked when she got ready to go out for the evening. She had been so lovely, like a fairy-tale princess to the small boy . . . so perfect.

"Harris?"

"Yes?" The young man blinked quickly. He was thin with legs and arms that seemed too long for his frail body. His light brown hair and pale blue eyes were nondescript. Nothing about him was distinctive, except for the missing digit on his right hand.

"I'd like an explanation, please."

"I didn't feel well. Catching the flu, I guess," he mumbled the lie. He really tied one on the other night and awakened with a terrible hangover. He could not sleep that night. Every time he closed his eyes, he would dream and with the dream came the voices again: Ben's voice, Mama's voice, the voices of the others . . . all screaming at him.

"I took a chance on hiring you without local references. Mrs. Gordon at the employment agency in Burlington convinced me that you were reliable. Up until recently, I agreed with her. I've had no complaints about your work. In fact . . ."

Although Amber continued talking, Harris was not listening. He was remembering how his mother used to pile her hair on top of her head like that. She had thick dark brown hair, too. Funny how he never noticed that before. Harris frowned as he recalled how his mother would be gone for a long time. Sometimes in his childish imagination, he worried that she'd hurt herself or gotten lost. He did not want to believe that she was living it up with some man and forgotten that she even had two sons. Harris had been left with his older brother, Ben. Harris's hands began to shake. No, he did not want to think about Ben or how Ben had hurt him. Ben made him swear never to tell their mother.

"Well?" Amber paused.

"I promise it won't happen again," he said, saying the first thing that popped into his head. "If that's all, I need to get back to the kitchen. Promised Mrs. Westmore I'd fix the garbage disposal today."

Amber knew that she had lost control of the interview, but she wasn't quite certain how it happened. To tell the truth, she honestly didn't much care. For once she couldn't get past her personal problems.

She had not been able to concentrate on much of anything but the man resting upstairs in her apartment. She was ashamed of her loss of control this morning. It was a foolish mistake to let Ray see her fear. How was she going to convince him that he was wrong about her—that she didn't need his protection, but his loving support?

"Miss Spencer?"

"Yes, you can go back to work. I'm warning you, I want to see a change. No repeat of the last week, or I'm afraid I won't be able to keep you on. I'd like to believe in you, Harris, I really would, but it all depends on you. I would like to be able to count on you."

"You can. I won't let you down," he said with a forced smile, his eyes chilling. He closed the door quietly behind him.

Amber sat for a long time staring at the empty chair in front of her. She sighed audibly, reviewing the interview in her mind. For just a second, Harris made her feel decidedly uncomfortable.

"You're just tired," she mumbled to herself. She was also sick of trying to figure out why Ray easily accepted her reason for being in bed with him. Shivers of remembered pleasure raced down her spine, but she refused to focus on them.

What was the point? Their lovemaking had happened so long ago. While he considered it a mistake, a temporary weakness that he would go to his grave regretting, Amber thought of it as a night of pure magic. She might have been young, but she knew how she felt about him. She would not have let it happen if she had not been in love with him.

Ray had been sleeping so peacefully when she brought up his lunch tray that she did not have the heart to disturb him. She left a note on his dresser and the covered dishes on the kitchen counter. He needed rest now, more than anything else.

"Come," Amber called in response to the knock on the door. She was on the last page of the psychological evaluation Wayne Adams, Ginger's husband, had prepared on one of their students.

"I need your John Hancock on these letters. Isn't it strange how the food truck arrives just as Mrs. Westmore is preparing to leave for the day?" Lynn Baldwin shook her head.

"Is it that time already? The children will be preparing to leave soon. You should have called me, Lynn. I could have helped put the food away." Amber frowned as she scrawled her signature.

"You were in conference with Harris. Nothing to concern yourself about—I took care of it. After that delicious clam chowder, homemade buttermilk biscuits, and apple turnovers Mrs. Westmore prepared today, I didn't have the heart to delay her by even a single second. The woman needs her rest so she will be here bright and early tomorrow morning. My dear, we couldn't have anything interfering with her creative processes." Lynn laughed.

Amber joined in. She'd come to depend on Lynn's good cheer, efficiency, and her sound advice. "Thanks. I owe you one," Amber said, returning the documents to the child's folder.

"Pardon my frankness, but you look like hell. Why don't you call it a day? Amber, you can't continue to do everything. You're wearing yourself down."

"I know. One quick call first. I need to talk to your husband. It helps that Alex is the head of the Early Childhood Department at the college. As soon as we have those student teachers in place, things should settle down nicely."

"The way he complains, I'm beginning to suspect those students may be more trouble than help," Lynn said, lifting a brow.

Amber laughed. "Oh, Lynn, what would I do without you?"

Lynn's eyes twinkled. She was ready to get down to the heart of the matter. "Tell me, how is your house guest? I've heard some interesting things. He's tall, dark, and sexy, in his late thirties, and available. I was hoping for a peek at him just to make sure Ginger didn't miss any important details. My . . . my, did he ever sound sexy on the phone this morning. Girl, I can't wait to meet him."

Amber blushed in spite of herself. "I should have known Ginger Adams couldn't keep her mouth shut, especially about a man." Amber did not really object to being the subject under discussion. Anything said between the three friends stayed between the three of them. Lynn and Ginger were interested in her happiness—which meant, to their way of thinking, they thought she should be married like they were. She had almost given up on her effort to convince them that her life-style suited her needs. If only they would stop competing with each other in hopes of finding her a husband.

"I will tell you the same thing I told your friend, Ginger," Amber said as she pointed a finger at her secretary. "Ray is an old and dear friend. He is family, Lynn." She paused to let that information sink in. "Unfortunately he's recovering from extensive surgery."

"That's a shame," Lynn said, noting her boss's troubled features. She would never forget Amber's kindness to her. She had given Lynn a chance, even though she had not worked since before her oldest child was born.

After taking time off to raise her children, Lynn found the job opportunities in the small college town almost nonexistent. Amber had given her reason to be proud of her own abilities. And for the first time, she was not just someone's mother or wife, but she was her own person.

"I just hope Ray stays until he's fully recovered," Amber grumbled worriedly, but knowing him that was doubtful. Measuring their time together in the last five years wouldn't fill a good-size teapot. That had been how they had managed to maintain their resolution by staying close but in their own special way.

"If you put your mind to it, I'm sure you can convince him he wants to stay," Lynn said softly, convinced that Amber was not being completely open about her feelings for Ray. They might see each other as family, but that did not explain the warmth in Amber's voice whenever she mentioned his name or the sparkle in her eyes. Whether she was willing to admit it or not, Amber was in love with the man.

As Lynn went through the open door toward her desk in the reception area, she said, "Oh, Jason asked me to tell you he has band practice after school every day this week and can't finish cleaning out the shed until Saturday, if that's all right with you."

"Saturday is fine," Amber said, punching out the number to the college and hoping Lynn was right and that Ray would stay until he was well.

"Are you sure you're up to this? Lynn will understand if we cancel. She frequently gives these cocktail parties." Amber's anxious gaze momentarily left the road in order to caress Ray's profile.

He stared out the window, concentrated on keeping his dark hungry eyes off the beautiful woman beside him. He considered himself to be a private man, normally comfortable with his aloneness. Yet he had turned to Amber during a weak moment, never doubting his welcome. His trust in her was absolute. She in turn had given of herself, asking for nothing in return. Their relationship was so simple, yet in many ways complex.

Beneath the concern, he had recognized the eagerness in her voice. This evening was important to her. She clearly was looking forward to sharing her friends with him. How could he refuse, especially when he knew that his consent had meant the world to her?

He said softly, "I want to meet your friends. Besides, you've been cooped up in the house with me long enough."

The sweetness of their quiet evenings together these past few weeks had been a rare treat, as well as an exquisite form of torment for him. His need for her rode him continuously, much more intense than ever before. What he could not understand was why it was so acute this time.

It was not as if they never saw each other. They spent time together. Yet since their reconciliation, their times together had never been like this. He felt a raw kind of hunger that often left him awake for hours, replaying every moment of the day that they had spent together. What was so different about this visit? Was it due to his close brush with death? Or had something changed between them that he simply was not aware of. Was it Amber . . . or was he the problem?

They were using Amber's small compact car for the trip to the east side of Shelly. Although the calendar said April, there were few signs of spring in the Vermont countryside. The ground was still covered with the frozen remains of winter.

Her soft laughter filled him with sweet warmth.

"I have no complaints." She was thrilled that he was finally on the mend, proud that her care had done this for him, and deeply grateful that he had stayed. She knew she would have been heartbroken if he kept his condition a secret from her and recovered on his own in D.C.

They chatted easily, discussing all sorts of topics yet nothing of any real consequence. She turned left onto Chandler Drive.

"The Baldwins' house is at the end of the subdivision. The redbrick house."

"You weren't exaggerating when you said the Baldwins know how to give a party."

A double row of cars lined each side of the wide circular driveway and the street. They were forced to park almost a block away from sprawling well-lit house.

"Lynn loves to go all out for these things, although she claims she is only returning a favor. Her husband, Alex, heads the Early Childhood Department at the college. I know you're going to like them both. They've become such good friends." Amber laughed. "She's a great organizer. I couldn't get along without her." She swung gracefully out of the car, putting a slim black-gloved hand into his wide palm.

"Apparently your secretary doesn't need the job," Ray commented as he eyed the stately lines of the exterior.

"You wouldn't hold that against her, would you?" Amber turned her face up to his, laughter sparking in her eyes. Her gaze lingered on his full, seductive mouth beneath the fall of that thick mustache.

"Never. You are looking awfully pretty tonight," he said softly. One large hand smoothed the fur on the turned-up collar of her black full-length mink coat after flicking the brass door knocker.

Amber's beauty and genuine warmth came from deep within and was something he'd come to value. As his body healed, his sense of urgency increased. Before too long he would be returning to the Middle East in order to complete his work. The difference this time was he did not want to leave. There was no need for him to remind himself that his life was very different and separate from hers.

Amber took in his tall, muscular frame with silent enjoyment. The dark brown tweed sport coat, cream cashmere sweater, and camel-colored dress slacks suited him. The tan leather overcoat seemed to barely contain the width of his shoulders and powerful forearms. He had lost weight during his illness. It was evident in his midsection and in the gauntness of his copper brown cheeks.

Lynn opened the door with arms stretched wide in welcome. The party was in full swing, encompassing Alex's colleagues, nursery school staff members, and a number of parents who worked for the university and had their children enrolled in the nursery school. In a community as small and friendly as Shelly, everyone knew everyone else. Amber was thrilled to introduce Ray around. And it had nothing to do with his celebrity status—it had to do with the man himself. He was not only someone she admired, but someone she liked and trusted.

Alex Baldwin was an intense, highly intelligent African-American man. He was a man of humble beginnings who had fought his way out of the ghetto with ruthless determination. His quiet strength was a perfect foil to his lovely, vivacious wife.

Alex and Ray hit it off right from the start, discovering a mutual interest in politics and fascination with antique weapons.

When Amber was sidetracked, Ray went in search of a bit of peace and quiet. He ducked inside of the room Alex had pointed out as the family room.

"Sorry," Ray said when he discovered the room was occupied. "Thought I'd just take a breather."

"Come on in," the teenage boy urged. "I'm Jason Baldwin. Just watching the Lakers and the Celtics. Boston has them by six points. You like basketball?"

"Love it. Thanks for inviting me in. I could use the break. Too many people for me. I'm Ray Coleman." He shook hands with the boy, then took one of the chairs in front of the wide-screen television. Across the room a rolltop desk stood beneath a series of windows. The drapes had been left open, adding to the sense of peace and tranquility.

"You're Miss Spencer's friend from Washington. Mom was telling Dad about you the other night. How ya feelin'? Heard you've been sick."

"Much better, thanks." Ray grinned, not the least offended. The small size of the African-American community enabled people to get to know each other. They really seemed to care about one another. No big city indifference here.

"I work for Ms. Spencer, like my mom does. I do errands and take care of the yard. I'm saving up for a set of barbells." The boy beamed with pride.

Ray estimated Jason was about thirteen. The small, painfully thin youth resembled his mother with that open winning smile.

"Will you look at that—another one for Boston!"

Ray was able to fully relax for the first time that evening.

"My older brothers, Chad and Brian, play basketball for Michigan State. Chad's on the freshmen team and Brian's a junior," Jason declared proudly.

Ray nodded. He liked the Baldwins down to the youngest member. "Are you planning to go out for the team?"

"When I get to high school. I'm still too small. Once I get those weights, man, there will be no stopping me." When Ray did not laugh at him, but nodded his agreement, Ray had unknowingly gained a friend for life. Jason asked, eyeing the other's powerful forearms and shoulders, "Do you work out with weights?"

"When I have the time." Ray offered a rare smile.

"Robert's Sporting Goods in town has the set I'm interested in. I read about them in one—"

"So this is where you disappeared. What's the score, son?" Alex came into the book-lined room, a wide smile on his light brown face. He was a stocky man of medium height, with salt and pepper hair and lively black eyes.

"Seventy, sixty-five, Boston. I was just telling Mr. Coleman about the set of weights in Robert's, Dad."

"I bet." He nodded with an indulgent smile. "Looks like a good game," he said, eyes on the screen. "Lynn has a spread set up in the dining room, Ray. She would have my head if she thought one of our guests missed out."

Ray would have rather stayed and watched the game, but quietly gave in to his fate. "Thanks for the company, Jason."

Neither man noted the shadowy figure disengage himself from a nearby tree he'd been propped against, or saw him lift the open whiskey bottle to his mouth. Harris drank deeply from it, oblivious to the cold as his heavy-lidded eyes remained steadfastly on the boy engrossed in the action on the television.

Once Ray and Alex were in the hallway, Alex chuckled. "Hope Jason didn't bend your ear too much. Like the other Baldwin males, that kid is basketball crazy. I don't know how Lynn puts up with us."

"Jason is a great kid. You're a lucky man," Ray said with a bit more wistfulness than he intended.

As they walked beneath the wide arch that led into the living room, Ray quickly scanned the room until he found Amber. She was in front of the brick-walled fireplace talking to the same guy she had been in conversation with when he'd slipped out earlier. He was the only one she'd neglected to introduce him to.

"Who's that with Amber?"

Chapter Six

"That's Elliott Wilham. He heads the Business Department on campus."

Ray suddenly realized that he had spoken to the man on three separate occasions when he'd answered the telephone. Amber had immediately excused herself and hurried into the privacy of her bedroom to take the calls.

Wilham was a medium height, medium-build brother. He was focused on Amber, with a distinct frown on his deep brown face. Amber looked up and spotted Ray, flushed deeply.

Ray didn't need a road map to recognize the signals. Although his facial muscles remained the same, his hands had curled tightly. It was one thing knowing there were men in her life, it was quite another to actually see her with one of them. Ray hadn't even considered the possibility of running into one of the men she dated when he agreed to this damn party.

Ray witnessed the possessive gleam in the other man's gaze as his eyes shifted from her face down to the upward tilt of her lush breasts—and Ray's cool control vanished in less than a heartbeat. He couldn't help wondering how serious she was about this guy. If so, why hadn't she mentioned Wilham to him? Were they more than friends? Were they lovers?

"Having a good time?" Lynn asked as she and Ginger joined the men.

"Great. You have a lovely home." Ray smiled, despite the sudden resentment and bitterness churning in his gut. Wilham's masculine hunger was unmistakable, for it rivaled Ray's own. It didn't take much imagination for Ray to put a name to his own annoyance. He was jealous.

No matter how much he loved and wanted Amber for himself, Ray knew she would one day share her life with another man. In fact it was his love for her that made him sincerely want her to have all the happiness he wasn't able to provide. So why did he feel the need to ram his fist down the other man's throat?

"Thank you." Lynn smiled even more. "Will you excuse us, Ray? I need to borrow my husband for a moment. Ginger has volunteered to help you fit all these names with the right faces."

Once they were alone, Ray assured Ginger, "I really don't need a baby-sitter."

"An attractive man needs a bodyguard, especially in a room filled with so many single women. How are you feeling?"

"Couldn't be better. Are you a native or transplanted?"

"Transplanted. My husband and I are originally from Ohio. We met in Columbus while we were attending Ohio State."

"Exchanging snow for more snow. Why not Florida?" Ray purposefully kept Ginger talking and his back to the fireplace.

"It was a matter of economics. Wayne was offered a partnership in a practice in Burlington. He's a child psychologist. We found this wonderful old house halfway between the two cities." She went on to tell him the history of her home.

Ray was only half listening. His visit to Vermont was a

matter of indulgence. He allowed himself the comfort of Amber's closeness, knowing that as his health and strength increased so would his sexual desire for her. He spent night after night with a raging hard-on in a bed just across the hall from Amber's. While he didn't plan on doing a damn thing about his own need, he knew Wilham didn't harbor a similar restraint. Damn it to hell!

"Where have you been?" Amber said, linking her arm with Ray's. Her black cashmere knit dress was splashed with silver beads across the neckline, while a black leather belt emphasized her small waist and soft curves.

Ray tried to steel himself against her particularly appealing scent and the tantalizing pressure of her left breast against his arm. His temper was raging, his arousal was painfully evident, and his nerves were raw.

"In the den with Jason. And you?"

"Talking nonstop." She laughed. "Having a good time, Ginger? It's a shame that Wayne is laid up with a flu."

"Hmm, I should be getting back to him. It's getting late."

"Ray, we probably should be going, also. Don't want you to overdo it your first night out. Are you ready to go?"

"Yes, I'm not much for these things. If you ladies will excuse me, I'll get the coats. What color is yours, Ginger?"

"Pink wool with black trim."

Once they were alone, Ginger said in an impatient whisper, "What are you thinking—spending so much time with Elliott and leaving Ray on his own? This place is crawling with available women. Don't you dare tell me it's no concern of yours—I know better. What were you trying to do, make Ray jealous?"

"No, you know me better than that. Elliott cornered me. He used the party to his advantage. I haven't been out with him in weeks." Amber pushed a thick wave of curls behind her ear. "There wasn't much I could do to get away from him short of making a scene. What I don't understand is why he can't take no for an answer."

"I almost feel sorry for the jerk. But I happen to know

two women in his department that he was sleeping with at the same time." Ginger shook her head. "Wonder of wonders. So it seems the old love bug has finally bit Elliott. Tough luck for him. You're not blaming yourself, are you?"

"Kinda. I dated the man for months. Ginger, I told him from the beginning that I didn't want the same things that he did. I made myself clear. I told him I wasn't interested in getting sexually or emotionally involved. A lot of good it's done me. Every blasted time he's called since Ray has been at the apartment, Ray has answered the telephone. Elliott had the nerve to turn possessive on me tonight, demanding an explanation about Ray. He even threatened to come over and tell Ray who-knows-what if I didn't start dating him again."

"That's blackmail! I hope you didn't let Elliott intimidate you."

"Of course not. I can handle him. It's Ray I'm worried about. Elliott was the only person in the room I didn't want him to meet. Do you think he noticed?"

"Be for real. He noticed, my friend. The man isn't blind nor is he stupid. Amber, you have to tell Ray about Elliott. The way it stands now, it looks as if you are trying to hide something from him."

"Hmm . . . Well, nothin' is going on between Ray and myself, either," Amber whispered, unable to conceal her keen disappointment. Ray was the one satisfied with the status quo. There was absolutely nothing she could do about it.

"That's your fault," Ginger scolded softly. She had seen the way Ray's eyes had followed Amber. He clearly cared for her. What was wrong with the two of them? Why were they so intent on maintaining a friendship when they were both crazy about each other? It just didn't make sense.

"Ginger, we can't get into this now. He'll be back in a second."

"No, he won't. Lynn stopped him before he could reach the hallway. She's introducing him to some late arrivals. Amber, I've seen your eyes when you look at Ray. After tonight, nothing that comes out of your mouth is going to convince me that you aren't in love with that man. When are you going to do something about it?''

Ginger was so right. She was deeply in love with Ray Coleman, had been so since she was a teenager. Neither time, distance, nor the man himself could change how she felt about him. What Ginger didn't understand was that some things weren't negotiable. They had made a pact five years ago when they reconciled . . . friends for life. Somehow she had to keep up her end of their bargain.

"Lately I don't know what's going on inside of me. Things were so simple—that was, until Ray appeared on my doorstep. I was so certain that I'd totally accepted our limitations." Amber frowned unhappily. "Oh, Ginger," she whispered, "living with him, being able to care for him, having him near has made such a difference in the way I feel about our relationship. What we've had isn't nearly enough. I can no longer settle for sharing only a tiny portion of his world. I want him to be the center of my life, and I want to be the center of his. Unfortunately Ray is satisfied with the way things are, and it's light-years away from me and the Green Mountains of Vermont.''

"I'm telling you, he didn't look too satisfied to me a few minutes ago when he was watching you with Elliott. In fact for a few seconds I'd say he was feeling downright hostile. He looked for all the world like the enraged male ready to lay claim to what was his. Amber, talk to him, find out what's going on inside of him. It's possible that he has changed also.''

"Do you think—" Amber stopped. There was so much Ginger didn't know about them. So much Amber couldn't explain.

Ginger evidently understood some of Amber's unspoken fears, for she said, "I want you to be happy. Deep in my heart, I believe Ray is the only man you are able to give yourself to. Something about him reaches into your soul. Wayne does that to me. I can't explain it, but I've come to accept it." Ginger went on to add, "I know advice is cheap and on every street corner. Can't life be so damn painful at times?''

Amber nodded. She suspected Ginger was thinking of the baby she and her husband, Wayne, had been unable to conceive. Amber had no trouble understanding the longing the two felt. The couple refused to give up hope of completing their family. They clung to the belief that someday they would have a child of their own. In the meantime, they shared their joy for life and of each other with their friends.

"I know I don't always say it, but I do so appreciate your concern," Amber said with a smile.

Both women smiled, hands clasped in friendship.

"Good, you found it," Ginger piped in, warning Amber of Ray's return.

Ray first helped Ginger on with her coat, then Amber. His hand remained possessively against Amber's shoulder blade as they said their good nights and walked Ginger to her car.

"Come on, let's hurry. It's starting to rain, and it's turning to ice," Amber said after waving Ginger off. She stayed close to Ray as they made a dash for the car.

The icy downpour fit Ray's dark mood. His body was tight with tension as he reached for the car keys. "I'll drive."

Amber's questioning gaze went to the harsh planes of his face. "If you're sure? It's been only three weeks since your release from the hospital."

"I'm fine," he said, helping her inside.

"You look a little tired, sweetheart." The endearment slipped out without her realizing it. "We stayed too late. I should have insisted we leave no later than nine." They were strapped into their respective seats with the engine running.

"Stop worrying." He caressed her cheek with the back of his hand, his voice low, sexy. He refused to give in to the negative force of his emotions. Even though he hated seeing her with the other man, he knew there was nothing he could do about it. He had no rights where Amber was concerned. "I liked your friends. Nice party. Nice people."

Amber smiled, settling back in what she thought was a comfortable silence. They were forced to go slowly on the slick icy road.

Surely, Amber thought, what they shared would eventually shatter and crumble away if the delicate balance weren't maintained. Each had labored diligently over the years to preserve the precious bond. She'd been so happy to have him back in her life that she'd gladly accepted the restrictions of their relationship. She hadn't allowed herself to consider the possibility of going beyond their agreement. Their entire relationship would be at risk.

Could she take the chance of losing it all? Was she strong enough to live with the results? They were so good for each other and good together—didn't that count for something? Yet all the doubts didn't alter the tender sweet hope she had carefully, secretly nourished. Perhaps it was time she faced the truth.

Like Amber, Ray was absorbed in thought. He knew he was putting far too much energy into trying to decide if Wilham and Amber were lovers. Not many men would continue to see an attractive woman month after month without a little s-e-x to keep things interesting. In fact, he knew only one such jackass . . . himself. Wilham wanted Amber, badly. That much was apparent even from across the crowded room. The question was, had he won her love and would he be able to make her his? Was marriage in the wind? Was that the problem between them?

Ray swore silently and profusely as he gripped the steering wheel forcefully. She had introduced him to everyone in the room but Wilham. Ray burned with outrage, needing to know why.

Hell, use your head, man! In another week or two at the most, he would be gone, leaving the way clear for the Wilham to lay claim to Amber. Ray grumbled to himself that his own presence wasn't much of a deterrent. How serious was she about this one? Is that why she hadn't introduced them? What had she been afraid of? Everyone in town knew he was staying with her. So why had she made such a point of not introducing them?

Although the rain had stopped by the time they reached the house, Ray said, "You go on in. I'll put the car in the garage." He let her out at the side door.

Amber switched on the lights in the back hallway, expecting Ray to follow. When she saw him heading back down the drive toward the front of the house, she left her purse on the bottom step, then hurried out after him. She had to run to catch up with him.

Ray heard her heels on the wet pavement. He waited for her to reach him. "It's too cold for you to be out here."

"Admittedly a warm fire and a cup of hot chocolate does sound appealing." She shrugged philosophically. "If you enjoy walking on a night like this, then so can I."

What could he say to stop her? That he preferred his own miserable company so he could indulge in a bit of self-pity, brood with bitter despair over what he could not change? He needed time alone to explore the potent rage and jealousy tearing him apart.

Who exactly was he trying to fool? His time with Amber, regardless of how brief, was special. It would make precious memories that could be stored away and then brought out during the empty hours when he couldn't sleep. He often lay awake ... thinking of her ... all she had said and done. He hungered for her softness, craved her womanly sweetness. His aroused body kept him awake long into the night, frustration mounting with each new dawn.

One single night was the sum total of their time as lovers. Yet the memory was as clear as if it had happened yesterday.

The air was poignant with the smell of freshly washed pine, the sky thick with clouds, the wind from off the lake whipping at their clothing. Although the calendar said spring, winter was not quite ready to let go.

Amber walked along beside him, puzzled by his continued silence.

"How's the Harris situation?" he asked unexpectedly.

"Much better, since our talk. He's living up to his end of our bargain. He still has the tendency to drink, but as long as he can control it and doesn't do it during the day while he's working, I can live with it. I don't like it, but I have to be fair. He has a right to a private life, away from the school. Do you think I'm being too hard on him?"

"Not for minute. You have the children to consider."

"They are my most important concern."

He held in a groan when she casually linked her arm through his. He told himself he didn't want to feel her softness. Told himself that he didn't want to be reminded of what he could not have . . . what might belong to Wilham. Yet he couldn't explain even to himself why he didn't pull away.

They walked on in complete silence. While he fought his instincts to claim her as his alone, she fretted that Ginger was right and there was a need to explain Elliott.

As they approached the woods, she urged, "A penny?"

"Hmm?"

"For your thoughts. Or is the going rate a dollar these days with inflation? You're so quiet. You're aren't in pain, are you?"

"No. I'm a little tired. I can't get back in shape by lying in bed all day, catching up on my reading from that stack of books on the nightstand." Although Ray strove to contain his bitterness, nevertheless some of it was evident in his tone.

"What's the rush? These past few weeks have been good for you. If you were at home, you'd be working nonstop on your book, rather than resting, regaining your strength. Admit it!"

"Probably."

"Ray—what's the matter? And don't you dare say nothing. Something is bothering you, I can feel it." She forced herself to ask, "Are you annoyed with me because of Elliott? I had a good reason for not introducing the two of you."

He stopped abruptly, to look pointedly at her. "I did wonder," he said carefully.

"It's complicated."

"I've got all night," he said tightly.

"You're not making this any easier."

"You've been dating him for a while, I suspect."

"Yes." She hesitated, knowing full well she did not want to get into this with Ray.

"Well? How serious is it? Are you making wedding plans that you haven't told me about?"

"No! What made you think that?"

"The brother has called several times since I've been in the apartment. Besides, he had you cornered for half the evening," Ray said, his hands balled at his side. He would like to slam his fist into something, preferably Wilham's too handsome face. "Should I have interrupted? I assumed his attentions were welcome."

"Elliott and I have enjoyed each other's company for the past six months or so. Lately he wants more from the relationship than I do. We stopped seeing each other just before you arrived. He was upset tonight because you've been staying with me. Under the circumstances I thought it best if you two didn't meet."

"What kind of relationship? Is that a polite way of saying you two are sleeping together? Is he your lover?" Ray asked bluntly, losing control of the battle with his emotions. Was she in love with the bastard? He had to know if another man had finally taken his place.

"Ray!"

"Just answer the damn question!"

Chapter Seven

Amber's chin lifted, her eyes flashing sparks at him. "I can't believe you asked me that question. You'd better not expect an answer because you won't get one from me!" She looked away from him, then said after taking a calming breath, "Ray, please. This is ridiculous. You know the ground rules we've been living with for the past five years. Good grief—you're the one who insisted on them. Or have you conveniently forgotten that also?"

No response was forthcoming. There was no simple explanation for his behavior and very little logic beneath it either. Damn it, he hurt—hurt in a way that didn't have a thing to do with his recovery or even rational thought.

"Ray?" Amber tugged at his sleeve, shivered from the cold. His silence was unsettling, even more disturbing than his smoldering temper. Was Ginger right? Was he as fed up with their present relationship as she was? "Why won't you answer me?"

"Are you sleeping with Wilham?" he repeated between clenched teeth.

"No, we're just friends."

"I know that look, Amber. Wilham wants you," Ray grated impatiently.

"What is wrong with you?" Amber wanted to smack him. Why was he acting this way? What difference did it make what Elliott wanted from her?

"Come on, Amber. Let's go inside. We're both going to have double pneumonia in the morning."

"Forget the cold. Don't you think it's long past time we really talked? I mean openly, Ray . . . about everything."

"No, I don't," he snapped, starting back toward the house.

"It's been twelve years!" she called after him.

"Leave it alone!"

"I can't . . ."

He walked away, knowing damn well he was not likely to forget the night he had lost control and took a mere child to his bed. He was old enough to know better. But he hadn't been doing his thinking with his head, either. Hell—his experiences with women weren't limited like hers had been back then.

Despite his best efforts, his thoughts flew backward to that night, the one and only time they had made love. They had shared more than the pain and grief of burying her brother and his best friend earlier that day. Ray recalled how his own hurt had equaled hers.

Brad had been like a brother to him. From the first they had developed a lasting friendship and had shared not only their thoughts but a passion for journalism. Naturally they had both accepted the danger they faced as nothing more than a part of the work. It was not unusual for them to go into war-torn parts of the globe. They'd accepted the risk along with the challenge.

Unfortunately Brad had been the one who had everything to live for . . . the one with the nurturing family. Ray had no one to call his own. His parents had died when he was still in his teens. His older sister, Catherine, refused to take him in and he was forced to endure the foster care system until he came of age.

In their grief, Ray and Amber had turned to each other for comfort. It was the singular mistake of his adult life. It should not have happened. She had been only seventeen, while he had been a twenty-seven-year-old man. It was true that she was preparing to leave for college in a few short weeks. Yet that did not change the fact that she was not even eighteen years old.

The bite of the cold wind brought him back to the present. What was he running from? The truth? There was no excuse for his behavior. He had violated not only Brad's trust in him but her parents' as well. He had not forgiven himself for that night, not even in all the years that followed.

The simple truth was, he had lost his head for the first time in his adult life, and he had done it in the arms of an inexperienced teenage girl. Because of his selfishness, he had come a hair's width away from ruining both their lives.

Amber called unhappily, "When are you going to forgive yourself? When are you going to forgive me?" Tears glistened in her lashes.

Ray heard them in her voice. He swore expansively, then hurried back to haul her into his arms. His chin rested against her forehead. "You're wrong. You were blameless. None of it was your fault."

"You didn't rape me."

"Damn near," he grated, recalling the raging force of his desire.

"We were in love." She stepped back so that she could see his face. "We were!" There was desperation in her voice as she fought to make him remember it all, and finally, hopefully . . . accept.

He knew exactly what he had been doing. She had no resistance against his sexual persuasion. He knew how to pleasure a woman . . . knew how to make her wet, eager for his lovemaking. What chance did a seventeen-year-old girl have against his hot male need?

"I'm so tired of being on that stupid pedestal you insist

on placing me on. I knew what was happening between us that night. I wanted it. I wanted you.''

"I had no business touching you. I didn't even have the decency make sure you were protected. You weren't even eighteen, Amber. You were barely out of high school! Oh, hell! I don't want to talk about this. Let it go, Amber. It's best to leave it buried in the past.'' He took her hand this time and pulled her along with him.

His stride was long, determined, and reckless on the icy ground. He stumbled over a snow-covered root. Amber's arms went around his waist in an attempt to steady him. They both went down.

A sharp twist of his body caused her to land on top of him thus cushioning her fall. His efforts may have saved her, but unfortunately he received the full impact of the fall. Pain shot like a searing poker across his midsection. He gasped, unable to swallow the sound.

Amber raised her head from were it rested on his muscular shoulder. "Honey?" Turning in his arms, she ran her hands over his body, her fingers touched the exposed skin of his neck, his lean hollow cheeks in an anxious caress. She asked, "Are you hurt, sweetheart?"

A grunt was his response as he fought to catch his breath.

"Ray! Talk to me. Should I call the doctor?" Amber was frantically raining quick kisses on his lean cheeks and neck.

"I'm fine," he managed tightly as her mouth brushed too close to his. "How about you? Were you hurt?"

"Don't worry about me. I wasn't shot up a few weeks ago. You don't sound fine to me. You were doing so well and now this. Please, let me take you inside. I just hope you haven't really hurt yourself."

She wiggled against him, trying to get up. "Ray?" she questioned, when his arms tightened around her.

"Be still for a second. Let me catch my breath."

"I knew it, you're hurt! If you hadn't lost your stupid temper, then none of this would have happened. You'd be—"

"Shush," he whispered, his mouth close to her ear, his

breath warmed her cheek, her throat. The pain was leaving, but in its place was a rush of exquisite yearning.

The softness of her breasts on his chest, the slender length of her thigh between his, sent flames of uncensored desire throughout his system, insulating him from the cold and dampness seeping through his clothing. The need to possess and claim dominated his senses. Apparently seeing her with another man had unlocked the door he'd kept bolted. He couldn't hide the prominent ridge of his erection against her stomach.

Ray slackened his hold on her, but he did not free her. Instead he clasped her by the waist and slid her up so that he could reach the delectible temptation of her beautiful mouth. Suddenly his need for her was all that seemed to matter. He had to taste her fully or die from the longing.

When she welcomed him, her lips opening under his, Ray took what he had denied himself for so long. There was no hesitation on his part. He ground his mouth against her soft full lips, his tongue thrust hotly in her mouth over and over again. He ravished her, savoring the sweetness that was hers alone. No other woman had ever tasted as good as Amber or felt so right in his arms. She belonged to him. He loved her . . . needed her.

Amber was molded possessively along his length. Her full breasts were pillowed on his broad chest, her mound bare inches from his aching arousal. As she inhaled his male scent, she trembled with the sweet pleasure of being back in his arms. The heady wonder of once again experiencing his blatant masculine appeal left her breathless with anticipation.

Yes . . . oh, yes, this was what she had waited an eternity for . . . what she had been created for . . . to love him and in turn be loved by him. The passage of time nor distance could not alter what they felt for each other.

As unexpectedly as the kiss had started, it ended. Ray tore his mouth from hers. He sat up then, wrenching with pain, but bringing her with him.

"I must be losing my mind," he mumbled to himself as

he eased her away so that he could rise. "Why did you let me do that?"

"Let you?" Amber said when she finally found her voice. She ignored the hand he held down to her.

"It was a stupid thing to do," he snapped, holding his side.

Amber sat where he had left her, having relished each moment spent in his arms but detesting his resentment. "The only stupid one around here is you, Ray Coleman. You're a stubborn mule! Once you make up your mind, nothing on God's green earth is going to make you change it," she yelled at him. On her feet now, she encircled his lean middle. "Can you walk?"

Ray nodded. He was exhausted and he did not have the strength to pretend otherwise. Their steps were slow, and they paused often allowing him to rest. The stairs were a bit of a problem. Ray moaned with relief when he was able to lower himself onto the sofa.

"Thanks." He tried to smile as Amber helped him remove his boots.

"You should get out of those wet clothes, take a hot shower, and then get into bed."

"Don't fuss, it's only a little after eleven. Besides, I couldn't sleep if I tried." Eyeing her wearily, he insisted, "I want this conversation finished tonight. Then we can both forget it ever took place."

"Mule!" She went into the kitchen, knowing better than to ask if he would see the doctor.

Once she had the percolator started, she went into her own room to change. She was relieved to hear the shower going in the bathroom. For once, Ray had taken her advice.

Her heart ached with grief, and her thoughts were so tangled with disappointment and bittersweet memories from the past. She knew he was right. It was probably best that they finish it tonight. He would not be the only one spending what was left of this night awake. So instead of putting on a clean nightgown, she changed into a pair of gold silk lounging pajamas.

When Amber came back into the living room, Ray was stretched out on the sofa, with his eyes closed. He had changed into close-fitting jeans and a burgundy silk shirt left open almost to the middle of his hair-covered brown chest. His long muscled thighs and bare feet were propped up on the sofa. Flames licked and danced playfully around the logs in the grate.

She carried in two steaming mugs. "Don't move. I'll take the other one," she said, when he would have swung his feet down from the sofa. She paused to hand him a cup. "Did you take anything for the pain?"

"Yeah."

His dark eyes heated, despite his ill humor, as he studied her golden beauty. Amber was his weakness. She alone could penetrate his defense, bring forth the wealth of emotions he had trained himself to keep under lock and key. That kiss should never have happened. For a few wonderful seconds, he had forgotten everything . . . the promise he had made to himself . . . the promise he had made her when she had let him back into her life.

After watching her all evening, desire had consumed him and combined with jealousy. The combination was worse than a narcotic. It blinded . . . it controlled . . . it destroyed. Unfortunately there was nothing he could do about the brief lapse other than try to forget and pretend it never happened. He comforted himself with the realization that she and Wilham were not lovers . . . yet.

Thankful that his equilibrium was once again firmly in place, Ray said, "The one thing I especially like about this part of the country is that there is almost always an excuse to have a fire."

She was curled on the opposite sofa, her legs under her. The grandfather clock chimed softly in the corner, while flames licked at the disintegrating logs in the grate.

Silence hung heavy between them. He could not fail to read the unhappiness in her eyes. He felt it, too. The painful memories that had been dredged up earlier were impossible to ignore. Neither of them needed a reminder of how they had managed to nearly destroy each other. Twelve years was a long time, but it evidently wasn't long enough.

She watched as he swung his long legs down, then added more logs to the fire.

Ray's inner turmoil was not on his face but in his brooding dark eyes. Finally, he said, his voice gruff from the rawness of his emotions, "You're angry with me, aren't you."

She shook her head but could not meet his gaze. "Would you care for another cup of coffee?"

"What I would care for is to know why you won't look at me. Was it the kiss?"

"That kiss has nothing to do with it. You know why I'm upset. What's the point in getting into it again? You won't talk to me about it. Frankly, I'm about fed up with pretending it didn't happen."

Neither of them said anything for a time. Ray was the one to break the silence. "Remembering won't serve any purpose other than reminding us both of the degree of selfishness and thoughtlessness I'm capable of. I don't want to think about it, and I especially don't want to talk about it," he ended dryly. "Can't we talk about something else . . . anything? Spring is late this year. I'd always assumed—"

"Stop it! Not once in all these years have we talked about this. Oh, what's the use!" She turned her head away for a moment in the hopes of composing herself. When she spoke again her voice was so faint that he could barely hear her. "Why can't you see how important this is to me? Ray, it hurts. It hurts knowing you would rather go through life pretending we didn't make a baby together."

Chapter Eight

"I'm not talking about blame, Ray. That baby meant the world to me, while you prefer to forget that I carried your child for nearly five months. I wanted our baby, Ray . . . I wanted it from the very beginning. Losing it was . . . horrible." Tears pooled in her eyes, but she brushed them aside impatiently.

Ray hurt, every bit as much as Amber did. Yet they had never been able to reach out to each other . . . comfort one another. The loss had been too great then as it was now.

They stared at each other, each afraid to move or to speak. The sound of a log falling, then settling among the flickering embers, caused them to jump, then look hastily away.

"Just because I don't think it's a great idea to drag up the past doesn't mean I can ever forget what happened. I cared, Amber. By the time I found out about the baby, it was over. You hated me, and I hated myself."

She had pushed him out of her life. They remained estranged for seven long painful years. It took a catastrophe—her parents' death—to bring them back together.

The sadness and grief continued to separate them as effectively as it had twelve years ago. Amber had kept it inside for too long. She knew she needed to talk about it, and she especially needed to talk to Ray about it. She longed to share it with him. Then maybe it would finally go away, and they both could get on with the rest of their lives.

While Amber bit her lips, staring at her tightly clasped hands, Ray stared with apparent fascination at the cooling liquid in his cup.

"I'm sorry, Ray. I was wrong to blame you for what happened," she whispered, trying to swallow the lump in her throat. "I've never stopped feeling guilty for pushing you out of my life the way I did. I was wrong. Please try to understand, I hurt so badly."

His voice was heavy with grief when he said, "You had every reason to blame me. I got you pregnant at the ripe old age of seventeen, then left you alone to cope with your parents and the loss of our child."

When he at long last looked at her he saw a quiet stream of tears trail down her soft brown cheeks. "No, angel. Please . . . don't." He felt the same bitter grief when he thought of what they'd lost, what they could never replace.

"I'm sorry," she choked out. "I wanted the baby. I wanted her so much," she sobbed.

Ray's head shot up with shock. A daughter . . . he had never known. He found the knowing made it that much more real, that much more painful.

"Amber . . ." His voice was raw with emotion.

She didn't ask for what she needed from him, but he gave it to her wholeheartedly. Ray rose and came to sit beside her, he took her into the muscular strength of his arms. Her head rested on his chest, close to his heart, as she sobbed out the anguish that they both felt so acutely.

As he rocked her, he whispered his own despair and grief of that precious loss. He wasn't aware of the moisture that filled his eyes, but Amber felt the dampness and knew. That knowledge soothed the wound deep inside. It made all the difference in the world knowing he also cared. Eventually she was able to compose herself, and she smiled at him.

"Thank you," she said quietly.

He nodded, not knowing what else to say or do. He was surprised at how much better he felt. Not that he could ever forgive himself or forget his part in it.

"Excuse me," she said. "I'll make fresh coffee."

Although he wasn't ready to let her go, nevertheless he dropped his arms. "Make it hot chocolate, or neither one of us will get any sleep."

Ray followed her into the kitchen, leaning against the counter, quietly watching her. He finally voiced what had been eating away at him for years. "What I still can't understand is why you never told your parents it was me. Why didn't you want them to know I fathered the child?"

"I couldn't! Oh, Ray, why hurt them? They loved you so much. It just wasn't necessary to tell them. I was away at college when I realized I was pregnant. It wasn't difficult to make excuses for not coming home. My parents didn't even know until the night I was rushed to the hospital . . . the night I miscarried."

As usual Ray had been overseas on assignment, and Amber resented him for not being there for her when she needed him the most. It wasn't until he was close to leaving South Africa that he realized there was a problem. Amber's refusal to even take his calls forced him to contact her parents.

"I'll never forget the shock I received when I spoke to your dad that day and he told me your news. I tried to tell him then, but I couldn't . . . I just couldn't." His voice was laced with despair and guilt, both familiar aches that had settled in his heart.

After that time whenever he visited the Spencers, Amber was conveniently absent, either away at school or away visiting with friends. Her parents never knew the truth. He often asked himself why couldn't he tell them. He always came back with the same answer: how could he when they treated him as if he were a part of their family.

"I'll take that," he said, gesturing toward the tray.

Once they were comfortably seated again on opposite sofas, Amber surprised him by saying, "I'm glad you never told them. What good would it have done? It took seven years for me to forgive you, and my parents' death, to bring us back together again." She longed to go to him, touch him, caress the fullness of his bottom lip beneath the fall of his thick mustache with her lips. She hungered for the taste of him as she ached to take his lip into her mouth and suckle. Yet Amber didn't move, knowing beyond doubt that he would not welcome her kisses.

The wind howled outside the window, rattling the panes, the fire crackled with life while the grandfather clock chimed loudly from the corner.

He looked at her intently. "When your folks died and you turned to me, I didn't question my good fortune. I was too grateful to be back in your life. Not once have you indicated a need to discuss that time or our estrangement following it. Why now? Why tonight?"

She swallowed, then said, "When I needed you after I lost Mother and Daddy ... you were there beside me through it all. You'll never know how much that meant to me. We've come full circle, Ray." She smiled at him. "I've grow up along the way. I can deal with the past, even the mistakes and the pain. You were not the only one who made mistakes. I made more than my share of them. And tonight ..."

"Yeah," he prompted, sensing there was more.

"Mind if I sit next to you?"

He hid his sudden amusement, instead patted the cushion next to him. He could see that she was nervous as she sank down beside him. He could have easily assured her that he would give her anything she wanted. He wasn't in the habit of denying her.

Normally he was a patient man, but around Amber his emotions were never predictable. Like that kiss outside.

The man in him was hungry for the woman in her. He had not planned on kissing her. Hadn't even suspected that his anger with the other man would make him suddenly possessive of Amber. He had no more rights to her than Wilham, probably less after the way he had hurt her in the past.

"Ray, I want something more. Something I'm not sure you're willing to give." She squeezed his hand where it rested between them on the cushion. "It's up to you."

"Anything," he promised rashly, tenderly brushing his mouth against her temple. Yes, he had changed. Although their kiss tonight had disturbed him, he nevertheless prided himself on the fact that he hadn't completely lost control. Not once since that fateful night twelve years ago had he unleashed the hunger he knew he had for her alone. He worked at keeping it hidden.

That hunger was the reason he'd seen so little of her over the years. Controlling the raw need was paramount to their continued friendship. That friendship meant the world to him. He wouldn't ever willing do anything to jeopardize it.

Amber laughed, a light tinkling sound that seemed to work its way into his very soul. Dear God in heaven, how he loved this woman . . . how he needed her in his life.

"A bit reckless, don't you think?" she teased, in spite of the fear languishing within her.

"Where you're concerned, I'm not exactly objective."

"I might want a cool million." She pressed a finger playfully into the cleft at the center of his deeply shadowed jaw. He needed a shave. The knowledge only heightened her feminine awareness of his blatant masculinity.

If only she were free to run her hands over his cheeks, along his throat, down his chest. She ached with a sweet need to feel the warm caress of his late-night beard against her bare skin over her achingly full breasts. Not for an instant had she forgotten the pleasure she'd found waking the other morning in his bed. Her head spun dizzily as his masculine scent filled her nostrils.

"I might not be the heir to the Spencer fortunes like you are, but I'm not doing too badly." He played along with her, even though his eyes searched hers. Was there a reason for this hell she had been putting them through tonight? He wanted to get to the bottom of it. "Stop stalling. What do you want?"

"You . . ." She watched a wealth of emotions fly across his bluntly carved African features. "I want us to be lovers again. I'm not seventeen anymore. I'm a grown woman with a woman's needs."

She wanted more kisses like the one he had given her outside. That kiss was different than any he had ever given her. The ones he had given the night they had made love were gentle, sweet in their tenderness as he took her virginity with slow expertise. He never faltered in his effort to consider her innocence and the need to take care.

What they had shared tonight on the cold icy ground was raw, potent with masculine need, hot and spicy with adult hunger. For the first time, Ray had held none of himself back. She tasted the essence and the power of the man. His mouth had practically devoured her while he rubbed the thick ridge of his sex against her mound. Shivers of desire raced down her spine even now as she recalled the excitement of being in his arms. She wanted that and more.

She had apparently given the matter a great deal of thought, Ray decided, as he pushed himself up and away from her. His flesh seemed to burn from where they'd touched. He struggled to ignore the way her full breasts lifted and fell with every breath she took.

His hands flexed, opening and closing as his thoughts filled with the image of her softness cupped in his palms, his fingertips stroking her large nipples. They were dark and plump like sweet berries—he didn't need to close his eyes to remember how they felt in his mouth, against his tongue. He had licked them, licked her until she lay gasping and trembling in his arms. Twelve long years and he hadn't forgotten what it felt like to be with her or to be buried to the hilt inside her body. She had been only a girl then. She was all woman now.

He didn't need to look at her to know there were physical differences. His iron control prevented him from allowing himself to wonder about those differences, let alone discover for himself those womanly needs she spoke about. He was already hot enough and hard enough to thoroughly enjoy the sizzling discovery. She had felt so good in his arms earlier tonight . . . so right. Her body fit his perfectly. She had tasted even better than he remembered. He wanted more. He was forced to remind himself that he controlled his body with his mind. His body did not control him.

"Don't say no until you've thought about it, please."

Lacing unsteady hands together in her lap, Amber's features were composed, but her heart was beating so loudly in her ear that she felt as if she were involved in a long distance marathon.

He went to the side table and poured himself a measure of scotch from one of the crystal decanters. He downed it in one gulp, enjoying the rush of heat to his belly. It matched the flames in his groin. The mere suggestion of making love to Amber was enough to keep him erect.

"Ray—"

"Ask Wilham, I'm sure he'll be thrilled to oblige," he sneered.

"That's not how you felt earlier. Besides, I don't love Elliott. I've already told you that I never even considered sleeping with him."

Ray would have chuckled, but for the life of him he couldn't find a damn thing funny about any of this. "I take it this offer doesn't include marriage?"

She nodded, her face flushed with embarrassment. She wanted marriage, but she wasn't about to do the asking.

"Amber, why? Why the need for change? Besides the possible destruction to our friendship, have you forgotten the risks I take day in day out? You know you can't handle that. I know I can't leave you not knowing if I've made you pregnant again. We both know that one day I might not come back.''

She shuddered as the image of her brother flashed through her mind. A young vital man cut down before his prime. She had not forgotten how close Ray had come to death this last time. She could never forget.

"I care about you. That's what's important. Nothing else matters,'' she insisted.

"In this case it's not enough.''

"I can handle the danger. I've lived with it for the past five years, haven't I?''

He shook his head. "It won't be the same. It will be much much worse if we become lovers.''

"Ray—''

"No, I don't believe you. You can't make me believe that you are strong enough to go through that kind of torment. Are you forgetting I love you? I won't willingly put you through it.'' He had seen the devastation she had suffered when Brad had been killed. How could he deliberately put her through that again and again? Each time he left on an assignment, she would be forced to wonder if this would be his last. The deeper the emotional bond, the deeper the fear.

"You said anything,'' she reminded him.

"You were right. I was being reckless.'' His hands trembled uncontrollably, forcing him to shove them into his jeans pockets. He wanted nothing more than to make love to her, over and over again until he could drown in her sweetness. He wanted to make her wet with need for him. And he wanted to take her with long and hard strokes, put a serious loving on her until she came apart in his arms, screaming his name in release.

Yet he knew he loved her too much to recklessly make love to her and then leave her alone to worry while he lost himself in his work. He had left her alone once to face a pregnancy alone. He was not about to make that same mistake twice. If necessary, he would protect her against himself, no matter what the cost to his own happiness.

"Ray, please, sit. Let's talk about this rationally."

He closed his eyes for a few seconds, hoping to find the calm within the raging sea of his emotions. He was a practical man, even somewhat pragmatic. He wasn't prone to rash behavior or thoughtlessness. So why did the thought of making love to Amber leave him weak with longing?

"Please."

"Okay." He sank back down, letting his head rest against the back cushions. "I'm listening." His neck was a knot of tension while he was aroused to the point of pain. All she had to do was look down and know a truth that he could not conceal.

"I have no way of proving that I can handle your job. Please, give me the chance. Don't I deserve that much?"

"Amber, be reasonable! Things have worked well for us. We see each other as often as we can manage. We're an important part of each other's lives. Why try and change a good thing? If we became lovers, there would always be the possibility of another pregnancy. I don't have to tell you that protection is not always foolproof."

He'd seen too many broken relationship and marriages among his colleagues. Men and women constantly torn between the demands of the job and needs of the family. Some broke under the strain, eventually they were all forced to make a choice: the job or family.

For years he'd tried to protect Amber from the potential danger inherent in his work. He did what he did out of a sense of duty, of rightness. In the process he willingly sacrificed having a home, a family, even love.

His life was a lonely one, but it had purpose, direction—his work was important to him. After this book there would be the possibility of a documentary and another book deal. His first book had hit the best-seller list with a vengeance. People had been moved by his pictures, touched by his commentary. His publisher had hinted that he might want to explore the political situation in Bosnia. It could mean months away from home, away from Amber.

Would it have been different if they hadn't lost their

daughter? Or if Brad had returned any other way than in a pine box? There were too many ifs. It was too late for him to change.

He couldn't become his sister's brother again, no matter how often she bombarded him with letters or phone calls since the release of his first book. Before his fame, as far as she was concerned, he'd been persona non grata.

He stared into the fire, his chest brimming with regret. He loved Amber, and because of his love he could not risk bringing her any further into his world. They had to maintain a certain measure of emotional distance between them.

Eventually he said, "I'm trying to be as honest and open with you as I know how. You felt my erection earlier. I'd be lying if I tried to pretend I don't want you, but the bottom line is you deserve better than I'm able to give."

Amber blinked back tears. Ray was the man she wanted, he was the one she loved. No one else made her feel the way he did. No one else filled her heart to the point of bursting.

"Is there someone else?" she whispered.

"What?"

"Are you involved with another woman?"

"What a thing to ask!"

Pent-up air rushed from her lungs as she concentrated on breathing normally. She had wondered for so long . . . frankly she had always been too afraid of his answer to ask the question. Now was not the time to get cold feet. She needed an answer.

"You're a healthy male. It would be terribly naive of me to assume you weren't physically and/or emotionally involved with a woman."

"I am not involved sexually with anyone."

He didn't need Amber to remind him of his potency. Sex was a physical necessity. It normally occupied a small portion of his thoughts. In the past when the urge came, he found a woman, just as he ate to appease his hunger. She didn't need to know that he hadn't wanted sex with another women in a very long time. He had chosen to remain celibate. Sex for its own sake alone had lost its appeal. Love was a different issue. Love was what he felt for Amber, and it encompassed all that he was and reached his very core.

"But you're turning me down. Pardon me for being stupid, but in my book that means you don't desire me sexually."

Golden brown eyes locked with dark brown ones. Ray was the first to look away, unable to bear her disappointment.

"You're wrong."

"You see our lovemaking as nothing more than a mistake. Maybe I happened to be convenient that first time. What about tonight, Ray?"

Blood pounded violently in his veins as his heavy shaft throbbed in anticipation.

"You weren't convenient, angel. I wanted you." That was all he could manage. A dozen years wasn't enough to dull the memory of that incredible pleasure she gave him. A lifetime was not enough time. His voice was rough with impatience. "Why are we still discussing this? You know how I feel and why."

Her voice was so soft he could barely hear, when she said, "Would it matter to know I haven't made love with another man? Our single night all those years ago was the one and only time I couldn't say no." Amber had no pride when it came to Ray. She loved him too much.

"I wish you hadn't said that." His voice was ragged with need.

"Why? It's true."

He couldn't remain near her a second longer without contradicting his beliefs. He went over to the mantel, stood with his back to her, then finally he forced himself to say, "One day the right guy will come along. You'll be glad you waited. You can have it all . . . career, home, marriage, and family."

"You are the one who doesn't understand, Ray. This was no hasty decision on my part. I've thought about it for a long time. I think it was the scare of almost losing you that prompted me to finally talk to you about it. There is no other man for me. I know you're going to leave again. I can live with that. I have my work, also."

Ray yearned to crush her against his chest, give her anything she wanted. She was making it so hard for him to fight her . . . fight his feelings. All he could think of was making love to her. Ray shuddered, wondering how he could fight her and himself, too. It was too damn much.

"No," he whispered, his voice gruff. He poked at a log with unnecessary force before he finally turned and said in a voice tight with emotion, "I do love you, but I can't make love to you. I promised myself when I came back into your life that I would never hurt you again." He left the room then, without a backward glance.

Tears of disappointment and hopelessness threatened to spill, but Amber held them back. They remained deep inside of her . . . unheard, unshed as she sat staring into the dying embers, her heart breaking.

Chapter Nine

In spite of the sharp stinging bite of the northern wind pouring in off the lake, sweat dampened Ray's upper body as he swung the ax with rhythmic ease. He wore a down-filled vest over a navy flannel shirt and corded jeans.

The blade splintered the pine log into even pieces. The pile of neatly stacked firewood continued to grow. As one week moved into another, he spent less time indoors resting. He started the day with a hard run through the woods, up and down the hills, and included a vigorous workout. He was determined to regain his strength. His days were full with working on his book, as well as doing odd jobs around the school.

He needed the diversion, especially after that late night discussion he'd had with Amber. He told himself physical labor was good for his spirit, but the truth was it allowed him to sleep when his increasing hunger for Amber would have otherwise kept him awake . . . hard and aching for what he told himself wasn't his.

Perhaps it was time he moved on. Leave while he could—before either of them ended up hurt even more than they already were. He'd stayed close to a month. Time enough for his wounds to heal—time enough to further complicate a complex situation.

"Hi!" Jason waved, his voice carried across the open field.

"You're early. Didn't skip school this afternoon, did you?" Ray lifted a brow, glancing at the gold watch strapped to his wrist.

Jason laughed with boyish glee. "No way. Ma would skin me. We had a half day. Teachers have a meeting this afternoon. Lucky, huh?"

Ray's craggy brown face creased into a rare smile. If their little girl had made it, she would be close to Jason's age now. The realization hurt. No matter how much time had passed, he still yearned for what might have been. They would truly have been a family. Ray's heart ached with regret.

"Can I help?" the boy asked, like a lively puppy, eager to please.

"Sure—that is, if the ladies don't need you inside."

"I'm done with my chores. Earned an extra five bucks, too, for cleaning out the pantry behind the kitchen. That's one job I don't mind. Mrs. Westmore thinks I'm too thin. She makes the best chocolate chip cookies in the state. Want one?" He reached into his pocket and offered one of the carefully wrapped treats.

"Thanks," Ray said, warmed by the youngster's smile. "Hmm, this is good."

They worked well together—Ray chopping, Jason stacking the logs against the outside of the toolshed. Ray found the boy's chatter refreshing. Alex Baldwin was indeed a lucky man. He was blessed with a warm and lively wife, as well as a son with so much life and intelligence that any man would be proud to call him his own. What more could a man hope to gain in this world?

Ray's thoughts flew back to the time when he had a family. His older sister, Catherine, had always been wrapped up in the glamorous world of fashion, pouring over fashion and movie magazines for hours, lost in dreams of one day becoming a world-famous model. Ray had also been full of hope, bursting with dreams of a bright future in journalism.

Ray had been only a few years older than Jason when his folks were killed in a car accident, victims of a drunk driver. Ray's world shifted dramatically. At eighteen, Catherine was more interested in following her own dreams rather than keeping what remained of their family together. She left Ray to the mercy of the foster care system. In so doing, she had cut all family ties to him for a lifetime. It had hurt like hell, but he had gotten over it and gone on with his life.

Ray was unable to tolerate the poor substitutes that were meant to replace the loving home he had once known. He had a tough couple of years, but he had managed to stay in school and out of trouble. Even now he missed his mother's gentleness and love. Mostly he missed the talks he had with his dad. There had been doubts, fears of inadequacy, that he had been unable share with anyone else. His parents' faith in him and their unshakable belief in education had been what had kept Ray in school even after they were gone.

His share of their insurance money, plus loans and odd jobs, had paid for his college education. His parents' loving support and belief in him was still a part of him. He carried it deep inside.

As he listened to Jason's monologue on the wonders of weight lifting, Ray recognized the boy's anxiety. Jason was small for his age and worried because he hadn't reached the height and weight of the other boys in his class.

"Do you think you can come into town with me someday? I'd really like to know what you think of the starter set I want to buy. Dad says I should wait awhile."

"I was smaller than you are now when I was your age." Ray hid a smile at the disbelief on the boy's handsome brown face. Jason eyed the powerful, distinctive muscles along Ray's shoulders and forearms.

"You're just saying that to make me feel better."

Ray shrugged. "The thought had crossed my mind, but I'm afraid it's the truth."

"How?"

With one booted foot propped on the tree stump, Ray leaned on an upraised knee. "Time. Now don't get me wrong, I enjoy a hard run and work out regularly. If I were you, I'd give it some time."

"What you're saying is that my dad is right." Jason didn't seem pleased.

"Yeah. Keep saving your money. By the time you have enough, you will have picked up some weight and might be further along than you think."

Jason grinned suddenly, nodding vigorously. "Okay. I figure I won't have enough saved until next year anyway."

Ray smiled, lifting the ax once more.

"I'd better get going. I promised Ma I'd pick up some lamb chops for dinner tonight. Or was it pork chops? Gee, now I've got to go back and ask her. I'd better get moving. See ya, Mr. Coleman."

"Ray," he said with a wave.

Despite the soreness in his midsection, Ray went back to work. He was out of shape. Soon he'd be leaving, finishing his work in the Middle East. Surprisingly he wasn't looking forward to getting back to work—for it would mean he had to leave Amber. That was something he didn't want to do.

He relished waking to see her cheery smile and sunny disposition each morning across the breakfast table. She brought joy to his days. He enjoyed talking to her or even listening to her. Ray couldn't think of anything he wanted more than simply being with her, except her sweet, sweet kisses and her unbelievably tight feminine heat.

Harris was furious. He'd trusted her! He'd thought she was different. Stupid! She'd betrayed him. Betrayed him just like the other beautiful bitch. She even looked a little like her. He should have know she wasn't to be trusted.

Yeah, she even looked a little like the other. They said she had been hit by a car. But he knew better. The whore had disappeared with some guy and left him with Ben. He'd fix her! He'd fix them both!

"Oops," Jason said, catching himself just in the nick of time from plowing into the kneeling man. "Sorry."

Harris slid the slender blade he'd been cradling in his hand down in his boot. He straightened from his position beside the colorfully painted bus.

"Hey, kid. What you doing here so early? Skip school?" Harris laughed, grinning at the youth, his pale blue eyes slowly running over the boy's small frame, lingering on his thighs.

Jason bristled. He didn't like Harris. There was something about him that made him uneasy. Nonetheless, he answered politely, "We didn't have school this afternoon."

"Where you going in such hurry?"

"I'm on my way into town. I have an errand to do for my mom."

"Long walk," Harris said. His smile widened as he switched a wad of gum from one side of his mouth to the other.

Jason shrugged. "I've got my bike." His ten-speed was propped against the side of the house. "Won't take long. Besides, Dad says the pumping will build up my calf muscles."

"I'm on my way into town. Want a lift on my bike?" Harris referred to his powerful motorcycle. "Bet you never had a ride on a Harley."

Ray worked until his arms trembled with fatigue and his side burned from the strain. Stopping to wipe the sweat out of his eyes, he looked toward the house. His thoughts were never far from the woman inside.

He'd worked hard at pretending they hadn't spoken openly about the past. That was something they had purposefully avoided in all the years they had been back together. He'd been forced to explore his own feelings of failure and disappointment he'd firmly believed were best forgotten, buried along with the crushed hopes of a shared future.

Since that night over a week ago, he'd gone over it again and again. He always came back to the glaring truth. No matter how hard he tried, he couldn't make himself stop wanting Amber. Long ago he had accepted that he needed her in his life, and he would never do anything to jeopardize what they had. Yet the knowledge that she wanted his lovemaking was agonizingly sweet. Ray's lips curled in self-mockery as he clearly recognized the wild sense of masculine joy that lingered within him because of it.

Damn it all—he was only human. For years there had been only one way for him to stay in her life. He had perfected the role of protector and close friend. Long ago he had reconciled himself to the limitations of their relationship. He survived by not allowing himself to dwell on his masculine needs.

There was a time in the beginning that he found he had to have a woman on occasion. Not any longer. He had been on an incredibly long dry spell with no end in sight. He hated celibacy. His normal sex drive was too high for him to welcome doing without. He discovered that he preferred to do without because he couldn't have the only woman he longed for. Amber had only to enter a room, and he reacted like a horny teenager. His sex would harden, demanding he put an end to this misery.

Suddenly she was telling him she had changed her mind. He could have her, could take her beneath him and bury himself deep inside her wet sheath. How in the hell had he managed to resist? Where had the determination come from when the need was so raw and his penis so unyieldingly hard?

He felt as if he were going crazy from wanting her. He was tired of being semi-erect all day long and fully erect during the night. The continuous ache was getting to him, weakening his resolve.

Did she honestly think that once the deed was done they could return to their old arrangement? He was a man! She couldn't have taken the nature of the beast into consideration, or she wouldn't have suggested such a thing. He was naturally aggressive, ruthless, and possessive. He would have to have her with him, not thousands of miles away in this sleepy college town. She was talking about a new kind of hell, couldn't she see that? It was better this way . . . better for both of them—for at least in Shelly she was safe.

Suddenly Ray's eyes gleamed with unexpected amusement. For all her soft ways and tender heart, Amber was just as strong willed and opinionated as he was. She was too independent, too intent on making her own way in this world to need a man. So far she'd done a fine job on her own. Apparently she found herself wanting something only a man could give her. She wanted him to do the giving.

"It isn't that simple!" he snapped, heading for the shed to lock the ax away from curious little hands. He loaded a canvas sling with wood, determined to ignore the way his body reacted when he thought of thrusting himself deep inside of her, his hands filled to overflowing with her breasts. Night after night he tormented himself with such blatant sexual thoughts of their lovemaking, trying not to remember, yet unable to stop himself.

What he felt for her now was so much deeper. He hungered for the mature woman she had blossomed into. He longed to know all her feminine secrets.

He was at the side door when he spotted a slim man crossing the road. John! Instead of entering, Ray put down the load against the house and headed down the drive.

John McClure paused on the walk, his sharp eyes taking in the jean-clad figure. He smiled. "Ray? I'll be damned. You look great!"

"Thanks. How are you?"

"Great! You gave us quite a scare. Sorry I couldn't get down to see you while you were in the hospital."

Ray shook the extended hand. "No problem. Brenda came. I appreciated it." John and Brenda McClure had often had Ray over for a meal when he was in town. Ray and John had met while working on the same case several years back, from different angles naturally.

"What are you doing in Shelly?"

"Visiting a friend of the family." Ray's dark eyes scanned the other's neat pinstriped suit and navy topcoat. "I could ask you the same. But it's obvious—you're here on business, unless you and Brenda suddenly tired of Arlington and decided to move the family into the country."

"Afraid not. This is business."

"What could be of interest to the Bureau in this nursery school?"

"Who's the friend?" John countered.

"Amber Spencer. She's the owner." Ray frowned. "What gives?"

John sighed. He knew Ray wasn't going to like this. "The lady may have a problem on her hands." John went on to explain his reason for being there in rapid detail.

Ray swore expressively.

John raised a brow but didn't satisfy his own curiosity about the exact nature of the friendship. He'd known Ray well enough to realize there was a special woman in his life, and she wasn't open for discussion. The question was, was it Amber Spencer? Instead John said, "It's great to see you on your feet, man. You were damn lucky."

"It was tough going for a while."

"When are you going back in?" Both men dedicated to their work knew it was not a question of if but a question of when.

"In a few more weeks, I should be back to normal and out of here. Come on in, I'll introduce you to Amber."

"Nice setup," John commented as they crossed the wide entrance hallway.

The busy hum of childish laughter and activity was everywhere. "The only time it's quiet is when the kids are down for their naps after lunch. Amber could be anywhere."

Ray poked his head into first the nursery and then the various classrooms. They were nearing the music room when a youngster came barreling out, smack into Ray's legs.

The little girl was screeching at the top of her lungs. Her rosy brown cheeks were streaked with tears.

"Hey, what's the hurry, little one?" Ray asked when the chubby little girl refused to let go of his legs.

Ginger was right behind her. "Ray," she sighed. "Thanks. I don't know how Becky managed to get to the door without me seeing her."

Ray chuckled, bending over to lift the sobbing child up against his shoulder. "Have you seen Amber?"

"She's in her office for a change," Ginger said with a smile, sending a curious glance to the other man.

"Ginger Adams, an old friend, John McClure."

While the two exchanged pleasantries, Ray took a clean handkerchief from his back pocket and coaxed the little girl into letting him wipe her face. Although she'd quieted somewhat with a small thumb firmly planted in her mouth, she refused to move from her perch against Ray's shoulder.

"Don't you want to go inside with Mrs. Adams?"

"Wanna go home," Becky insisted petulantly.

John looked on in amusement.

"Becky's angry with me because she didn't have a second turn to play the drum," Ginger explained patiently.

Ray nodded. "Becky, if you go back inside, Mrs. Adams might let you have another turn. Would you like that?"

Becky's large brown eyes moved from the big man to her teacher. Finally she nodded her head, long braids bobbed around her shoulder. Ray handed her over.

"Thanks." Ginger waved, going back into the room.

As the two men walked on, John shook his head. "Cute kid."

"The place is full of them," Ray said dryly.

"Yeah, that's what I'm afraid of."

Chapter Ten

From where Amber stood at the wide window, she had an excellent view of the lake. Goose pimples beaded her arms. She ran her hands up and down the sleeves of the magenta cashmere sweater she'd teamed with cream wool slacks that morning. She wasn't really cold. Her thoughts kept returning to the unpleasant interview she had with Harris earlier that afternoon. Amber told herself that Harris should be the least of her worries.

It was Ray who was the real problem. Ray was the one who hadn't budged from his refusal the night of the cocktail party. Amber was beginning to despair that he ever would. Night after night she would lie awake hoping, praying he'd come to her. He never did. Nor had she gone to him.

It wasn't that she thought of herself as a coward. She felt as if she were woman enough to tempt him. But that was not how she wanted it to be. She wanted the decision to be his alone, without any coercion on her part.

She must find a way of making him understand how much this meant to her. This wasn't a rash decision on her part. Perhaps she hadn't explained it to him clearly enough. Maybe she had become too emotional. Was that why she'd failed to convince him? The way things stood between them now, the issue wasn't even open for discussion.

Time had become her enemy. With each passing day, he regained more of his strength. Soon he would pronounce himself fit and able to leave.

The knock on the open door broke into her thoughts. She half turned toward the sound. Her eyes lit with pleasure as she took in his strong, distinctly African features. He was a throwback to the tall, strong warrior able to take care of himself and his woman. Her smiled was welcoming.

"Got a minute?" His wide shoulders seemed to fill the width of the doorway.

"For you, a whole five. Lynn had an emergency, so I'm taking care of the phones. Jason fell off his bike and twisted his ankle. She took him over to the hospital to have it X-rayed. Oh, I'm sorry. I didn't realize you weren't alone." Amber blushed prettily as she realized she hadn't so much as seen his companion. Talk about having eyes for only one man.

Ray made the introductions. "Amber Spencer, John McClure. John and I worked on the same case a few years back."

Amber offered her hand, having recovered her natural grace and poise. "It is a pleasure, Mr. McClure. How long are you going to be in the area? I certainly hope you can stay for dinner. I'm sure you and Ray have a lot of news to catch up on."

"Unfortunately, Ms. Spencer, this isn't a social call. I ran into Ray out front. May we speak privately?"

Amber blinked in surprise before she said, "Yes, of course. Won't you sit down, please." She indicated the chairs in front of the desk as she took her chair behind it. She tried not to show her confusion as she watched Ray close the door. He ignored the empty chair in favor of leaning against the window frame over her left shoulder.

A knot of tension welled up in her stomach as she asked, "How may I help you, Mr. McClure?"

He admired her cool elegant beauty. One look into her large golden eyes explained Ray's fascination with the lady. Such warmth and feminine strength were rare qualities and could prove impossible for a man to resist, especially difficult for a man like Ray. He lived his life on the edge. She was the one, John decided, as he noted the way Ray hovered protectively in the background, like a great cat, his relaxed stance deceptive.

John reached into his jacket pocket, flipped his badge down on top of her desk, then casually took out a small notebook and pen. "You run an efficient and profitable business here, Ms. Spencer. How many people do you employ?"

Amber answered without hesitation, yet added, "Mr. McClure, you have me thoroughly confused. What possible interest could our small school be to the FBI?" Amber sent a quick look in Ray's direction. He hadn't moved. In fact, his behavior was every bit as baffling as John McClure's.

"We're interested in one of your employees. He may be the individual we've been trying to locate. We would like to put a trained agent inside the nursery school. Someone to keep tabs on his activities. We need your cooperation."

The men waited. Each seemed to be preparing himself for feminine hysterics. Although Amber felt inclined to fulfil their expectations, the tremor in her voice was the only concrete evidence of her accelerating alarm.

"Who are you looking for?"

Ray's heart swelled with pride as he watched her. He could feel her distress, yet she maintained control of her emotions. She had endured more than her share of heartache in one lifetime—she didn't deserve this.

"Foster Harris. My information indicates he has been in your employ for approximately eight months. His job involves driving the school bus that's used to transport the youngsters to and from their homes. He also handles minor repairs on the vehicle and the premises. Is that correct?"

"Yes." Amber nodded numbly. "What do you think he has done?"

"Child molestation and murder."

Amber gasped in horror.

Ray was there. His large hand grasped her left shoulder, squeezing tenderly, hoping his nearness would help her. "Are you all right?"

"No," she whispered tightly, "but that is the least of my concerns. You honestly believe Harris is responsible for crimes against children?" Her hands were trembling so badly she had to clasp them together in her lap to keep them still as she silently prayed, *Please don't let this be true. Let it be some terrible nightmare that will soon disappear.*

"Yes. Unfortunately I can't prove it."

"Then you could be wrong?"

"It's possible. Are you willing to take the chance?"

"We could be talking about two different people with the same name," she said wildly, her chest heavy with dread.

John pulled out a black and white photograph of the man she had come to know as Harris. He was younger, but there was no doubt in her mind it was the same man.

"He's only twenty-two but has been in and out of mental hospitals since he was ten. He was responsible for the death of his older brother, Ben, but because he was a juvenile and considered criminally insane, he was institutionalized. He's been on his own since he was eighteen. He's a loner and has managed to stay on the right side of the law. I know he is my man. I just have to find a way of proving it before he takes another kid down."

"You could be wrong!" Amber was quivering so badly, she didn't even notice when Ray went to the closed secretary in the corner of the room and poured brandy from the crystal decanter into one of the glasses stored inside.

"Drink." With a look, he cautioned John to give her a moment to recover. "More?"

"No," she said, biting her lips to hold back the tears lodged in her throat.

"Okay?" Ray's face was etched with lines of concern.

She nodded, looking into his eyes. She seemed to gain strength from his closeness. There was an unmistakable message in his dark eyes. An offer of assurance that they would make it through this . . . make it through together.

Her gaze slowly returned to the other man. "I'm sorry. This is all so upsetting."

"I've been working on a string of murders, all teenage boy, runaways. Same MO—sexually molested before being killed. One youngster in Seattle, one outside of Denver, another in Wisconsin. There is nothing to connect Harris to the murders except for way they were killed. The same way he admitted to killing his brother, deep slash at the throat then left to bleed to death."

Amber shuddered. "Why are you in here talking to me? You should be out arresting him!"

"Angel, that's why John is here. He'll set a trap for him, stop him cold. It's important that Harris not know he's under suspicion. It's also damn good insurance to make certain he doesn't hurt one of your kids here."

Her eyes went wide with horror. "Surely you don't think he's hurt one of the children?"

"All we know is they're too young for his taste. Our guy goes for boys between the ages of ten and fourteen."

Ray could feel her sag beneath his hand as she released the breath she'd been holding.

"Now about putting someone inside the nursery school . . ."

"I'm afraid it's too late. You see, I fired Harris earlier this afternoon."

"Thanks Ginger," Ray called as he backed the bus out of her driveway and into the street. He switched on the windshield wipers, deciding the steady downpour reflected his dark mood. "Damn that little weasel."

It had taken all Ray's resolve to convince Amber to rest, while he and Ginger took the children home. The operation had gone smoothly in spite of his brooding anger. Whether Amber was able to admit it or not, she was a bundle of raw nerves after the interview with John.

"Of all the rotten luck," Ray mumbled to himself as he accelerated up the steep, deeply rutted two-lane country road. Amber didn't deserve this kind of heartache. She had worked hard to make a success of the school. He couldn't help wondering if the small community would rally to her aid, or would it turn against her.

His protective instincts had reached new heights. He didn't have to be told how little it took to ruin a good reputation. Her only mistake had been in giving Harris a chance. Anyone who knew her couldn't doubt her innocence in all this. Regardless, all too soon, rumors would fly. Human nature being what it was, Ray wouldn't be surprised if Amber ended up shouldering the blame for this mess.

Ray's hands had tightened on the steering wheel as the bus crested the top of the hill. The left rear tire suddenly blew, sending it skidding on the wet pavement over the double yellow line and into the oncoming lane. Ray gave the wheel a hard jerk to the right, narrowly missing the approaching taxicab and sending the bus into a skid that caused it to fishtail several yards along the muddy shoulder before it went bumping down the rocky incline. It eventually came to a stop against a boulder.

Ray lay hunched over the wheel, too shaken to move. By the time he decided the strain along his arms and shoulders was due to tension rather than injury, a flashlight was being aimed through the partially open window.

"You okay, young fella? I saw you swirling out there like a salmon headed upstream."

"Yeah," Ray said, shouldering open the door.

"Maybe you shouldn't be moving." The elderly cab driver shone his light over Ray.

"I'm okay. You aren't hurt, are you, Mr. Morgan?" Ray asked, realizing he was the driver he'd narrowly missed.

"Fine, just fine. My reflexes are as good as they were thirty years ago," Mr. Morgan said with pride. "What happened? You been over to Jose's? Had one too many beers?"

"Unfortunately, no. Tire blew." Ray lifted the collar of his leather jacket against the bite of the cold wet rain. "Would you shine that light over here?"

The front tires were buried in the mud. It was the rear left that held his attention. He dropped down on his haunches for a closer inspection.

He swore under his breath when he found the long gash along the wall of the tread. The tire had been deliberately cut, not deep enough to cause a flat, but enough to create a dangerous situation. It didn't take much of an imagination to figure out who and why. From what Amber said, Harris had been furious when he was dismissed. There was no doubt in Ray's mind that he was capable of such an act . . . none whatsoever.

"Miss Spencer ain't gonna be none too happy about this," Mr. Morgan said, studying the cracked headlight and the bent front fender.

"Mmm," Ray acknowledged absently. He inspected each of the other tires in turn.

"Can I give you a lift to Miss Spencer's place? Figured that was where you was headed."

"Thanks. But I could use a lift into town."

"Town, you say?"

"Yes, to the sheriff's office." Ray's wide mouth was grim.

Bushy white eyebrows shot up in surprise. "Sure thing." He started back to where he had left his cab, leaning heavily on a cane. "It's gonna cost plenty, especially if you want me to drive back out here. Mike's Garage stays open until eight, but Matthew Junior is most likely to be at dinner by this time of night. That young fellow ain't got no wife to keep supper waiting for him. Some say he's sweet on Miss Spencer." He chuckled.

Having pocketed the keys from the ignition, Ray locked

it before he joined Mr. Morgan in the cab. "Matthew Junior?"

"Sheriff Matthew Brown. His daddy, Matt Senior, held that job for close to thirty-six years or more. His boy's had the job some six years in the fall, I suspect. Yes, sir, old Matt was madder than hell when his boy ran off and joined the Marines. Barely eighteen, he was. Why I remember just like it was last week when Matt Junior was no higher than his daddy's . . ." The elderly driver was just getting warmed up as he set the car into motion.

Ray wasn't listening. He was livid. The so-called accident hadn't been meant for him. Harris had no way of knowing that Amber would not be driving tonight. It had been sheer luck that he had been behind the wheel. Ray wasn't the type to take threats casually, especially when they were directed at the most important person in his life.

"The ungrateful bitch!" Harris mumbled over and over again to himself as he paced the dust-covered hardwood floor.

He'd been a fool to trust her . . . believed she liked him. The first chance she had she'd sacked him. Too drunk to drive her precious brats! Just who did she think she was dealing with, some punk kid?

His long fingers flexed on the handle of the sharp slender blade. It was her fault. If she hadn't put so much pressure on him, he might have made it work this time. He had done a good job. In over six months not one slip. He'd done his work, kept his nose clean. Only recently had the nightmares started. He dreams were filled with accusing voices . . . Ben's, the others. He needed the booze in order to sleep. She hadn't given him a chance to explain. She wanted him to face the black endless hours of the night with nothing to blunt the pain. The nightmares were too horrible to face sober. Ben lurked in the dark, ready to hurt him over and over again.

"You're dead, Ben . . . dead—I should know!" he yelled,

pounding on his chest. Harris stumbled over a loose board, the knife clamoring on the hardwood floor. Using the chair to catch himself, he grabbed the open whiskey bottle from the table and helped himself to another healthy swig.

Why didn't she give him a chance to explain about the dreams? Those dreams had spooked him. It had been months since he'd been bothered by them. Suddenly they were back, night after night filled with the cries of anguish . . . sounds from the grave. They were dead, all of them. He'd seen to that. So why wouldn't they leave him alone?

He'd wake up in a cold sweat and reach for the bottle. He drank only enough to enable him to fall back to sleep. Liquor dulled the pain. Why couldn't she see that? He had to get some sleep if he was to do his job the way she wanted it. Why couldn't she understand that?

He hated her. She was pretty like the witch that had brought him into this world. "Couldn't trust the pretty ones."

Ben . . . Ben was dead. Harris was free. Or at least he was free until the rich bitch had sent the law after him. When he'd gone back to the rooming house, Mrs. Kennedy told him about the stranger asking questions about him.

Now he had no job, no place to live, all because of her. It didn't matter. They wouldn't find him. He wouldn't let them taken him back. Never again would he let them lock him away! Before he left, he'd fixed the pretty witch— make her pay for what she'd done to him.

A smile suddenly lit his pale blue eyes. "Let them look for me." He laughed. They'd never find him. He would be leaving this place, but first he had to get the boy. He'd been wanting the boy for months now. There wasn't one reason why he couldn't have him. He had nothing to lose, thanks to Ms. Amber Spencer . . . not a damn thing.

Chapter Eleven

Amber was up to her elbows in soapsuds as she scrubbed the kitchen floor. A half dozen pots simmered on the stove.

"Expecting the Redskins?" he asked as he fought to hide his own anger and frustration.

"You're late. Dinner should have been on the table an hour ago." Amber sent an overly bright smile his way—a smile that didn't conceal the unhappiness reflected in her eyes. She'd been so keyed up that it was either cook and clean the apartment from top to bottom or worry herself half to death. She suspected Ray would not have been thrilled to return and find his mattress airing on the front porch. "How does collards, pot roast, candied yams, creamed corn, and corn muffins sound with deep-dish apple cobbler for dessert?"

"Fantastic!" he said. His troubled eyes studied her. He knew he had to tell her but not just yet. Didn't she have enough to worry about? If only he could have gotten his hands on that slimy piece of lowlife. Harris wouldn't be able to hurt another child when Ray finished with him.

"Can I help?"

"Yes, you can wash the dishes, later. Dinner can wait

fifteen minutes, time enough for a quick shower if you like and for the floor to dry."

After his call on the sheriff, Ray had arranged for the bus to be picked up and taken to the local garage. He'd also called John McClure and learned that Harris had bolted.

Amber chatted nonstop through the meal about the possibility of expanding the school. Not once did she mention Harris or John McClure. Ray listened with an ever increasing sense of helplessness. She was hurting, yet she refused to share her pain or fears with him.

They were having dessert when he felt forced to admit, "I ran into a little trouble on the road. It was after I'd taken the children and Ginger home." He didn't want to tell her any of this. What choice did he have?

"What kind of trouble?"

"A blowout, of all places on that hill outside town."

"The children—"

"Are fine. I was on my way back when it happened."

"I don't understand. The bus has new tires. I had them replaced less than a month ago."

It hurt him to say it as much as it would hurt her to hear it, but it had to be said. "One of the rear tires was slashed."

For a time neither said anything, they simply looked at each other. Her eyes filled with horror.

She finally said, "You think Harris is responsible for this, don't you?"

"It was no accident, angel."

"Oh, no—how could he do such a thing? What about the children? They could have been hurt . . . even killed!" She shuddered with terror. "What about you? Were you hurt?"

Ray took both her hands into his.

"I'm fine. The bus has been taken to the garage. Front end needs some work. We were lucky, honey."

Amber's eyes filled with tears. "Ray, how could he do such a hateful thing?"

Ray dried her face with his napkin. "He's sick and dangerous. He is no longer a threat to you or the community. He's gone, honey. He's on the run. Your involvement with Foster Harris is over. As selfish as this sounds, I'm going to say it anyway. I for one am grateful. I don't want you anywhere near someone like him. It's over, angel."

She shook her head, trying to dispel the swelling sense of fear that had been her companion since John McClure's visit. "If only it were," she whispered. Unable to sit still a second longer, she began clearing the table.

"It's true," he insisted.

Amber didn't answer. Ray took dishes out of her hands and set them on the table before he clasped her by the shoulders and steered her into the living room.

"Sit." He pointed to one of the wingback chairs positioned in front of the curved windows.

"But—"

"But nothing. The cleanup is my responsibility, remember. You relax. You're as tight as a drum."

Amber was too upset to argue. She leaned back, giving in to the comfort as Ray's strong fingers massaged the tense muscles of her neck and shoulders.

"Better?"

She nodded, forcing a smile in an attempt to appease him.

"Talk to me, angel. Let me share this with you."

He had no idea why it was so important to him that she believed in him and share her problems with him. It just was. She didn't have to face this alone. He was here for her. All she had to do was reach out to him.

"Please . . ." He was as startled as she to hear the gruff plea in his deep voice.

She slid forward, just out of reach. Her shoulders hunched tiredly. "You're wrong. It's not over, Ray. I have to find out if he's hurt one of our children."

"How?" Ray asked, crossing to the side table. He filled two crystal brandy snifters. She still hadn't answered when he handed one to her. "Drink it."

She sighed heavily. "I called Wayne Adams, Ginger's

husband. Do you remember my telling you about him? He's a child psychiatrist, plus teaches classes at the college."

"I remember. Drink."

She obeyed. She could feel it burn all the way down to her stomach. "Naturally Wayne couldn't exactly assure me that Harris didn't harm one of the children." She paused, unable to conceal her fear. Tears threatened to spill. She took a deep breath, forcing back the anguish inside of her. She wouldn't break down. She had to get through this. Her voice was clear although a bit uneven when she said, "Wayne has given me a list of symptoms to look for in the children. I plan to have a staff meeting on Monday morning before the children arrive. The teachers must be informed. Also I intend to notify the children's parents and—"

"Amber—what are you thinking? That kind of action will only alarm the community and for no good reason!"

"No good reason? I think what that evil man has done is reason enough."

"Angel, we have no proof he's harmed anyone. What purpose would sharing your suspicions serve? The authorities have been notified. At this point these suspicions— and that is all they are right now—will only upset a great number of people unnecessarily. Give yourself some time to think about this. Amber, this could ruin your school's reputation."

"You think that matters to me now? We're talking about something that could impact on the children's entire lives. Nothing is more important than those kids. Nothing!" She glared at him as if he were the enemy. Suddenly realizing what she was doing, she said softly, "I'm sorry, I didn't mean to yell at you."

Her fear was running wild, but she could not help it. First she'd cooked enough food to last for months. Then through dinner she'd shoved food at Ray while her own plate remained untouched. She had spent the entire meal rearranging her food in neat piles, hoping he would not notice her lack of appetite. Now she found herself screaming at him, when all she really wanted was to bury her face against his chest and cry her heart out. Just the possibility of that horrible man touching those precious children made her sick to her stomach.

Ray's emotions were running as high as Amber's, only his were raw and directed at a single man. The bastard deserved to suffer for the anguish he had left behind. Amber was hurting. Ray literally ached to ease her worries. But all he could do was offer his support, and that didn't seem like a hell of a lot.

"Amber, let's take this one step at a time. The authorities are aware of the situation. John has seen to that. From what you say, Wayne Adams is an expert. Let him do his job. Let him find the answers."

Hot, bubbling water swirled over Ray's tired muscles as he leaned back against the rim of the tub. He absently massaged the soreness in his shoulders and midsection.

"What a day," he mumbled to himself, eyes closed. Unfortunately the tension and frustration that had plagued him through the long evening weren't as easy to eliminate as the discomfort in unused muscles. His temper hadn't benefited from idly watching Amber suffer.

Although she voiced some of her worries, she hadn't opened up to him or allowed him to share the fear, the grief, and the guilt she was experiencing. She had shut him out and claiming exhaustion had gone to bed. Why wouldn't she let him help?

She alone could touch the tender feelings inside of him that others claimed he didn't possess. Her smiles were as refreshing as sunshine after weeks of endless rain. For more years than he had cared to count, he'd gone about his work, comforted by the knowledge she was safe.

Now suddenly a creep like Harris had crawled out from under a rock and threatened her happiness. What really hurt was that for the first time since their reconciliation he couldn't seem to reach her. He had failed to protect her.

He had talked and talked, said all that he could to comfort her. Yet she held her pain inside like a shield. He had seen it, felt it, but she had not allowed him close enough to share it with her. Ray had never felt more frustrated in his entire life.

As his thoughts returned to the blowout, he shuddered from the depths of his anger. It wasn't uncommon for him to come face to face with death. But this vendetta was not directed at him. It had been meant for Amber ... his Amber. The thought of it left him shaking with cold-blooded rage. He had never hunted another man before with the sole purpose of destroying him with his bare hands—that was, until tonight. Ray knew that if he had been able to find Harris, he would be a dead man.

What was wrong with him? Why hadn't he had Harris investigated when she initially expressed doubts about the man? Where was his mind? All it would have taken was one lousy phone call, and a man like Harris would never have gotten close to Amber. He swore savagely.

Ray, having switched off the whirlpool, paused in the act of drying himself. Amber's muffled sobs of anguish came from the next room. He pulled on and belted a short dark green toweling robe as he crossed on bare feet to the connecting door.

When she did not respond to his knock, he went in. Light from the bathroom spilled across the carpet, illuminated where she lay curled on the bed, her arms clenched the pillow, her face pressed into it. Her whole body shook with her despair.

Ray's heart contracted with despair as he crossed to her side. She needed him, and that was his single consideration as he dropped down beside her. "Baby ... don't," he whispered in a tender voice. Soothingly he rubbed her back.

Unable to control the turbulent emotion racking her slender frame, Amber sobbed even harder. Ray could not bear it. He reached for her, lifting her until her damp cheek rested on his chest and her slender arms encircled his waist as she accepted the comfort of his strong arms.

"Shush . . . shush, baby. It's all right," he said, close to her ear, his large hands pushing the damp, cottony-soft curls away from her face. "It's not the end of the world. None of this is your fault."

When her sobs intensified, Ray picked her up and carried her to the oak rocker by the window. The heavy drapes shut out the sight of the night. He sat with her on his lap, slowly set the chair into motion, cradling her as if she were a small child. Her pain was his pain, she was his world.

As her heart-wrenching sobs eased somewhat, he murmured soothingly, "Baby, you'll make yourself sick. Stop. He's not worth it." Ray wiped at the tears that seeped through her lashes, with tender large blunt fingertips.

"It's all my fault. I should have kn-o-w-n," she hiccupped, burying her face between his shoulder and neck. Her full breasts pillowed on his chest.

"No, Angel . . . don't."

"I should have kno-ow-n."

"How could you have known?" Spotting the tissue box on the sidetable, he mopped at her damp face.

The tears had slowed somewhat but not the anguish. "It's my responsibility! Those precious babies . . . their parents trusted me to care for them . . . to . . . to protect them."

"Now listen to me!" He cradled her jaw in the palm of one wide hand, forced her to look at him. "None of this is your doing. You depended on a reliable agency, one with a good reputation. They didn't know, either. Harris lied to them, he lied to you."

"But—"

"No buts. You aren't responsible for that monster's behavior. Look at the facts. As far as we know, he's never been alone with any of the children. There was always an attendant on the bus to help with the kids, right?"

"Yes . . ."

"In the school the children are always well supervised."

"You don't think he hurt one of them?"

"No, I don't. When could he have gotten to them? You and your staff take excellent care of the youngsters. Besides, John said his preference is for teenage boys. More than likely he only picked this area to hide out for a while, make some money before moving on."

"Oh, I hope so," she whispered, wanting desperately to believe.

"Amber, face it. We may never learn the whole story. Baby, let's be thankful that as far as we can tell he hasn't done his worst."

She smiled through her tears. "I'm so glad you're here. I don't think I could handle this alone."

Ray shivered when her soft lips brushed over the base of his throat. Her softness was not lost on him. The thin silk of her yellow gown enhanced, rather than concealed, her loveliness, her round bottom fit snugly against his sex.

Although he told himself she was only expressing her gratitude, nevertheless his voice was a throaty groan when he said, "You're stronger than you're giving yourself credit for, angel." Her face was still buried in the place where his neck and shoulder joined and her soft breath warmed his skin. She smelled of crushed rose petals.

"I can't help feeling responsible."

"If you must blame someone, blame me. I should have had him investigated when you first raised doubts." His mistake could have proven fatal for her. The incident with the tire verified just how dangerous Harris was. If anything had happened to her . . . Ray's arms instinctively tightened around her, bringing her even closer to his large frame. He was determined to ignore the unmistakable proof of his arousal. His shaft was thick with desire.

"Oh, honey . . . no." She looked up into his eyes, caressed his cheek. "You had no way of knowing."

All he knew was that she had been hurt. Somehow he should have prevented it. His voice revealed an acute anger that was directed inward. "I didn't protect you! None of this should have happened."

Amber felt his anger and heard his frustration. "Ray . . . please. You weren't here. How could you have known about Harris? Be reasonable. When you arrived, you were in no condition to properly evaluate anyone. You were shot, for goodness sake!"

There was no excuse, as far as Ray was concerned. Her happiness and well-being were too important to him. His carelessness could have cost her her life.

"Honey, you have no idea how glad I am that you're here and not halfway around the world. I need you." She snuggled against him.

Ray seriously doubted that Amber realized how deeply her softly spoken declaration had affected him.

"How about some hot milk? Might help you sleep." He tried but failed to force his gaze away from the soft curves beneath the silk cloth. The creamy golden tops of her shoulders and slender throat were left bare by the gown's ivory-colored lace scalloped-edged neckline, which was gathered into a wide band at her waist. Her legs were curled across his thighs. Her soft bottom was snug against his hardening sex.

"Please, just hold me." She was in desperate need of his warmth, his strength. If she thought of the havoc her scented body was having on his nervous system, she gave no indication.

"I don't think that's a good idea." He voiced a logic and reason he that he did not feel. "I want you," he said, his voice rough with pulsating desire.

Chapter Twelve

No matter how he tried, he could not tear his eyes from her lush beauty. He did not have to strain his imagination to recall the hue of her engorged nipples sweetly beading the cloth. He knew the richness of her soft golden skin, knew how high and ripe her breasts were, knew the precise thickness and length her dark pretty nipples would reach when she was aroused. Perspiration dampened his forehead, hunger knotted his stomach, while his sex was painfully ready for Amber.

When Ray slid his hand beneath her soft thighs in order to lift her from his lap, Amber sighed at the sweetness of his caress. Her legs parted slightly—and his hand, instead of clasping both her legs, ended up between her baby-soft inner thighs. He closed his eyes as his entire frame quivered in response to that accidental caress.

Amber, inhaling his clean male scent, recognized the husky tremor in his tone, saw the burning sparks in his dark eyes, heard the shallowness of his breath, and felt the rapid beat of his heart. Yet it was the distinct masculine pressure of his unyielding sex that caused her own heartbeat to race. Oh, yes, he wanted her, ached to be inside of her just as much as she yearned to have him there. She moved her hips against his engored penis, unwittingly pressing her thighs together and effectively trapping his hand.

"No," he groaned thickly, fighting the need to stroke the hard ridge of his shaft against her lush behind.

Her breasts felt swollen, heavy with want of his hands . . . his mouth on them. Her golden brown eyes sizzled in response to the dark flames in his gaze.

"Ray, do you remember the first time you touched me? You caressed my breasts . . . took them into your mouth. Oh, honey, do you remember? I've tried to forget, but I couldn't. How could I ever forget the feel of your mouth on my body?" She trembled in his arms, pressing her lips against the ultrasensitive side of his throat just below his lobe.

With sudden insight, he understood why he had been able to remain in control of his senses these past five years. It was quite simple. It was because Amber allowed it. One look into the depths of her eyes told him she wanted him as much as he wanted her. And this time she would have him because he could not contain the force of his need for her.

He lowered his head until his mouth covered hers, opening over hers and taking with it all the pent-up longing tearing at his soul. His tongue plunged into the sweetness of her mouth, rimming her teeth, sliding over the fleshy smoothness inside her lips, before stroking the velvet roughness of her tongue with his, over it, around it, against it, drowning his senses in her sweetness.

Ray's thought processes seemed to have stopped functioning. His heart and his body ruled his world as he rose with her in his arms, crossing to the bed. He was so painfully aroused that the feel of her as they came down on the bed together nearly drove him out of his mind. Somehow the belt holding his robe closed had disappeared. Ray hadn't noticed. All he could focus on was Amber.

It had been so long . . . so long since he had allowed

himself the sheer luxury of expressing his feelings for her. Holding her, touching her, was like heaven on earth, he decided as he crushed her against him. His body shook with the power of his need. He had to have her, every delectable inch of her.

He pushed the fabric down her arms, peeling away the bodice that hide her beauty from him. Impatient to see her, all of her, he yanked the gown away from her body.

"Baby," he moaned as his dark eyes caressed every bare inch of her. Her breasts were larger than he remembered, the years added a lushness to her slender figure. Her waist seemed smaller, her hips and thighs more sweetly rounded. The brown curls shielding her femininity were thicker. His pulse beat wildly in his veins as he stared at her, finally accepting what could not be changed. There would be no turning back for either of them. She was his woman—had always been his, just as he belonged to her.

"You're even more beautiful than you were as a girl. You're all woman, Amber . . . my woman." He stared into her eyes, waiting for her response, yearning for her agreement.

Amber was beyond words, lost inside of the whirlwind of what he made her feel. She trembled, whispering his name.

She tightened her arms around his waist, clinging to him.

His heart pounded with his excitement, thundering like the rhythmic power of a thousand African drums. He felt powerful, felt like one of the countless ebony warriors who lived before him, ready to claim what was his alone.

Battling the force of his emotions, his trembling fingertips were gentle on her face as he caressed her. He followed the soft curve of her cheeks to trace over the fullness of her lips.

When he moved to rise, she held on to him. "Where are you going?"

"I won't take you without a condom."

"Wait." She caught his hand, halting his movement.

Opening a drawer in the nightstand, she reached inside and handed him what he needed. At the fierce question in his eyes, she smiled. "I bought them for you. I meant what I said the other night. I want you. I want everything to be right this time."

His kisses were fierce, almost volatile as he crushed her mouth beneath his. He bit her lips, then licked the small hurt away. She gasped at the sweet pleasure. When he slid his tongue deep inside to stroke her tongue against his, he whispered her name with a hot urgency. Amber nearly cried out when he bent his head to lick the sensitive flesh along her neck, pressing his full masculine lips against her soft golden skin a split second before he licked her.

She could not suppress a moan as she arched her body and lifted the achy tips of her breasts toward his mouth. Ray shuddered in anticipation. He wanted . . . he needed to be inside of her. Amber clearly craved the pleasure only he could give her. She had waited long enough—they had both waited for this incomparable pleasure.

He bent to his task, first kissing her breasts then he cupped her in each wide palm before he squeezed her incredible softness. He played with the sensitive tips of her breasts before taking one into the hot warmth of his mouth, applying such a marvelous suction. Amber's cries of pleasure added to his own enjoyment and caused him to tremble with urgency. He wanted her and he wanted her now.

But she was not ready for him and he knew it. He was so painfully aroused, so close to losing the last bit of control, that he knew of only one way to quickly prepare her for him. He pressed hot hungry kisses down her soft frame, not stopping when she gasped as he reached her sweet thighs. There was no hesitation or indecision on his part.

Ray knew what he wanted, knew what she needed from him. He parted her thighs to caress the fleshy folds of her sex, before opening her to the hot invasion of his tongue. He was thorough in his efforts to give her the utmost enjoyment, he laved her until she shattered into a heart-stopping climax, gasping his name as she begged him to fill her emptiness.

He quickly prepared himself, thrilled by her thoughtfulness. There was no doubt in his mind that she wanted him as much as he wanted her. His penetration was slow and difficult—as ready as she was for him, he took care not to hurt her. She was too small to accommodate him easily. He groaned at the sheer pleasure he felt as he stroked her with the broad crown of his sex. He gritted his teeth as he fought against his body's demand that he get on with it.

Amber whimpered in frustration, moving against him, needing more. She arched her body hoping to force him to complete their union. "Please . . . I need you."

He growled his frustration, but he held fast to his determination. "Shush, baby. Be patient. I don't want to hurt you." He soothed her with his kisses.

"Ray . . ." she said, lifting her legs to encircle his lean waist. "Love me."

Ray surged forward until he was surrounded by her wet, tight heat. He closed his eyes against the rush of swelling emotions. He had no choice but to acknowledge the depth of his feelings for her. He was deeply, irrevocably in love with Amber. In fact, he had never stopped loving her. The sheer pleasure she gave him was like none other. The force of his emotions seem to heighten his desire, thus compelling him to give her all the love he had to give. It was impossible for him to hold any of himself back from her. Amber instinctively tightened around him, causing Ray's entire body to shudder from the erotic massage.

His control was quickly disappearing. His strokes were unrelenting as the pleasure intensified. With each driving force, he gave more and more of himself. "Amber," he groaned, his eyes tightly closed as he focused on her. "No . . . not yet." He felt his climax approaching. He fought against it, held himself still. It seemed as if he'd waited an eternity to have her like this, but his body was greedy for the long-denied satisfaction. Even though his senses threatened to flare beyond his control, Ray was a man governed by self-control. He inhaled quickly, determined to rule his body with his mind.

It was a wasted effort, for Amber's sweet heat was his undoing. As she rubbed the achy tips of her breasts against his chest and tightened herself around him, milking his hard length, Ray convulsed from the exploding force of his release.

Amber held him tight, thrilled by his keen enjoyment. It felt so right . . . so good. They belonged together. Surely he couldn't doubt it now, after what they'd just shared. She rejoiced in the fact that she had given him complete satisfaction.

Ray held on to her while his heart rate slowed. He could not remember feelings so good or so infuriating. He'd lost it at the end. He had climaxed, yet his lady had not. That realization weighed heavy on his heart.

"Amber," he said, stroking the damp hair at her temples.

"Mmm?"

"I'm sorry, baby. I lost control."

"Don't. It was wonderful. You were wonderful." She pressed her kiss-swollen lips to his.

Ray's response was immediate despite his impatience with himself. She was trying to make him feel better, trying to soothe his male ego. Ray wouldn't have any part of that. He lay with one arm flung over his forehead, deep in thought.

His continued silence frightened her. Amber craved his assurances, his love. Did he regret their making love? She finally whispered, "Talk to me."

A hard rush of air left his lungs before he said, "I came in here to comfort you and wound up making love to you. This was not supposed to happen."

"Don't say that," she said, her heart breaking.

"It's true."

"I see nothing wrong with wanting or needing you. Ray, it was time . . . long past time. Nothing happened that we both didn't want to happen. I needed you tonight. I needed your love." She stroked his back. "Baby, you were here for me. Please, let's not worry about the past or even the future." She pressed a kiss against his jaw. "We're here together right this second. Must we solve all our problems tonight? Can't we just enjoy being close?"

"Sooner or later, Amber, I have to leave. We both know that. Putting off the inevitable won't make it any easier."

She pressed her fingertips against his lips. "Shush . . ." She followed the lines of his chest with her soft lips pressing sweet little kisses on his damp skin. "It felt so right having you inside of me." She paused to kiss his full lips. "Was it good for you?"

Ray moaned as she caressed him. She had no idea what she did to him. She had his pulse racing. "Amber . . ."

"Was it . . . good?"

"Yes," he groaned thickly, his palm smoothing over her hips.

"Mmm," she crooned into his ear. Her sweet tongue was so hot on his chest, circling his nipple, sucking. When she lifted her head, she whispered, "I want us to be together . . . whenever, however we can manage it." She met his dark troubled gaze.

"What about next month or the one after that when I'm gone? What about then?"

"I'm not a little girl anymore. I'm a woman in need of your lovemaking. Can I have it?"

"You can have anything you want. The problem is, are you prepared to accept what an involvement with a man like me means? The success rate of married journalists isn't good."

"I don't remember proposing."

"You know what I'm trying to say."

"Stop being my protector. Be my lover."

"I don't want you hurt."

"I know," she whispered as she kissed him, her soft hand caressing down the hard muscular lines of his body. When her fingertips played in the thick crisp hair between his thighs, his breath quickened alarmingly. His shaft lifted and hardened in readiness.

"What are you doin'?"

"I want to touch you, caress you."

"It's too soon for you. I don't want to hurt you again tonight."

"Let me . . ."

Ray trembled, unable to refuse her anything.

"Baby . . ."

"Yes . . ." He couldn't think of anything he wanted more than her hands on his body.

Amber's own breathing accelerated as she caressed him slowly, shivering at his deep throaty groan when she sheathed him in her small palms and stroked her hands over him from the broad peak of his shaft to the thick base. When she cupped his heaviness below he growled his pleasure, covering her hands with his and showing her how to drive him out of his mind.

Amber had never felt more alive, more desired. Her smooth limbs curled over one of his hard muscled thighs. Her skin seemed to burn from contact with his.

Unable to bear any more of the sweet torment, Ray caught her hands and placed them on his chest. He slid his arms around her waist and lifted her up until he could take her breast into the warm wet recesses of his mouth without straining. He locked on to her hard sensitive nipple, sucking until she whimpered, trembling from head to toe—only then did he turn his attention to the other erect nipple.

He rolled over until his large frame covered hers. Her thighs were parted but not nearly enough to suit him.

"Open for me," he said, guiding her thigh up until it rested on one of his shoulders. "Sweet . . . baby . . . sweet," he whispered throatily, his mouth returning over and over again to hers.

With quick, sure movements he tore open a small foil packet and prepared himself for her. Their gaze was locked when he carefully filled her wet sheath. She moaned, her voice husky with feminine pleasure as he took her with purposeful, strong thrusts. One long-fingered hand caressed her clitoris as he ground himself against her, giving her the hard friction she craved.

"This time is for you, baby, for you," Ray said between tightly clenched teeth.

Amber cried out his name, tingling from his mastery. He was so wonderfully male. "Ray . . . please." The pleasure was building to alarming proportions. She was so close to spiraling out of control. Amber clung to him. Ray's breath quickened—his mouth, his hands, his manhood all seemed to be focused on one critical goal . . . pleasuring Amber.

"Yes, that's it, baby," he whispered throatily. He was panting as his lungs fought for more air. It took so little on her part to set his teeth on edge and send his blood pressure soaring.

Her small hands splayed out across his back and smoothed over his warm flesh before it curved into the powerful lines of his shoulders. Ray felt his whole body tighten with delicious expectation as she met him thrust for pulsating thrust.

"Ray . . ." she chanted in a desperate plea.

He tongued her, sliding down the length of her golden brown throat. He lapped at the scented hollow where her pulse beat wildly; it matched the heavy thump of his heart. He moved on to the valley between her breasts, bathing her skin with the rough heat of his caressing tongue. Ray inhaled deeply, his head filled with the erotic scent of their loving.

She trembled with pleasure as his large hands cupped her breasts, reshaping them while enjoying their weight, their softness. Desire sent sparks of pure heat through her entire system as he took his time, licking her large dark brown nipple thoroughly before he eventually took it into his mouth to suckle. She could feel the powerful sensations deep in her womb. She cried out, reveling in his strength.

When his blunt fingertips returned time and time again

to caress the tiny center of her feminine passion, she cried out in uncontrollable pleasure. They shared many hot sweet kisses, one right after the next.

"Angel, my angel," he crooned in a rough whisper.

Amber pressed her lips to his, exchanging hot, sweet kisses with him. His arms tightened around her. She cried out his name as the pleasure seemed endless. There was no beginning, no end—just an endless road of sizzling hot pleasure as he took her with deep hard thrusts. Her entire body tightened around him an instant before she came apart in his arms, her soft frame quivering uncontrollably. Perspiration beaded his upper body as he rode out the crushing waves of joy that washed over her.

"Ray!" she screamed. Her heart-shattering release was his undoing. He soon followed in her wake, pouring forth his masculine offerings. They were both slick with perspiration as their bodies cooled.

She held on to him as she thought of how much she loved him, needed him. Some things a woman never forgets. Ray was her first lover . . . her only lover. Being with him now like this was pure magic. Twelve long years was a long time to wait, but finally she had him where she wanted him most—back in her life. She told herself she could cope with being separated by thousands of miles—that she could manage not seeing him for months at a time. What she could not bear was things going back to the way they had been.

Slowly he rolled onto his back, taking her with him by the aid of one strong arm around her waist. He held on to her, for he couldn't even consider letting her go. His large hands were tender as he caressed the lines of her back as he watched her sleep. Her head was on his shoulder, her soft frame on top of his. Frowning, he wondered how in the world he would be able to leave her when the time came. There was no doubt in his mind that it would come . . . it always did.

Chapter Thirteen

"Morning, angel," Ray said softly, leaning down to place a kiss on Amber's neck as she stood flipping pancakes on the grill built into the stove.

"Breakfast is ready," she said, offering him a nervous smile from over her shoulder. "That enough?" She placed a heaping plate in his hand.

Ray frowned, failing to gauge her mood. "What's wrong?" he asked, placing the plate on the counter so that his hands were free to cup her shoulders and turn her around to face him. Her golden brown eyes were clearly troubled. "Is this about Harris? Or is this something to do with us? I didn't hurt you, did I?"

Amber's smile brightened, and her soft gaze lingered on his fully drawn African mouth. She had no regrets where they were concerned. She did not want him to have any, either. She raised on tiptoes, her hands gliding upward to lock around his neck. Her mouth was warm, pliable under his. "How did you sleep?"

"It's you I'm concerned about. I had hoped to wake with you beside me, baby . . . your head on my shoulder, your soft breasts on my chest."

He held her against him, not wanting to let her go. He still could not get over how deeply she pleased him. He could not remember ever climaxing so powerfully or feeling so whole afterward. It was like no other experience with any other woman. No, that was not quite true. He recalled how deeply gratifying it had been the first time they'd made love. He had not made love to her as thoroughly as he would have liked to due to his guilt because of her innocence. He had been ashamed of his feelings . . . ashamed of his keen hunger for a mere girl. He had taken her only once that first night.

Last night had been different. He had taken her several times, even waking during the night hard and aching, his body still very much a part of hers. The temptation was irresistible, and he had made love to her yet again, his passion almost as keen as it had been that first time.

She was no longer a girl. Amber was woman enough to fill his arms to perfection and keep him purring in and out of bed. He needed her love, he decided, as he shivered at the way her tongue all too briefly slid over his lips before she turned back to the stove.

Unfortunately a night of sweet loving had not altered his doubts. He still feared that she would not be able to cope emotionally with the high risks he routinely took on the job. Damn it, he didn't want her hurt because of her love for him. He knew how she felt, just as she knew how he felt. Would the time ever be right for them?

It was not until he was seated that he realized she had not answered his question. "Amber, how are you feelin'?"

"I'm fine, just a little shaken. So much has happened since John McClure appeared at my door yesterday afternoon. Eat, honey, before your breakfast gets cold," she said, carrying a full platter of breakfast food to the table.

He barely gave her time to put down the platter before he whispered, "Talk to me, baby," sliding an arm around her small waist and pulling her into his lap. His mouth settled against her throat. "Any regrets?"

Amber trembled from the heat of his mouth. His mustache tantalized before his lips settled over hers for a long, hungry kiss. "None," she whispered breathlessly.

"Do you have to go to your office today? We could play hooky . . . spend the day in bed," he said thickly, his arousal snug against her soft bottom.

"I wish," she said dreamily.

The telephone rang, interrupting their fascination with each other's eyes.

"A little early, don't you think? I wonder if that is the garage calling about the bus."

"I just hope it's not bad news. I can't take any more surprises," Amber said, rising to pick up the extension. "Spencer residence."

"Good morning. May I speak to Ray Coleman, please. Tell him Rita is calling."

Amber handed over the telephone without a word. When she tried to move away, he tightened his arm around her and held her fast while possessively studying her soft mouth.

"Coleman," Ray said absently.

"Ray, darling. I've been trying to find you everywhere. Your secretary was no help at all. I finally gave up and called your agent. Is it true you've been shot?"

"I'm fine now. What can I do for you, Rita?" he said impatient to be off the telephone.

"We have a problem with the show. I need you to look at several of the photographs before we hang them. Darling, the showing is tomorrow night, everything must be perfect," Rita Caldwell purred in her rich southern-accented voice.

"You don't need me for this. Call Walker."

"Ron Walker is your agent, not the photographer. Darling, I need you. You are coming, aren't you, my love?"

Ray could tell by Amber's set features that she could hear every word of the conversation.

"Darling, I know how important the Healing Hunger photographs are to you. They must be perfectly displayed. No one can handle this but you."

Ray scowled. "Okay. I'll see you this afternoon. Bye," he said, hanging up the telephone.

"You're leaving." Amber's voice betrayed her. The bitterness that she kept deep inside was evident.

"It's business. That was Rita Caldwell, the owner of Caldwell Gallery in D.C. There is a problem with a couple of the photographs."

Amber pushed herself away from him. She was heading for the front door.

"Where are you going?"

"To work."

"What about breakfast?"

"I'm not very hungry."

"Amber, you can't leave like this."

"Like what?"

"You're angry."

She turned until she could look into his eyes. "I'm not angry. A bit disappointed . . . yes. I just didn't expect you to leave so soon." She had also expected him to at least tell her about his show. They had been friends, for heaven's sakes. Suddenly she realized she was not sure what they were now. Everything had changed. The alarming part of all this was she was the one who insisted on the change in their relationship, on the intimacy . . . not Ray.

"I'll only be gone overnight. The showing is Saturday night. I had no plans to attend." His brooding gaze never left her troubled features.

No, just to see Rita Caldwell, Amber thought nastily. She had seen the beautiful African-American gallery owner in the society pages of the *Times*. Her instincts told her Rita Caldwell was interested in more than displaying Ray's photographs.

"Amber?"

"I have a lot to do today. Do you need a lift to the airport?"

"Nah, taxi is fine."

"Will you stop in the office before you leave?"

"Of course." Ray watched the seductive sway of her

sexy bottom until she disappeared from view. Rita's timing stank. Ray wasn't ready to be away from Amber, not even for one night.

Amber was almost sound asleep on Saturday morning when the downstairs bell rang. The insistent banging on the door forced her eyes open.

"I give up!" she said with a sigh. First the stupid crank call, now this.

"I'm coming!" she called, pulling on a rose-colored velour robe and tucking her feet into fuzzy pink slippers. She was all thumbs as she fumbled with the lock on the apartment door before racing to the bottom landing. Cold air rushed in when she swung the rear door open, completely forgetting Ray's warning to take care.

"Come in, quick. It's freezing out there."

"It looks as if we caught you in bed," Lynn said, followed in by Ginger.

"It's time I got up." Amber covered a yawn, waving them in. "Go on up." She took time to relock the door before following.

"Forgive us for waking you so early on a Saturday morning, but we had to see how you were," Ginger said as they hung their coats in the foyer.

"Well?" Lynn asked, taking Amber's hand. "How are you?"

"Much better than yesterday. I was really out of it the other night. I'm glad you came."

Ginger asked, "Is Ray back?"

Amber couldn't prevent the blush that stained her cheeks. "He should be back this afternoon." He'd been gone one day and already she felt lost without him.

"I guess you didn't get much sleep last night, huh?" Lynn guessed.

Amber nodded, opening the drapes. "Would one of you put the coffee on for me while I dress? I won't be a minute. There's cheese Danish in the fridge. Help yourselves."

"Take your time. We'll find everything. I for one love to putter around in other folk's kitchens," Lynn said with a giggle.

When Amber returned some ten minutes later, having showered and dressed in a blue fleece-lined jump suit, her friends were comfortably seated around the dining room table with coffee and warm Danish in the center.

"Good, you found everything. Lynn, how's Jason?" Amber poured herself cup.

"Just fine, thank goodness. It was only a sprain. I left him wolfing down his breakfast as if he hadn't been fed during the last year, declaring he would be sure to come around later this afternoon to finish some job he started in the shed. I told him it could wait until he's better. Kids!" She threw her hands up in a gesture of frustration.

"You tell him I said not to show his face around here, at least until after the weekend. Nothing is as important as his health." Amber smiled. "You know, Lynn, he's really a great kid even if he is a bit overzealous."

Ginger and Amber shared an understanding smile, while Lynn beamed with maternal pride.

"How are you, truly?" Ginger looked searchingly into Amber's eyes.

"We were worried about you, honey," Lynn said softly.

"Stop . . . both of you. I'll get past this. I know I will." She sighed wearily. "But I don't have to tell either one of you how upset I was after John McClure's visit. I'm sure you two were feeling the same. Frankly, I'm still having trouble believing Harris is the one the FBI has been looking for all this time. It gives me goose bumps just thinking about it."

"Me, too." Lynn shivered.

"It's possible they could be wrong about him. But just the idea that we've had a suspected child molester and killer working with us daily is frightening," Ginger said, cringing.

The doorbell sounded for the second time that morning.

"If that's Jason, send him home immediately," Lynn directed.

"Will do," Amber called over her shoulder as she hurried out.

This time she remembered to pull back the curtain covering the window to identify the caller. "Mr. McClure," she said, opening the door.

"Good morning. May I have a few moments of your time?"

"Of course. Please, come on up. You can join us for coffee." Amber ushered him upstairs and made the introductions.

"May I speak to you privately?"

Amber unconsciously stiffened. "That isn't necessary. Ginger and Lynn are colleagues, as well as friends. They know everything. Besides, they may also be of some help to you."

"Very well." After retrieving a small notebook from the inside pocket of his suit coat, he hitched up a pant leg as he joined them at the table.

"I'll get another cup," Lynn offered.

"Don't tell me Ray's still in bed?"

Amber couldn't prevent a quick flush of embarrassment nor could she hide the tremor in her hand as she poured the hot liquid into a cup. While Ginger answered, saving her from having to make the explanation, Amber decided it must have been the way the inquiry had been phrased that brought forth an unexpected rush of the memories of the night they'd made love. So much had been left unsaid between them. There was plenty of time for that. This trip was just a small interruption. He would be back before the evening meal.

"I just have a few questions. Has Harris contacted you since we last spoke in your office, Ms. Spencer?"

"No."

"No request for money? Back pay?"

Amber shook her head. "Lynn gave him his last check before he left Thursday."

"Ladies, has he ever mentioned any family?"

They shook their heads.

"Is it—" Ginger began, but Lynn interrupted, "Come to think of it, he did say once that Amber reminded him of his mother. Apparently she looks a little like his mother, same color hair and eyes, I think he said. It was when he first came to work at the school. I'm sure he said his mother was killed when he was still a boy. I know it sounds silly now, but at the time I didn't want to pry."

"What I would like to know is why you haven't arrested the man. It sounds to me as if you have enough evidence to arrest him," Ginger said, her voice full of impatience.

"He's disappeared. That's why I'm here. He knows we're after him."

"So why are you here badgering poor Amber? She's been through enough without these endless questions."

"Believe me, Mrs. Adams, if we knew where to look we wouldn't be here. Don't worry, it's only a matter of time until he resurfaces."

"I hope you're right. Whenever I think of the harm he might have caused, I see red." Ginger cringed. "Before yesterday I wouldn't have believed it was possible to be so wrong about someone."

Amber's eyes were brimming with sorrow and confusion. "I kept thinking there had to be a mistake. But after what happened the other night . . . Ray or one of the children could have been seriously injured or even killed on the bus. What kind of a monster could do such a thing?"

If John McClure was surprised that she was aware of the incident, he did not show it. He made the explanation. It was Amber he asked, "So you do think Harris was responsible?"

"Who else would have reason to do such a thing? I don't have many enemies. And he left angry, declaring I had cheated him out of a good job. He refused to accept any responsibility for his own behavior." Her voice trembled with emotion when she said, "If only I hadn't hired him in the first place."

"Stop blaming yourself, Amber. As far as we know, none of the children have been injured," Ginger reminded her.

"Thanks, ladies, for your help. If you think of anything that might be useful, please—no matter how seemingly trivial—give me a call." He extracted a business card and quickly jotted down a number on the back. "This is my home phone number. If I am not home, my wife will know how to reach me."

He was thoughtful as he followed Amber out. He recognized what he'd seen in Ray's eyes. Ray was in love with this woman. John would be the first to agree that Ray deserved some happiness. He only hoped Amber was strong enough to deal with the hazards the job entailed.

His mouth pulled down at the corners as he thought of his own situation. His wife claimed he was never home and that the children did not know him. She had threatened to leave because of the constant separations and the dangerous nature of his work. Yet their love for each other somehow kept them together despite the odds. And that magical ingredient was what he hoped Ray had found with this lovely lady—for without it, they did not have a chance in hell of making their relationship work.

Amber broke into his thoughts when she said, "I can't wait until this is behind us."

"Is there anything you need before I leave?"

"Just find Harris before he can hurt anyone else."

Chapter Fourteen

Ginger and Lynn were clearing the table when Amber returned from seeing the FBI agent out.

"You don't have to do that."

"No trouble. Lynn said. "It's been a nightmare, hasn't it?"

Amber could only nod in agreement.

"Perhaps you should think about getting away for a while. Easter break starts next Thursday. The school will be closed for two weeks. A cruise would be just the thing," Ginger suggested, once they were all relaxing in the living room.

"What a great idea!" Lynn echoed.

"Absolutely not. I couldn't possibly enjoy myself."

The two women exchanged a worried look. Lynn was the one who said, "Amber, you have to stop blaming yourself. None of this is your fault."

"I'm not! It's just—"

Ginger broke in to say, "You most certainly are. That can be very destructive. I think you and Wayne have hit on the perfect solution. The series of workshops on sexual abuse for the children's parents is a positive step. We will all feel prepared to deal with this issue.''

"Alex is excited about it, too. He and Wayne were on the phone for hours last night. This morning he made some calls. He knows people knowledgeable in the field who may gladly volunteer their services to the school.'' Lynn added quickly, "So you see, there is nothing to worry about.''

Amber's throat locked with emotion. "I don't know what to say.''

"You don't have to say anything. The nursery school has been an asset to our community, not to mention the leg up it has given our lives personally. We're family, sisters. We're going to help you through this,'' Lynn ended with a smile.

Amber knew that logically she had no reason to feel guilty—nevertheless, she knew she would not be able to draw a peaceful breath until Harris was behind bars where he belonged and Wayne had spoken to every child in the school and given them the thumbs-up sign.

"Perhaps this isn't the time, but I have some good news. I thought you two would like to be the first to hear about it,'' Ginger beamed.

"Personally I can't think of a better time. What is it?'' Lynn demanded, eyes sparkling.

"The adoption agency has found our baby. In a few short months we're going to be parents. Oh, I am so excited!'' Ginger confessed.

Both of them rushed over to hug her. Everyone talked at the same time.

"This is wonderful!'' Lynn said, tears in her eyes.

Amber declared, "We'll give you a baby shower.'' They were so excited that they were laughing and crying at the same time.

"It's been so long. We'd almost given up.''

"Aren't you glad you didn't,'' Amber said. "This is the best news I've heard all week . . . all month!''

"Tell us everything,'' Lynn insisted.

"The birth mother is a senior in college. She hadn't planned on having children and was eager to place the child in a good home. She is in her third trimester. We met her and her boyfriend. We plan to be there the day the baby is born. Within a few days, baring any complication, we'll be taking our baby home. Isn't it exciting? I can't wait to start the nursery. There is so much to do. I want everything to be perfect."

They were engrossed in a discussion of the baby when the telephone rang.

Excusing herself, Amber twisted around in order to reach the extension on the table behind the sofa. "Hello?"

"Did you get any sleep last night?"

"Ray." His name came out in a gentle rush of air, leaving her breathless with pleasure. "How are you?"

Whatever Lynn had started to say was forgotten as both women shamelessly watched the way Amber's face lit up with pleasure.

"Missing you. And you?"

"Doing the same," she said softly, oblivious to her audience.

"Good." His voice was deep, gravelly. "Come to me, Amber. Fly in this afternoon. I'll have a ticket waiting for you at the airport for the twelve o'clock flight. Bring your prettiest dress. We're going to a black-tie show at the Caldwell Gallery. One of your favorite photographer's work will be on display."

"You changed your mind about going," Amber murmured, wondering if the lovely gallery owner had anything to do with the change of heart. Thank goodness she had sense enough not to ask.

"Will you come?"

"Yes," she said without hesitation, disregarding her hurt feelings. He had wanted her there with him, didn't he? And what about Rita Caldwell? Was she the reason Ray had changed his plans?

"Good. See you soon."

"Well?" Ginger prompted as Amber hung up the phone.

"That was Ray."

"Really? I never would have guessed!" Lynn laughed playfully.

"More coffee anyone?" Amber was determined to hide her confusion. A one-man show and he was just now asking her. What caused him to change his mind? Amber's mind kept flitting back to the telephone call from the woman just the other morning. The assertive way she asked for him indicated that Rita Caldwell was used to having her way.

Lynn and Ginger exchanged an exasperated look. "Should I strangle her, or would you like the pleasure?"

"Me first," Lynn volunteered sweetly. "Girl, you have ten seconds to tell us what is going on between you and that man—one, two, three . . ."

"What makes you think there is something to tell?"

"Talk!" the two said at once.

"I don't know why either one of you seems surprised. You both know I've been hopelessly in love with the man for years." Amber blushed in spite of herself. The other night in his arms had been sheer magic.

"For heaven's sake—girl, will you open your mouth and talk," Lynn said impatiently.

"I'd been upset after learning about Harris, so when Ray told me about what happened with the bus, I just broke down. He helped me through it. One thing led to another, and we ended up in bed together." She smiled at the admission. "I couldn't continue to fight my feelings for him, and apparently his defenses were down as well. He seemed to need to be with me as much as I needed him."

"They made love!" Ginger squealed like a teenager.

Amber giggled when she looked up to find both of her dear friends faces lit with excitement.

"All I can say is, it's about time!" Lynn added. "I told you the man was wild about you."

"Was it worth the wait?" Ginger asked recklessly.

"Definitely." Amber's answer caused a peal of laughter.

"And now you're going to meet him in D.C. I say go for it, girl!"

"Wait a minute. Perhaps it's time to proceed with a bit more caution. We don't want to scare him away," Ginger speculated, chewing on her bottom lip.

"Have you suddenly lost your mind? The man wants her in Washington. She's goin'. End of subject," Lynn broke in.

"Naturally. That's not what I meant, Lynn. I'm thinking about the future. Has he declared himself?" Ginger wanted to know.

"If you mean, am I planning the wedding, forget it. No—we live in two separate worlds. Ray travels constantly. He is away more than he's in the States. My life is here, in Vermont, at the nursery school. All I want is to be with him whenever I can." What about Rita Caldwell—just how did she fit into the puzzle? Was she also in love with him?

"What does Ray think? Somehow I don't think he's indifferent to the two of you spending so much time apart," Lynn speculated. "Perhaps he wants more?"

"What we have is enough for me," Amber revealed. "He was very reluctant to change the relationship that we've had for so long. He doesn't think I can handle being emotionally involved with him, especially considering knowing the risks he must take because of his job."

"He could be right. It won't be easy, Amber," Lynn said, watching her closely. "I wonder how long this will be enough for you."

Ginger said, "She's in love with that man. It's only natural to want to be with him and someday wear his ring."

Deep in thought, Amber moved to the fireplace and absently traced the marbled veins. "Maybe . . ." she finally said, with troubled eyes.

Lynn and Ginger exchanged a concerned look. Ginger was the first to speak. "Does Elliott know?"

"About me and Ray?"

Ginger nodded.

"No, and I have no intention of discussing it with him. We were never anything more than friends."

"That's what you said about Ray and look what happened," Lynn reminded her. All three giggled.

"Come on, you two can help me decide on what dress to take. Ray's having a showing at the Caldwell Gallery. I plan to knock his eyes out."

"Wow! Caldwell Gallery is on the same level as some of the New York and London galleries. I saw Rita Caldwell in the society pages of the newspaper. She's very beautiful and very rich."

Amber refused to voice her worries. Their relationship had changed drastically. They were lovers now. There would be no turning back. She was going to him because she needed to be with him just as much as he seemed to need and want her there. If Rita Caldwell wanted him, she would have to go through Amber to get to him.

It was only after his fingers began to ache from the way they were clamped around the receiver that Ray remembered to return it to its cradle. He hadn't so much as considered Amber's reaction to the late invitation to the showing. Nor had he allowed himself to dwell on the delicacy of the bonds holding their new relationship together.

He was troubled. What he had not told Amber was that the news out of the Middle East was bad. He would be flying back tomorrow. They would have only one more night together.

It could not have come at a worse time. Not for one second did he delude himself into thinking that his leaving would not affect their relationship. It might destroy it.

He'd lived too many years, seen more than enough solid relationships fall apart, for him to believe theirs would be the exception. There weren't any guarantees floating around. Time and time again, he'd watched as good men were forced to retire from the work they loved. Or worse, they'd refused to alter their deadly occupations and ended up divorced, isolated from the women they adored and children they loved.

It was not only the constant separation that destroyed the closeness, but the ever present element of danger that was a necessary part of the work. Some women would put up with the life-style for a time. Ray had found it safer to just not get involved.

That had all changed the instant he and Amber had become lovers. Everything was different because of Amber. She alone could touch his heart, his very soul. Amber . . .

"Damn it!" he said, scowling at the antique clock in the corner of his living room. They needed more time . . . time to love each other . . . time to understand each other . . . time to come to a deep appreciation and acceptance of each other. That could not happen in a single night.

His eyes slowly scanned the tastefully furnished bronze room as if he could see it as Amber would. Persian rugs from India, rock crystal objects from China, the Syrian certosina mirror embellishing a Regency serpentine chest, an antique Egyptian mask on the mantel, African carvings from all over the continent, seventeenth-century Japanese lacquered chest-on-stand, and English armchairs. All had been collected during his travels in a vain attempt to make a real home for himself, just as the investments he'd made over the years were an effort to prove to himself that he was good enough for a Spencer.

Although Ray was a wealthy man, it no longer mattered as it once had. He had nothing to prove to anyone. He was at the top of his field, and he was paid well for the risks he took. His thoughts were not on the challenge ahead.

After twelve long and lonely years, he'd allowed himself the luxury of making love to the only woman he had ever cared for deeply. Had he come to terms with all that entailed? Perhaps he had looked after her and been her friend for too many years. Suddenly he was hungry for more, much much more.

Amber hinted that she was strong enough to deal with

the long separations and the ever present possibility that this was the time he would not be returning. Unfortunately she would be given the chance all too soon to test her strength.

Chapter Fifteen

The Dulles International airport was crowded. Amber, concentrating on her search for a particular dark, tall, broad-shouldered man, jumped when Ray said, "Hey, foxy mama, need a lift?"

She whirled around, heart pounding with excitement, causing the woman behind her to make a hasty sidestep in order to avert a collision.

"Ray," she breathed, her golden brown eyes sparkled with love.

"Took you long enough," he complained, brushing his lips over her cheek before transferring the strap of her garment bag from across her slender shoulder to his wide one. He was determined to ignore his aroused body, which was making demands that he had no way of accomplishing anytime soon. All he could think of was getting her home and into his arms. He needed her heat, needed her sweet fire.

"We circled the airport for an hour before we were cleared to land." She linked her arm through his. A small makeup case was in one hand, her purse tucked under her arm.

He nodded, steering them through the crowded terminal. "Any baggage to claim?"

"Nope." She smiled. "I travel light."

He cocked a dubious brow.

"Well, occasionally."

Ray chuckled throatily. "Good flight?"

"So-so," she said, looking around with interest.

They were approaching the parking garage when she asked, "How are you feelin'? Any pain?"

"Nothing for you to be concerned about. How are you feelin'? Still blaming yourself for this Harris mess?"

She frowned. "I can't help feeling responsible. After all, I'm the one who hired Harris. Since we still don't know for sure if he harmed any of the children, I can't stop worrying about them. At least the despair I was feeling the other night has passed, thanks to you. I needed you, and you were there for me."

"Amber, you have every right to be upset—but, angel, remember you aren't responsible for another person's actions."

"I know. It's so hard, especially when I think about what could have happened to you or the children when that tire blew." She shuddered, unable to finish.

"Nothing happened."

"It could have!"

"It didn't. Tell me, how did it go today? Any news? Have you heard from John McClure?"

Amber told him about the FBI agent's morning visit.

"You're awfully quiet," she said thoughtfully.

Ray shrugged but didn't comment as he led her toward the sleek black Jaguar parked at the end of the next row.

Once he finished with the luggage and settled himself behind the steering wheel, Amber placed her hand over his, preventing him from turning the key in the ignition. "Ray, what is it?"

He gave her a questioning look.

"Are you sorry you asked me to come?" Amber asked, her heart pounding with fear. Rita Caldwell's sexy southern

voice replayed inside her head. If she looked even half as
good as she sounded, Amber decided she was in a world
of trouble.

"What are you talking about?"

"You haven't really looked at me, not even once. You
certainly haven't touched me, let alone kissed me. I don't
call that peck on the cheek a kiss." She blushed with
embarrassment, suddenly preferring to study her pink-
lacquered nails than meet his dark gaze. It had made perfect sense to her, but it ended up sounding so stupid,
almost as if she were begging for his attention—more to
the point, his love.

For an instant Ray forgot to breathe. His voice was husky
with desire when he asked, "Feeling a bit neglected?" He
cradled her small brown chin in his warm palm.

"Yes, I suppose I am. The other night was all my doing.
I tempted you. You probably wouldn't have made love to
me if I hadn't fallen apart and cried all over you." She
tried to turn her face away, but he wouldn't let her.

"You're wrong. Don't you remember how badly I wanted
you? Oh, baby, there was only one reason we made love
and that was because we needed each other." When she
couldn't meet his gaze, his voice dropped even more, the
tone deeper, rough with need yet smooth as silk. "Girl,
there is no reason for you to hide those beautiful eyes
from me. I've missed you, baby. I am so very glad you came
to me. But I don't think a parking garage or the airport
terminal, for that matter, are great places to make love to
you. I'd prefer a bit more privacy when I show you just
how hungry I am for you." The last was whispered into
her ear, before he pressed his mouth against the sweetly
scented place below her earlobe, then teased it with hot
flicks of his tongue.

Amber shivered in reaction, the brief caress sent chills
racing down her spine. "A tiny kiss," she requested, desperate to feel his mouth on hers. She wanted to drown in his
taste, and her nostrils were overwhelmed by his male scent.
Her eyes flared with a feminine hunger she did not attempt

to hide. She wound her arms around his neck. Her fingers caressed his clean-shaven brown cheek, his thick ebony mustache, and his full sexy mouth. "I've missed you so much."

A nearby car door slammed, a horn blasted as another car applied brakes loudly. Ray did not really hear them for his entire focus was on his woman. Yes, she was his. He had made that decision the other night when her tight body milked him dry. There was no other woman for him. He was secretly thrilled that she desired him.

Ray chuckled softly. Tiny lines around his eyes and mouth fanned out as he grinned. His Adam's apple bobbed as he swallowed with difficulty, his mouth a breath away from hers. Ray's senses simmered toward a rolling boil. He was so painfully aroused, it was all he could do not to take her hand and have her caress his sex. He was so ready that he didn't need anything more than privacy in order to give her the hot and deep loving they both craved. "Amber . . ."

She leaned into him, her full breasts so soft against his arm that he found himself reaching for her hand, but stopped himself just in time, a split second before he would have curled her soft fingers around his pulsating shaft and urged her to stroke him from the broad base to the ultrasensitive tip. Instead, he pressed her hand against his wool-covered chest and trembled from thoughts of the intimate caress he was forced to deny himself. He comforted himself by inhaling her sweet scent. When she said his name, and her velvety soft tongue brushed down his throat lingering at the base, he groaned from the pleasure.

He required no further urging. His lips quickly covered hers, claiming what was his. Plunging his tongue into the honeyed depths of her mouth, he stroked her tongue with his own as he threaded his fingers into her lush brown curls. Oh, she was so sweet, so very sweet. He felt the way she trembled in his arms, her enticing nipples pouted against the silk of her sweater. He didn't dare caress her.

A few stolen kisses in a crowded garage could not begin to eliminate the man-sized ache he had for her.

His voice trembled from the intensity of his emotions, when he said, "Let's get out of here. I'm so weak for you, baby, I could take you right here . . . right now. I don't think either one of us wants that."

She was barely able to nod. She felt as if her brain had stopped functioning, and all she could do was feel. For so many years they had camouflaged their true feelings for each other. Now suddenly all the pretending was over. Amber found she needed his assurance that he still found her as desirable as he had the other night. She could not bear it if their loving turned out to be a mistake. It would break her heart, especially now that she realized how deeply in love she was with this man. There was only one man on this earth for her . . . Ray Coleman.

During the drive from Arlington into Georgetown, Amber told him about Ginger and Lynn's visit, and the Adams's plans to adopt.

"That's great. You have certainly made some wonderful friends in your new home. Shelly has been good for you."

She nodded. "I know. I feel very fortunate that neither Lynn or Ginger turned their backs on me. It has been a rough few days."

"I think you'll find, given time, the community will stand behind you. You're not to blame for any of this."

"I hope you're right—I mean, about the community. We must have their support to keep our school open. I suppose it would be foolish of me not to face the possibility that some people will never believe I wasn't part of this."

"Don't start blaming yourself again. I thought we worked through that the other night."

"Yes, but—"

"You're taking this much too seriously . . . too person-ally," he insisted, his voice taut with tension. He could feel her pain and he hated it . . . hated that she was suffering.

"I can't help it. This is not just a business to me. I care about the children. Their entire welfare matters to me. I

can't just take their trust or their parents' belief in me
lightly. It *is* personal, damn it. If Harris hurt one child, he
hurt us all," Amber said, fighting tears.

"How was the faculty meeting on Friday?"

"Difficult but enlightening. Everyone is willing to do
whatever it takes to support our children," she said with
apparent relief.

Ray was relieved. It bothered him knowing that he had
to leave before this Harris thing was settled. He didn't like
it one bit. He couldn't ever remember feeling so torn up
inside.

"How lovely," Amber said as they came to a stop outside
his town house.

It was among the richly restored Georgian and Federal
period structures in Georgetown, which housed elegant
boutiques, art galleries, restaurants, and nightclubs.

He urged her through his towering front door, into the
foyer, and into his empty arms.

"Finally," he groaned, lifting her until her feet were
several inches from the floor. He whirled her around,
caught up in the thrill of having her at long last in his
home.

Giggling, her arms locked behind his neck, her fingers
caressing his close-cut natural: "Are we alone?"

He lifted a brow. "I'm not that hard a taskmaster. Meg
does not work weekends," he said, referring to his secretary
who worked out of his home office.

"Wonderful," she practically purred.

He teased the sensitive place just below her ear, his nose
buried in her fragrant hair. Slowly he let her soft body
slide down his. He felt her tremor as her soft mound ever
so briefly came into contact with thick ridge of his sex.
Amber's eyes matched the passion in his own gaze. Yes,
she was where she belonged with him.

Swallowing with difficulty, he said, "Come on, let me
show you around."

He took her on a tour of the downstairs rooms, watching
with pleasure as she gently handled the artifacts he'd col-

lected from all over the world. Her presence in his home filled his heart with gladness.

"Honey, your home is lovely."

By the time they had returned to the foyer, his need had almost completely eroded his self-control. After one night in her bed, he was hooked on her sweet kisses . . . her tight, wet heat. "Did you miss me?" he asked, watching her closely but made no move to touch her.

"Oh, yes . . ." she said.

Her answer seemed to satisfy him, for he dropped his head in order to take her mouth with a masculine need that could not be ignored. Amber quivered with longing, opening her lips to the insistent pressure of his tongue. His arms were like bands of steel as they crushed her to him.

Dear God, he didn't want to leave her. For the first time in his professional career, he felt no excitement for the job ahead. What he wanted . . . needed more than anything else in the world was right here, in his arms. Ray's kisses were possessively insistent as he accepted how intricately his happiness was intertwined with her. He was one huge ache, throbbing with an acute hunger to lose himself in her sweetness.

She stroked his lean cheek tenderly. There was a kind of desperation in his eyes, in his kiss, that she didn't understand. "Sweetheart, is something wrong?"

"Let me love you . . . now," he said between hot tongue-thrusting kisses.

She shivered from the desires he alone could ignite. "Yes . . . oh, yes." Her hands were beneath his sweater. Her fingers curled into his shoulder blades as she rubbed the hard tips of her breasts against him. She needed him inside of her, filling her, claiming her, loving her.

He swept her up into his arms and quickly mounted the narrow flight of stairs that would take them to his bedroom at the end of the hallway. His still tender midsection ached from the exertion, but he could tolerate the discomfort. What he couldn't handle was being without her.

The four-poster bed creaked beneath their combined weight. Wrapping arms and legs around each other, they shared kiss after sizzling hot kiss.

"Hurry," she panted as they impatiently undressed each other.

He was not satisfied until her breasts filled his hands. His skin was dark against the pale brown richness of her skin. She was so soft, so soft, he marveled. He stared down at her, his breath sending chills of excitement to the hard tips of her breasts.

"Beautiful," he said, then he followed the curve of her breast with his tongue, then licked the hard nipple before taking it into his mouth, sucking.

She moaned from the pleasure, clenching his head to her body. She cried aloud when the suction seemed to intensify. Ray took his time tasting her, then teased her by worrying the sensitive peak gently against the sharp edge of his teeth. Amber gasped his name as the passion that ran wild through her system seemed to accelerate while his stroking fingertips moved through the damp thick curls between her thighs.

"Oh . . . oh, baby, you're so sweet, so wet," he whispered.

She made inarticulate gasping sounds in her throat as he tugged at her nipple, drawing circles with his fingertips over the tiny heart of her feminine yearning. "Please . . . please," she begged. He didn't stop until her slender frame shuddered, awash in pleasure.

"Oh, Ray," she said, kissing him. She pushed her tongue between his lips, plunged into the moist warmth of his mouth. Her hands weren't still—they caressed his nipples, gently tugging at them until he groaned in response. Her soft hands stroked over his hair-covered chest, moving toward his taut stomach, careful of his wound. He growled his excitement when her slender hands stroked the coarse dense hair that surrounded his sex. Her fingertips played in the thickness while he held his breath—waiting, hoping for the feel of her soft, soft hands palming his shaft, stroking him.

She was so close . . . so close to where he wanted her.
When she curled both hands around him, he gasped her
name. "Amber . . . yes . . . yes." His whole body craved
her full caress. His swollen shaft thickened even more,
pulsating as she stroked him, paying particular attention
to the ultrasensitive broad crown. His hand briefly guided
hers, applying the firm pressure that he craved.

"Yes . . . oh, yes," he said, his deep voice rough with
need as his hips moved against her encompassing hands.
It felt so good . . . so good. Suddenly he said tightly, "No
more." Taking her hands away, he pressed a tender kiss
into center of each palm. At her questioning eyes, he said,
his voice thick with desire, "I don't want to come until I
am inside of you."

He paused, reaching for the condom on the nightstand,
long enough to prepare himself. No matter how badly he
ached to be inside of her, he would never make the same
mistake twice of leaving her pregnant and alone. With his
weight balanced on his elbows, he licked her lips and
caressed her soft breasts. The pleasure was so great that
his mouth ravished hers.

When she said, "I need you," he knew he couldn't wait
any longer, he had to be inside of her.

He had to have her. Taking as much care as he could,
he guided his heavy shaft against her petal softness before
slowly moving deep inside of her, penetrating, filling her.
They both moaned from the pleasure of their joining. All
too soon, powerful sensations eroded his control, forcing
an avalanche of even greater sensations. Ray established a
rhythm that thrilled them both. When Amber tightened
around him, he called out her name.

His thrusts were deep and hard while he stroked the
highly sensitive pearl at the top of her mound with his
fingertips. Amber's moans of excitement increased Ray's
pleasure. He did not slow his movements but continuously,
persistently, determinedly loved her until they shared a
incredibly exciting climax as one.

They clung to each other. Their uneven breathing was

the only sound in the room. Gradually it slowed, his body still very much a part of hers. His hands caressed down her back from her nape to her soft bottom.

Forcing himself to move, he slowly eased from her magical heat. He sprawled on his back, holding her close against his side.

"You were wonderful."

He quirked a brow at her, then teased, "So were you."

Amber smiled at him, lacing her fingers through his. She absently traced his mouth from beneath the fall of his mustache. He had the most beautiful mouth.

"I was too rough," he said with a frown. He'd lost control toward the end and was unable to slow his hard thrusts.

"If you keep scowling like that, Ray Coleman, I'll start imagining all sorts of things—like you're not pleased with our lovemaking."

He smiled that slow devastating smile of his that made her heart race. It was no different now, even when her body still tingled from his lovemaking.

The late afternoon sunshine filtered past the partially opened brown and gold flecked drapes. The room, done in shades of brown, from darkest mocha to the palest beige, suited him perfectly, Amber decided as she snuggled against him.

"Fishing for a compliment?" He grinned broadly.

"You bet!"

He chuckled, brushing his lips over her kiss-swollen lips. "I missed you so much last night. I couldn't sleep for wanting you."

"I missed you, too," she said, then was forced to cover an unexpected yawn.

"Tired?"

"Mmm," she yawned again.

"Why don't you close those pretty brown eyes—get a few hours rest."

She did not feel the gentle caress of his mouth against her cheek. She was already asleep.

Chapter Sixteen

Ray's smile was exquisitely male as his dark eyes followed her as she descended the stairs.

"Well?" Amber said softly.

His eyes glowed with appreciation as she slowly whirled for his inspection. The black silk dress lovingly followed the sleek lines of her gently rounded frame. Soft padded shoulders, deep V neckline, a wide black sequined belt secured the overlapping front. The dress moved when she did, stopping just above her knees. She wore black leather pumps with snakeskin toes and heels. A cloud of soft brown curls framed her face and pooled on her shoulders. Diamond and onyx square-cut earrings were her only jewelry.

He crossed the room, arms outstretched. When he finally spoke, he had to get past the constriction in his throat. "Girl, you take my breath away." He inhaled her sweet scent as he pressed his lips against her cheek, his hungry gaze lingered on her beautiful mouth covered with deep red lipstick. His shaft thickened as if time were not a consideration, and need his only barometer, as he enjoyed her beauty.

A few hours in bed had not eliminated the hunger he had for her. Need continued to mushroom into a deep craving that couldn't be easily or quickly ignored. They had been apart too long. In spite of the carefully made plans for the gala evening ahead, all he could seem to concentrate on now was how much he wanted to be with her, just the two of them.

The thought of having to leave her pierced him with acute disappointment. This would be the first test of their love. Could she handle the separation? How would she cope with the distance and the danger? Everything was different now, more complex because they had become lovers. Their emotional ties were stronger now than they had been at any time in the past five years.

He still had not been able to tell her that this was their last night for a while. He had found himself wanting to put it off for as long as he could, wanting only to see her eyes sparkling with happiness exactly as they were now.

Her smile took his breath away and left him reeling from the impact. How could one woman be so perfect for him and yet be so fragile?

"You look very handsome yourself, sir." She stroked the satin lapels on his black dinner jacket.

Ray's hard features softened as he grinned boyishly. "Ready?"

He represented all that Amber considered wonderfully male. The very feminine part of herself responded without censor to his very masculine essence. It had nothing to do with the way his suit fit the width of his shoulders or the taut lines of his lean waist and hips or even the hard muscled length of his legs. The stark white shirt and black bow tie only added to his dark raw beauty. He was all man from the top of his thick close-cut natural to the tip of his Italian loafers. No woman in her right mind could resist him, Amber decided. It had always been this way for her. And she had come to realize it always would be.

He reached for the black cashmere shawl she carried and placed it over her shoulders. His hands lingered at her nape.

All she could do was nod—her throat had locked as her

emotions swelled. Their intimacy had proved to her that being with him was more wonderful, more exciting, than she could have imagined. He had taken his time, focused his attention on her needs. Loving him was worth the difficulty it had taken to convince him that they could be both friends and lovers.

At long last, they were together . . . really together in the way she longed for them to be. All else paled including the worries over Harris and the nursery school.

The air was filled with the fresh smells of spring. The night sky was clear and intensely blue. Surely no woman had ever felt more loved or desired. He had not said the words, but she had felt the force of his emotions. He cared for her deeply. Somehow she had to convince him that she was strong enough to handle the danger he faced each time he left. If she wanted him, then it was something she must do to keep him. The problem was she had her own doubts.

"You're going to really like Rita," Ray said momentarily taking his eyes from the road. "She has been a great friend. She's done an excellent job of promoting my work, even when I'm halfway around the world."

"Why have you discouraged me from attending your showings?" she asked, determined to hide her hurt feelings.

"You know that I have been very careful over the years to keep my private life separate from my professional life. The showings have nothing to do with us. It is enough for me that you are there when I need you."

"I would have liked to have gone to your showings to support your work." She refused to let the subject drop, well aware of his determination to protect her from the unpleasant side of his work.

He squeezed her hand. "I never intended to shut you out. The showings are for the children. The money goes back into helping them with food, clothing, schooling, whatever is needed."

"How long have you been doing this?" she asked, her heart filled with pride. Ray was such a special man.

"Since Rwanda ..." He suppressed a shudder at the horrors he had seen and photographed there—so many lives lost to war and disease and starvation.

"What made you change your mind about attending tonight?"

"Rita convinced me that my presence would make a difference. I found I could not refuse."

Amber tried to ignore the twinge of jealousy she felt whenever Rita Caldwell was mentioned. It was ridiculous, considering she had never even met the woman. The gallery owner just seemed too caught up in Ray. Did she wish to be part of his personal life?

"I hate these things," he grumbled.

"I know you don't care for parties, but I can't think of a better cause," she softly encouraged.

"Yeah."

"Have you ever been to one of these showings?"

"No. I detest the crowds, the personal questions, and the speculation about my private life. My sole purpose tonight is to ensure that the children and their mothers in these war-torn places aren't conveniently forgotten, and their plight is no more than a sound bite on the evening news. It's important that they aren't exploited, but their lives are made better." He frowned in concentration, warming to the topic. "Someone must take note of what war does to women and children. So many are left homeless and hungry. In today's global society, starvation should not be an issue. Look at Somalia and Rwanda—Haiti—to name a few. It is an outrage."

"I'm so proud of you," she whispered, stroking his hand where it rested on his thigh.

Ray nodded, deeply touched by the sincerity and warmth in her voice.

"Do you think there will be any reporters?"

"Baby, this is Washington, D.C. The political machine never sleeps, which means neither does the press. I just hope I don't regret bringing you tonight. Our relationship is private, not for public scrutiny," his said tightly. "I would have preferred that we spent this evening alone. I don't want to share you with anyone."

Her skin and eyes glowed as she said, "Nothing can spoil what we have. I'm floating on a cloud of happiness. Oh, sweetheart, I'm so looking forward to sharing these next few weeks with you."

Although he remained silent, his hands tightened on the steering wheel and a muscle jumped in his jaw. They had tonight. Tomorrow he would be boarding a plane that would take him back to Lebanon.

"Washington in the spring is the most beautiful city in the world." Amber sighed contentedly, then turned to him with a wide grin. "Do you remember the night you and Brad built that bonfire on the beach and drank that hundred-year-old bottle of scotch Dad had been saving for a special occasion?"

"How could I forget? Your dad nearly killed us that night. We got smashed. How did you know about that? You, little girl, were supposed to be asleep."

"Even kids have ears. Dad wanted to ground both of you for the next twenty years. Fortunately you two had to head back to university."

Whenever Ray remembered the incident, it brought back the warmth and sense of belonging he'd experienced that night. He had not experienced that kind of caring since his own folks' death. Andrew Spencer treated Ray no differently than his own son. The sharp tongue-lashing had been issued to both of them. The underlying love and concern had lasted through the years.

"Mother and I were the ones forced to listen to him rant and rave for a solid week. Is this it?" She leaned forward as far as the seatbelt would allow.

"Uh-huh." Ray eased the car to a stop, almost two full blocks away from the entrance to the impressive two-story building. Rita Caldwell was renowned for her lavish parties, and her showings were social events. Both sides of the street were lined with cars.

"This is exciting. I can't wait to see your work." Her eyes twinkled like diamonds. "I'm so glad the world has finally realized how talented you are."

Ray's heart raced. Her faith in him and her love were what kept him going. It was the fuel that pumped blood into his veins. He smiled, brushing his mouth against the side of her neck. His deeply hooded eyes lingered on her full tinted lips. His voice was husky with emotion when he said, "Thank you."

"Brad would have been so proud of you," she said candidly, refusing to let the painful loss inhibit the simple truth. Ray loved and missed her brother just as much as she did.

Ray's breath caught in his lungs as he swallowed the hard lump in his throat. That simple acknowledgment coming from her meant the world to him. There was nothing she could have said that could have pleased him more.

Ray found himself shaking his head in wonder. He knew he was blessed to have this warm generous lady in his life. He had almost lost her once. He was unwilling to take any chances where she was concerned. Amber was his heart. Ray fought the urge to sample the sweet honey of her lips. The taste of her lingered in his mind, serving to inflame his senses and settle in his groin. He almost laughed out loud. One kiss from her luscious mouth, and he'd really give the capital's gossip columnists something to improve their circulation.

"Ray?" she inquired when he made no move to get out of the car.

He sighed, consoling himself with the promise that they would be here for only a short time, then they would have the rest of the evening to enjoy a late supper and each other.

The wide gallery's double doors were opened by a uniformed butler. The elegantly appointed interior was furnished with exquisite antiques. A picture of Ray graced a gold easel in the lobby. There were warm rose-beige tinted walls and matching carpet underfoot. It was crowded with what seemed like wall to wall people.

Clearly the entire main floor of the gallery had been exclusively devoted to one man's work, Ray Coleman. Amber gasped at the huge black and white photograph of a young mother struggling to protect herself and her child from an angry mob. Her eyes filled with tears at the hopelessness and despair depicted on that woman's face. There was a starkness, an earthiness, to the piece that was very much a part of his personality.

"Ray, darling." Rita Caldwell hurried over as quickly and gracefully as her petite frame could carry her. She threw her arms around his waist and pressed herself against him. Her lips lingered on his in greeting. "I'm so glad you made it. As you can see, it is simply a madhouse tonight. Everyone who is anyone in Washington is here, darling." She paused long enough to motion for the uniformed maid to take their things.

Ray's arm slid possessively around Amber's waist as he pulled her close, then he made the introductions. "Rita Caldwell, Amber Spencer."

"Good evening." Amber smiled, determined to hide her surging feelings of annoyance. She reminded herself that the petite African-American beauty with her flawless rich brown skin was no threat to her. Her long black hair was coiled into a sleek French roll, while diamonds sparkled at her ears and her throat. Her dress was heavy cream-colored silk and clearly haute couture. She barely glanced at Amber, dismissing her as unimportant. Amber valiantly told herself that Rita's kiss meant nothing more than a friendly gesture.

Rita merely nodded then smiled at Ray, hooking her arm through his as she urged him forward and away from Amber. "Darling, the Powells are here and they are dying to meet you. I think they have their eye on the 'Child at Peace.' Come help me convince them they can't live without it. Please, Ms. Spencer, excuse us."

"Amber?" Ray hesitated.

"You go on ahead, I want to look at the work here."

Ray frowned. "If you're sure."

Amber nodded and watched as Ray disappeared into the next room with Rita clinging to his arm. Amber found herself alone, champagne glass in hand. Sighing, she slowly studied each photograph, trying to gauge his mood at the time it was taken and determined not to feel threatened because Ray had left with a flawlessly beautiful woman. She told herself that she had no reason to be concerned, just because Rita Caldwell hung on to Ray as if he were the last black man in America.

No, damn it. It was not like that. Ray was here to raise money for his charities. The children in Africa and Haiti needed all the help he could give them. Yet there had been no mention between them of being in love or maintaining an exclusive committed relationship now that they were lovers. The lovemaking started by accident, a result of a momentary weakness on his part.

If he had not heard her crying, he would never have come into her room that late at night nor would he have had reason to comfort her. She was not blind to the truth, no matter how much she wanted things to be different. He loved her, yes—but there was a question that remained unanswered in her mind: was he in love with her? Until she knew the answer, Amber decided with a heavy heart that she had no more rights to him than Rita Caldwell.

Forcing her thoughts away from her problems, she discovered that his photographs were totally captivating yet painful to behold. Her tender heart ached from the despair she saw. She felt compelled to contribute. Amber purchased the photograph of a tear-stained little boy, his face haunted by death and despair as he stood in the road alone surrounded by the horrors of war.

She was making arrangements with one of Rita Caldwell's assistants to have the photograph shipped to Vermont when Ray approached her from behind, his wide palm settled on her back, her wrap over his arm.

"Let's go," he whispered close to her ear.

She swung around in surprise. "So many of these people are here to meet you."

He frowned. "Wrong. They are here to impress each other." He took her hand and led her down a hallway. The rear doorway open into an alleyway.

"But . . ." she said as she ran with him to the street and down the block. She was nearly out of breath when they reached the car.

He did not say another word until they were both belted into their respective seats. "I need to be alone with you. Any objections?"

Amber shook her head, lifting her face for his all too brief kiss.

They were both quiet for a time as they drove through the city. Ray was the one who broke into the quiet. "Well?"

"Huh?"

"What did you think of the work?"

"Oh!" She laughed. "Your photographs are fabulous. Such depth, such perception, such emotion," she marveled. "You are so talented. I couldn't help it—I bought one."

"Really," he said, his voice gruff with emotion. Somehow he knew she would understand why he did what he did. He had not realized until just then how much her approval meant to him. "Which one?"

" 'The Boy in the Road.' I had to have it."

Ray smiled, thoroughly pleased. When he stopped at a traffic light, he dropped his head so that his mouth could linger briefly on hers, but her sweetness was overwhelming, and it took the sound of a blowing horn behind them for him to break the seal of their mouths and return his focus to his driving.

Amber forced herself to say, "Rita has a wonderful gallery. I was very impressed."

"Yeah," Ray said absently.

Amber longed to ask questions, such as how long had they known each other and if they had ever been lovers, but she did not. She had no right to invade his privacy. They were lovers, friends. They did not own each other.

He looked at her momentarily, wondering what she was thinking. She seemed so quiet, almost lost in thought.

He had said they were friends, but it didn't look that way to Amber when Rita kissed him. Amber longed to demand an explanation, shout her outrage. Thank goodness, she caught herself in time. She reminded herself yet again that she had no right to be jealous . . . no rights whatsoever.

Ray had decided their time together would be of the finest quality. Amber deserved the best. Ray planned to see to it that she got it. Her body was made to be draped in satin, covered by the finest silk. He would give her no cause to regret the changes in their relationship.

How much longer could he put off telling her? He would have to tell her, even when his gut told him that it was too soon to spring this on her. They needed time. Unfortunately time was something they did not have.

Chapter Seventeen

"You look beautiful tonight," he said softly.

They shared a curved velvet banquette in one corner of the softly lit dining room.

"Thank you." Thoughts of the gallery owner were finally pushed to the back of her mind. Her common sense was firmly in place. If he wanted to be with the other woman, he would be there now. Ray was man enough to do exactly as he pleased. He'd never had a problem getting or keeping women.

They had been through a lot together—the worst being the seven years they were apart. His only solace had been his work. He'd become the best in his field. He had made a name for himself. His work had been heralded, but his personal life had suffered. Money in no way compensated for the loss of the woman he adored. Time nor distance could ease the pain or disappointment. He used other women to ease his sexual needs. He was left wanting, needing what only Amber could give him. He didn't like to think of that emotionally empty time when she had shut him out of her life completely. Now finally they were really together, lovers as well as friends.

"We've managed to waste a hell of a lot of time, haven't we, angel? To think I've been sleeping alone in that guest room of yours when we could have been together."

"It's in the past. For the next few weeks we are going to be inseparable. Did I tell you yet how happy I am that you invited me here?" She was so close that a wayward curl clung to his sleeve.

"Yes, but I don't mind the repetition. How is your prime rib?"

"Perfect. How about yours?"

"Perfect." But Ray's mind was not on food. He was hungry, but he was hungry for Amber. He wanted to be alone with her, with the door locked and bolted against the rest of the world. They'd wasted so much of the evening already. Time was disappearing. He'd put off the inevitable for as long as possible. He did not want to risk spoiling their last evening together for some time. How many hours did they have before he must board that plane? His silence was rooted in selfishness. He wanted it all. He wanted her smiles, her laughter, but most of all her precious love.

His stomach was knotted with tension as he drained his wineglass. If the truth be known, he was afraid—afraid of her reaction to the news that he was leaving. She claimed that she could handle a love affair with him. Neither of them expected her to be put to the test so soon. What if he were wrong, and she was not strong enough to deal with the danger he faced day after day? Then what?

He was so used to protecting her from the harsh reality of his job that quite frankly he was not sure he could stop. He did not want her hurt again. Wasn't it tough enough that they had to deal with being separated so often? He wanted what they had to last. Yet he would be a fool if he did not face the fact that this could very well be the beginning of the end of their happiness. Hell—he did not want it to end . . . not ever.

"Honey, what's wrong? You're scowling. Are you in pain?"

"I'm fine. Have any room for dessert?"

Amber was not quite convinced that something was not wrong, although she did not press the issue. "I caught a glimpse of the dessert tray. It looks sinful." She smiled playfully at him.

He grinned. "Mmm, we must keep that in mind. More wine?"

"Please. Did I tell you I like your friend John? How long have you known each other?"

"Seven years. We met when we were working on a international drug-smuggling case. One night he felt sorry for me and took me home for one of his wife Brenda's home-cooked meals. I've gotten into the habit of seeing them at least once or twice while I'm home."

"Tell me about his wife."

"She's nice." Ray did not add that he wished there was enough time for them to meet.

"What does that mean? Does she work outside her home? You mentioned kids, how many?"

"Three little girls. I believe she and John met in college. Good people."

"And?"

"They had twins last year. Brenda quit her job to stay home with the babies until they're a little older. She came to see me while I was in the hospital when John couldn't get away. Unfortunately they're going through a rough time in their marriage. Basically she's raising their kids alone with John away more than he is home. It's hard on them both. They are close to filing for divorce."

"That's too bad." Had he told her about the McClures as some kind of warning that what they had now was all that they could ever have? Was it his way of protecting her from future hurt?

Amber instantly realized that she should be far more jealous of his job than Rita Caldwell. It would eventually take him away from her. He would be completely absorbed in it, so much so that he wouldn't give much thought to anything else, not even her. Time was not on their side. How much did they have? Two weeks . . . possible three?

Amber could not help wondering if he had ever thought of marrying. She nearly voiced the question when their waiter picked that moment to asked if they would care to see the dessert tray.

Ray asked, "Amber?"

"Nothing, thank you."

Ray ordered coffee and after-dinner drinks for them both.

"You're not worrying about the school, are you?"

"A little. Although I do feel much better about the whole Harris thing. I believe Wayne has found the answer. He and Alex are organizing workshops for the children's parents in order to help them deal with the problem. The hope is to give them concrete ways of handling this and helping the children. Until we're absolutely sure that none of the children have been violated, it must be done."

He nodded in understanding. "This is so hard on you. I don't want you to be hurt by this." He hated like hell that he had to leave when things were still so unsettled at the nursery school. How could he support her when he would be hundreds of miles away from her. Ray, toying with her fingers, said, "Come on now. We agreed not to have any serious discussions, remember?"

"Yes." She shivered delicately when he pressed his mouth into the open center of her palm.

"Did I please you this afternoon?" he asked softly, seductively.

"Oh!" She blushed.

He chuckled huskily. "Did I?"

"Yes . . ." she whispered.

"You've got stars in your eyes. I hope I am responsible for putting them there."

"Absolutely."

Ray laughed, studying her mouth. "I bet you were the most beautiful girl at your high school prom." He caressed her cheek when he said, "I would have given anything to have been able to see you that night."

Eyes wide with surprise, she said, "You were overseas at

the time." Watching him smile, she teased, "You know, Mr. Coleman, you don't smile nearly enough."

"I'll try to remedy that. There is music and dancing next door in the nightclub. Come on, I have an overwhelming need to take you into my arms." The timber of his voice was low, blatantly sensual.

Even if Amber was not ready, the sparks in his dark eyes would have convinced her to reconsider. She wanted to be in his arms as much as he wanted her there.

Ray led her through wide oak double doors and into the other room, where small candlelit tables encircled a marble-veined dance floor. Tall windows overlooked the garden.

At last Ray sighed his pleasure as his hands locked behind her narrow waist, and he could feel her along his entire length. With her arms resting on his shoulders, Amber relaxed, her curves melting into the hard angles of his body. She heard the rush of air leave his lungs as her soft breasts pillowed on his chest. His body heated as he thought of her as she had been this afternoon . . . in his bed beneath him.

"I feel as if I've waited all night for this moment," she whispered, her breath caressing his throat.

His arms tightened as they swayed with the music. The sound was hot, intoxicating, and intensely sexual, pure jazz. No hotter, Ray decided, than the blood coursing through his veins. His body pulsed from the rhythmic force of his aching shaft. He had always had a strong sex drive, but never to this extent. He could not get enough of Amber. No matter how many times they made love, he still wanted more. He'd been without a woman for a long time, simply because he did not want anyone but Amber. He'd left her sore from his relentless need that first night, and tonight would be no different. He felt if he did not have some of her sweetness soon, he would crack into a thousand hungry pieces. Forget this candlelit dinner and romance—he needed her. His control was slipping.

The breath rushed from her lungs as his thigh moved

even more firmly between her legs. She gasped his name, unknowingly rubbing against his hard muscled thigh. They had made love only this afternoon, yet her breasts felt so heavy with longing, desperate for his attention. That secret part of her throbbed with yearning to be filled by Ray.

"This was a mistake," he said roughly into her ear. Unable to stop himself, he took her tiny earlobe into his mouth for a hot tonguing and tiny bite. One of his hands was spread wide against the small of her back while the other was scant inches above the lush swell of her behind. "This is insane. We are in the middle of a crowded dance floor, and I'm reacting as if we were alone in the town house. Amber, I want to make love to you . . . with my hands . . . with my mouth. I'm tired of wondering what you have on under this damn dress. Come home with me . . . now."

Amber's entire body trembled in response to him, but before she could speak he groaned. "Angel, tell me you will let me have you. I need to hear that you want me deep inside of you, loving you, as much as I want to be there." He fought down the urge to stroke his erection against her sweet heat.

"Ray . . ." was all she could manage to say, and it turned out to be a husky caress filled with need.

He stepped back, cupping her elbow, and urged her ahead of him. They threaded their way across the dance floor. They slowed only long enough for him to hand some bills to their waiter and collect her wrap.

"Your answer was yes, wasn't it?" he asked as they waited for the car to be brought around. The night air wasn't doing a thing to cool his arousal. He'd been wired as tight as a fist full of dynamite on that dance floor, ready to explode if he hadn't managed to get them out of there.

Amber's soft laughter tingled like sweet chimes against the gentle breeze. She laced her fingers through his. "Oh, yes."

* * *

"Better," Ray whispered into Amber's ear as the two of them moved to the sultry rhythm of Herbie Hancock pouring seductively from the stereo.

A single lamp was the only source of light in the room. His suit coat and tie had gone the way of her purse and shoes, onto an armchair in the corner.

"Much." She brushed her lips against the base of his throat, pleased as his big body responded with a deep shudder to her gentle caress.

Silk rubbed against silk. Amber caught her breath. Heat, delicious heat, caused her breasts to feel swollen, and their ultrasensitive tips ached as they brushed against his wide chest.

Amber's soft hands trembled as they slid up over his shoulders and clasped at his nape. She arched her back and allowed her body to sway with his, shifting from one leg to the other, her sex nestled against the muscled firmness of his thigh.

The fire kindling merrily in the grate couldn't begin to compare to the internal blaze flaming inside of Amber. She wanted him and didn't understand his hesitation. At the restaurant he had practically made love to her on the dance floor. Now he clearly had himself under ironclad control.

The showing followed by a romantic meal and the long drive back to his townhouse had all been wonderful. She didn't need the fancy trimmings. What she needed was Ray. "You planned a very special evening for us, sweetheart. I loved every minute of it, but I'm so glad we're finally alone." She pressed closer.

Ray groaned, loving the feel of her. His body, heavy with longing, demanded that he take what was his. Yet he waited . . . expectantly . . . hopeful that she would show him how badly she wanted him. His male ego was not calling the shots. He was hungry for her, but his hunger would have to wait a while longer.

He had been quaking with need their first night, and again this afternoon, that now he was unsure if the love-making had been all his own doing. It was time for her to show some initiative, give him the assurance that she wanted him as much as he wanted her. The trouble was he was unsure if he could bear the wait. His sex was so painfully hard now that he could barely stand the wanting.

She followed the firm lines of his jaw, first with her soft lips, then her sleek wet tongue. Ray shuddered, dropping his head, allowing her complete access to his mouth. With parted lips, Amber brushed his mouth with hers, soft silky strokes designed to titillate, to tantalize.

The moan he released from deep in his throat sent her heart soaring. Busy exploring his fleshy bottom lip with her tongue, she soon sucked it into her mouth, causing desire to rush wildly throughout his system and his heart to hammer crazily in his chest. When she finally eased her tongue inside, past his strong white teeth and into the heady recess of his mouth, Ray trembled, close to losing control.

Determined to let her set the limits and take as little or as much of him as she wished, he steadied himself. Ray was thrilled when Amber boldly stroked his tongue with her own then sucked it into her own sweet mouth. By the time she pulled his shirt free and smoothed her hands from the base of his spine up his muscular torso, he was shaking from head to toe.

"Amber," he said gruffly, effortlessly lifting her off her feet and pressing her hips into the throbbing strength of his arousal. Vaguely he wondered if it were possible for his blood to boil in his veins—he was flooded with such heat. "Twelve years we were apart. How did I manage without you for so long?" His bewilderment was clearly evident as was his raw male strength. He was all man . . . her man.

He had not felt so vibrantly alive in years . . . an essential

part of her life. Even years of separation had not permitted
him to forget what it was like to be deep inside of Amber,
sheathed in her moist, tight silken warmth. He had tried
to do without her—how he had tried. Yet he had never
been able to stop loving her or wanting her.

"Please . . ."

"Amber . . ." His love . . . his heart—the sound of her
name sent echoes of pleasure resounding inside his head.

"Oh . . ." She shuddered as he licked the top swells of
her breasts exposed by the neckline of her dress.

She was sweet . . . so sweet. Effortlessly she made him
forget all his resolve. An accidental brush of her hand over
his skin, a ready smile that came so naturally to her, could
ignite a fire inside him that was almost impossible to contain.

"Tell me . . . tell me what you need," he growled past
the constriction in his throat.

"You. I want you, baby." At last she told him what he'd
been dying to hear. If by some off chance that he did not
comprehend her meaning, she went on to say, "Inside of
me, loving me." There could be no room for misunder-
standing.

Ray tightened his hold on her until her soft length fit
perfectly along his big frame and caressed along the hard
ridge of his sex. He slowly lowered her, then he bit her
lips before parting them and taking her mouth in a wild
declaration of love. Eventually he pulled back, far enough
so that he could unsnap the belt at her waist and unhook
the overlapping front of her wrap-style dress.

"How, baby, do you want me to love you?" he moaned
against her throat as he pressed his lips there, the brush
of his thick mustache offering an exquisite caress.

"Touch me. I ache for your hands on me, your mouth,"
she whispered barely able to breathe, let alone think coher-
ently. Why was he teasing her this way? He knew how to
pleasure her. He had proven that this afternoon. Her climax had been so strong, so shattering.

"Oh, angel," he said as he shoved the dress off her

shoulders. He ran his hands over the smooth lines of her shoulders and upper arms. "You are so beautiful." He left a trail of kisses down the creamy golden length of her throat to her collarbone. "Such soft pretty skin . . ." He bathed her skin with his tongue.

"Ray," she gasped out, unable to catch her breath.

"So damn sexy," he said, running his hands down the slippery satin black bra, bikini panties, and garter belt cut to reveal far more than they concealed. With his thumb he traced the lace-edged bra to the valley between her full breasts straining against the front clasp. He pushed the straps down her arms and released the clasp, his broad-fingered hands waiting to cup and squeeze her softness. His mouth was hot and heavy on hers, his tongue insistent, demanding her total surrender. He worried each elongated peak, using the tips of his fingers to tug and squeeze her nipples as her breath came in quick uneven pants.

Amber's hands went to his throat. She worked to free his buttons as she longed for the feel of his bare chest. Pushing the shirt away, her hands went to his trim waist while Ray's hands smoothed over her ribcage down to the soft skin of her concave stomach. He did not even consider stopping. He was rewarded for his efforts when he reached the bounty of her womanly hips.

He cupped her softness and lifted her until he could feel her against the hard evidence of his passion. His fingers stroked along the leg opening of her panties to the junction of her thighs, before moving on to the ruffled garters. He slid a finger along the top of her lace-edged black stocking before gently squeezing her upper thighs.

"Oh . . ." she panted.

He unhooked the garters and rolled the thin silk stockings one at a time down her legs. Amber tingled in every spot he had touched, no matter how briefly. She probably would have fallen if her hand wasn't braced on his shoulder as he stooped and lifted each foot in turn. He did not slow until that enticing bit of lace landed in the chair along with the rest of their things.

Her eyes were closed when she felt first his warm palm, then his mouth, on her breasts. He followed the outer curve, lifting, reshaping, then cradling the fullness of her softness in his large hands.

"This is what I've been wanting to do all evening," he said, opening his mouth over a hard sweet dark nipple, circling it with his hot tongue, scraping it against his teeth before sucking it. He was insistent and relentless in his effort to please her. Whimpers escaped from her throat, and she trembled in his arms. He, the source of her pleasure and torment, was driving her absolutely mad with unfulfilled yearnings.

She shuddered as he moved to the other breast, not sure of anything but her overwhelming love for him. Desire radiated outward like a starburst, from her love-filled heart along her weakening limbs as far down as her toes and fingertips—it encompassed her entire being and settled heavily in that empty place between her thighs. She pressed her legs together, hoping to ease the ache raging inside of her.

He kissed her, relishing her sweetness. Dear God, how could he leave her behind? How would he survive without her? She was his heart, his soul.

"Please," she pleaded, when he freed her lips only to return to her breasts. Her hands pushed impatiently at the fabric of his slacks. Why was he still dressed? She needed to touch him . . . to caress his hard length.

Ray took his time, concentrating with unbelievable patience on one dark sugar-sweet nipple. Amber was ready to scream when he eventually moved back to the other. She had never felt more alive, more beautiful or desired.

Her nails sank into the hard muscles of his back as her legs gave out on her. Ray caught her, slowly lowering her to the plush oriental rug.

She opened her eyes in time to watch as he practically ripped his slacks from his body. His eyes were glued to her loveliness as he peeled off briefs and socks in a careless sweep.

She gasped at the raw power in his big dark copper frame. Would she ever become used to his male beauty? It didn't seem possible, for Amber was as needy for him as he was for her. She had to touch him, caress him, pleasure him. On her knees, she ran her hands over his thighs and taut buttocks.

"You're beautiful," she whispered. He was as dark and strong as the African warriors she'd read about. She shivered with excitement as she pressed her soft open mouth against his rock hard stomach where he had been wounded. Her lips were like a healing balm against his flesh.

There had been no time to prepare himself for the sweetest caress as she ran the wet velvet of her tongue down his body. Even if there had been time, Ray doubted he could have managed as wave after wave of pleasure washed over him with an overwhelming force as she slowly, lovingly caressed his heavy male sex from the crown at the broad tip down the entire pulsating length of the shaft to sponge the fullness below.

Ray growled out her name, unable to bear the keen pleasure as his heart raced with uncontrollable excitement. He was a heartbeat away from completion when he pulled her away. He thrust his tongue into her mouth, offering one scalding hot kiss after another. "Do you know what you've done?"

She shook her head, her eyes wide with doubt. "I'd hoped to please you."

"A lit match to a powder keg wouldn't have been more effective." He poured all the love he was unable to put in words into his kisses. Love that had languished deep inside of him for years had erupted, pouring forth . . . all for Amber. Finally he was able to show her how he felt.

He released her mouth only to lap at her navel, causing ripples of sexual tension to streak across the surface of her skin until it reached the heart of her feminine desire. She was panting as he caressed her soft inner thighs. She parted them, eager for his touch . . . his manhood.

Square blunt tips of his fingers moved slowly through the thick dark brown curls, enjoying the softness of her mound. Eventually he parted the womanly folds that hid her secrets from him and stroked the moist heat he found waiting for him. Her soft moans of enjoyment and need seemed to increase his own enjoyment. He loved everything about her—from her own exquisite feminine scent to her damp heat as his questing fingertip eased deep inside of her womanly center. She clung to him, gasping from the spiraling pleasure as he stroked her deeply.

Ray ignored his own pulsating hunger to bury himself inside of her incredibly tight sheath. There would be time for that later, he told himself, but now he wanted to return the exquisite pleasure she had given him. He increased the sweet torment by caressing the tiny pearl at the top of her mound while continuing his strokes deep inside of her.

"No more, Ray, no more."

"Yes, my angel, more." He replaced his hand with the hot, wet strokes of his tongue. He thoroughly enjoyed her sweetness.

"Ray!" she screamed.

He refused to be rushed, he focused only on giving her the utmost pleasure. She spiraled away from herself, and Ray hung on as she reached a quick heart-stopping climax.

Amber had barely caught her breath when he took time only to protect her, then repositioned himself and plunged deep inside of her, filling her to the point of bursting with his masculine strength. It was a long time coming, but finally she was his and he was hers. They claimed each other with each hard, long stroke. No man could love or need her more than he did. No woman could love him so perfectly. His mouth covered hers possessively, and her arms and legs held him close.

They both cried out when he slowly withdrew before thrusting powerfully, deeply. They both trembled from the sheer pleasure of being one.

He pressed his mouth to her ear and told her just how

much he wanted her . . . how she excited him . . . how thrilling it was for him to be inside of her. His voice was gravelly, rough with desire.

They were two souls, two hearts, sharing one special love. While Ray claimed her as his own, Amber cried out as she climaxed yet again. She felt as if she'd burst into a zillion colored crystal lights as she convulsed in his arms. Ray gritted his teeth as her inner tightening rippled along his length. Suddenly his control crumbled, and he plunged over and over again as he convulsed in her arms—his hoarse shout the only sound in the room as his arms tightened even more around her.

Chapter Eighteen

Amber was cold. She turned, reaching for Ray and the warmth of his body, but she found his side of the bed empty. He was standing at the window, staring down into the street. Her voice was filled with sleep when she asked, "Can't sleep, sweetheart? Is the wound bothering you?"

"I'm fine," he said, unconsciously pressing a hand against the injury. "Go back to sleep, angel. It's late."

With a shoulder braced against the wall, his arms were crossed comfortably over his chest. He studied the late night traffic on the street below.

Something was wrong, she could feel it. "Are you sorry?" she asked in a tight voice teaming with worry.

"That we're lovers?"

"Yes," she said, holding her breath as she waited anxiously for his answer.

He did not turn when he felt, rather than heard, her approach. "What made you think that?"

"That's the problem, I don't know what to think. Something is keeping you awake."

He gazed at her from over the width of one shoulder. Sighing softly, he murmured, "Angel, have you taken up mind-reading?" He moved to press a kiss into her hair as he placed an arm around her waist and pulled her close.

"Not exactly. I've an idea," she whispered, pressing the cushiony softness of her breasts against him.

Ray chuckled. "I love you."

"What did you say?"

"You heard me. And don't pretend surprise. You've known how I've felt about you for years." His voice was filled with emotion. He stared down into her small African-featured face.

Going up on tiptoes, she captured his bottom lip between her teeth, bit him playfully, then tenderly sponged the hurt with her tongue.

It was impossible for him to resist her. He responded with all the yearning that had been locked inside of him during the empty years they'd both been busy pretending they didn't care about each other. Such a waste. Finally he accepted the truth. Amber was essential to his emotional survival. He had no life without her.

The trouble was he had to leave again, and he knew his leaving would hurt her. That was the last thing he wanted. That was why he'd put off telling her. Their time together was running out. Their time together could be measured in mere hours.

"Honey . . ." She was supported by his lean hard strength. "Say it again. I need to hear you say it."

"No way. Once is plenty. No sense in inflating your ego."

For once her laughter did not lift his spirits.

"I want you to promise me—no matter where I am—that you'll let me know what's going on with you. I want to know everything. I don't want to be left in the dark. Promise me, Amber."

"What do you mean? You sound as if we're not going back tomorrow together. Didn't you complete your business?"

Ray closed his eyes. When he opened them, he said,

"No, honey. We have only what is left of the night. I have to leave in the morning. I'm going back to Lebanon."

They were standing so close that it would have been impossible for him not to hear the catch in her throat or feel her body stiffen. His arms tightened protectively around her.

Amber turned her head, hiding her face in the space between his shoulder and side of his neck. What she could not hide was the quivering in her limbs.

"I'd hoped we had more time." She prayed her voice was steady, that it didn't reveal her anguish.

No! She did not want him to leave. She did not want to live each day imagining the danger he might be facing each and every day he was away. It was too soon. He had barely recovered from his injury. "Does this have anything to do with the problems with the peace accord?"

"Yes, with the new man Netanyahu in power in Israel the political climate also changes with him. After Rabin was assassinated, Peres was the likely replacement. That didn't happen. I'm interested in how this change will affect the population of not only Israel but Lebanon and the Gaza Strip—the entire Middle East.

She wanted to yell, what about our lives? What about our love? Damn it! All they had was now. She bit down hard on her bottom lip to keep from letting go of the anger, frustration, acute disappointment, and fear that had just invaded her world. She felt them all, but angry disappointment at this moment was the most powerful. It tore at her self-control.

They had been through this before, many many times. Oh, she knew what was expected of her. If he thought his leaving was too upsetting for her, or if he thought she was too frail to handle the danger he faced, he would leave her in order to protect her from himself. She did not want that. She could not bear him withdrawing from what they had so recently found together. They needed time to see where this new intimacy would take them . . . time to just love each other.

But Amber knew she did not have much choice. She must say the words, had to say them even if it killed her. She knew he was watching her, closely, with eyes that saw too much. He was gauging her reaction. Was this a test? His way of determining her strength, her ability to cope with the pressure that his job was imposing on them? Dear God, please don't let her fail, she silently prayed. Her intuition told her that if she showed the slightest bit of weakness, they would have no future. Ray would not hurt her over and over again. No matter how deeply they cared for each other.

If she let her true feelings show now, then later when he returned he would go back to being her best friend. It would be as if the last few days had never happened. She could not bear that. It would be the same as losing him.

"Amber, please. I need to know if you are going to be okay with this. I won't hurt you. No matter how much we both want things to be different. Amber? Do you understand what I'm trying to say?"

She knew perfectly well what she must do, but she chose a diverting tactic, thus giving herself time to gather her strength. "You've known all evening, haven't you?"

"Yeah. I wanted to tell you earlier. I couldn't. It would have spoiled our evening. Tonight was magic, wasn't it, angel?"

"Pure magic," she whispered.

The time had finally come to prove to him she was strong enough . . . strong enough to face losing him without tears or without recriminations. With tightly closed fists as she fought back tears, she knew she had no other choice if she wanted him. She had to make herself say what he wanted to hear.

"What about your injury? Are you strong enough to go back to work?" she forced herself to ask calmly.

"Yes, besides I have a job to do," he said bluntly.

He was leaving in the morning, leaving her behind to face the situation at the nursery school alone.

"Amber?"

She brushed her mouth over his skin near the highly sensitive spot near the base of his throat, hoping not only to distract him but herself as well. "You feel so good." Her soft fingers caressed down his body, tangling in the thick nest of curls below his waist.

"No," he whispered, trying to focus on the problem they must face. Yet his large frame quivered with glorious expectation, and his shaft lifted eager for her caress.

"Yes . . ."

He caught her hand, stopping the movement up and down his length. "I need to know how you feel about this."

"I'll be fine," she said, pressing her mouth to his. She stepped back, catching his hand in hers. "Come back to bed. I want to be in your arms."

Ray was disturbed by the turmoil inside of him. He hated the thought of being separated from Amber. He did not want to leave. For the first time in his professional career, there was no excitement in the challenge ahead.

Separation was nothing new to them. In fact, they'd been apart more times than he cared to remember, the absolute worst being their estrangement. Not since their reconciliation and decision to remain friends had his heart been so heavy and his spirit been so weighed down. Naturally there had always been a certain amount of sadness when they parted.

He considered it an inevitability—a prelude to the loneliness that would haunt his nights and overshadow each day until he returned. With their lovemaking came feelings more intense than ever before. He felt as if he would not be able to breathe easy until he could see her, be with her, make love to her once more.

As they walked hand and hand through the airport terminal, he had no choice but to accept the bitterness of his emotions. He was dreading the isolation, which did not make much sense considering he had been comfortable with his solitary existence his entire adult life. Everything was different now. He never felt like this before, and he did not quite know how to handle it.

The only comparison he could make was after the loss of his parents and his sister's rejection of him. He realized for the first time that he had no family whatsoever. Every new step he would take in this world would be a step alone. Although now he had Amber, leaving her was harder this time around.

His ruthless hunger had begun even before he had opened his eyes that morning. It started when he'd felt her softness along his side. They'd awakened late, but he had nonetheless reached for her with an unforeseen desperation. He'd made love to her as if it might be the last time.

Ray refused to accepted anything less than her total surrender. He'd taken his pleasure from the way she had cried out time and time again in a earth-shattering climax; only then had he allowed his body to claim his own longed-for release. He couldn't remember being so hard or feeling such a violent sweet climax.

They showered and dressed together, unwilling to be apart even for a few minutes. The turmoil inside of him had raged as the time for their separate departures draw closer. Now it was almost a tangible force squeezing his vitals, tearing him apart.

"Have you got your ticket?" he forced himself to ask.

"Yes, sweetheart." Her amber-colored eyes and lovely features were radiant with happiness, her smile warm and loving.

She'd been like that all morning he thought gloomily. Not once had she displayed the tiniest bit of unhappiness. If he had not known better, he'd have sworn she was eager to be on her way back to Vermont. Elliott Wilham's territory. Hell! Her good cheer was beginning to grate on his nerves. Not that he wanted her miserable, but a couple of farewell tears would be okay, Ray decided moodily.

"You'll contact John McClure if something seems out

of the ordinary, won't you? This won't be over until Harris is behind bars."

"If you are trying to frighten me, you're doing a remarkable job." Amber looked at him with wide-eyed concern.

"No, baby. I just want to make sure you are protected. It wouldn't be such a bad idea to have all the locks changed. There is no point in asking for trouble. If I didn't have to leave, I'd see to it myself. You do understand why I have to go, don't you?" Even as he said it, Ray couldn't believe he had vocalized the question.

He was so desperate for her to be strong ... strong enough to handle the inherent danger with his job. He did not want them to have to go backward. He wanted them to continue to be lovers as well as friends. Yet he also accepted that if it was too stressful for her, they would have no choice but to sever their physical intimacy. He would not cause her pain.

"Of course I do. Honey, I don't expect you to give up your work for me. I would never ask that of you. Nor would you ask it of me." The idea was outrageous. He was a highly acclaimed photojournalist, for heaven's sakes. She was nobody's fool.

He sighed heavily, stopping. "This is as far as they'll let me go."

"I'm going to miss you."

"Yeah," he said roughly, dropping her bags and pulling her into his arms against the cradle of his thighs. "Prove it."

Amber pressed her mouth against his, forgetting the foot traffic flowing around them. His lips were soft and dry and so so tempting. She ran her tongue over his fleshy lip before sliding inside to seek his warmth, his magic. His chest rumpled with his response as his breath quickened. He crushed her softness to him for a painfully brief moment before he recovered his senses and eased her away. His hands had tunneled beneath her short peach wool coat to clasp her around her narrow waist. Tenderly he caressed her spine beneath the soft layer of her apricot-tinted silk blouse.

"I love you." His voice was gravelly from the complexity of his emotions, his mouth on her throat. "Remember that."

She stepped back so that she could smile up into his beautiful dark eyes. "I'll remember. Please be careful, my heart. I want you back in one piece."

"Ditto," he said before giving her another hard, sweet kiss. "Promise you'll call John if there is a problem?" When she did not answer fast enough to suit him, Ray said tightly, "I don't want you taking any risks. You should see about getting a locksmith out there first thing tomorrow morning, get every lock on the property changed. Promise me, Amber."

"I promise," she said, terrified he might detect some small tremor. Their entire relationship hung on her ability to keep her true feelings from him.

"You'll call John?"

"Yes, Ray. Don't worry about me."

"It will all work out, angel. Just keep the faith. Now get going before I change my mind and lock you in my town house." A ridiculous thought, considering his own plane was leaving in less than an hour. As it was, he had to make a fast trot across the airport to reach his gate for his international flight. It didn't matter. He had to make certain that Amber was safe.

"Sounds wonderful." She gave him another hug. "I love you," she said before stepping away and waving goodbye.

She continued on through the metal detectors alone. She didn't glance over her shoulder to where she knew he stood watching. She didn't see the puzzled frown marking his harshly drawn features, nor did she see the anguish in his brooding gaze as he followed her until she disappeared from sight, his hands balled at his sides, the knuckles taut with tension.

Ray never saw the slow trickle of tears gliding down her cheeks, tears she held inside since first learning that he had to leave. She knew she should be proud of her acting ability, but she didn't have the energy. It had been taken up by her keen sense of loss. It wasn't until she was strapped into her seat by the window that the slender thread holding her self-control snapped. The anguish battering her heart poured out.

"Are you all right?" the stewardess asked as she checked to see that all the seats were in an upright position for takeoff.

Amber waved the woman away, averting her face. With the seatbelt sign on, she couldn't even seek the privacy of the lavatory. The tears were coming fast and furiously. No, she wasn't all right! She knew she wouldn't be all right until Ray was back ... safe. The pain that ripped at her heart wasn't new. She had experienced it time and time again whenever he left for an assignment. But this time was different. It was raw, excruciating. It was because their relationship had changed, they had become lovers. Her love for him had deepened even more.

She gained what comfort she could from the knowledge that she'd managed to hide her true feelings from him. He had enough to contend with without the added burden of worrying about her. She prayed silently for his safety.

The flight ended none too soon for Amber. She was glad that she had driven herself to the airport rather than asking Ginger or Lynn to meet her. She just wasn't up to any kind of inquiry, even one laced with a large dose of love. She had enough of pretending with Ray to last her a lifetime. She couldn't even face polite conversation when all she really wanted to do was curl up into a ball of misery and pull the covers over her head.

The long drive from the airport in Burlington into Shelly did one good thing for her, she decided. It had certainly tired her out and hopefully would allow her to get some much needed sleep. She was exhausted by the time she turned into her own drive.

"Home at last," Amber mumbled to herself as she slumped dejectedly over the steering wheel. Every muscle ached. She quite literally understood what bone weary meant. It didn't take much effort on her part to realize her fatigue was due to emotional distress rather than a physical cause.

She was alone yet again. Would he come back this time? His last brush with death had been too close for comfort. He could have easily been killed. Didn't he realize that? Why didn't it matter? Why must the job always come first with him?

For weeks she'd worked hard not to let herself imagine the danger he faced as a matter of course or acknowledge that he might not return. Her exhaustion had caused all her defenses to crumble. There was nothing inside of her to block the terror clawing at her nerves.

Frankly she deserved an Oscar for the performance she'd put on for him, especially that farewell scene at the airport. It was a classic. Angela Bassett move over, Amber Spencer was taking her place. Not for an instant had she revealed the despair mushrooming inside of her.

"No more!" she told herself. She was better off concentrating on the sweetness of the night they'd shared—a time of passion and love.

Well, sitting out here won't accomplish anything, she thought tiredly. He would be fine. Very soon they would be together. For now he had his work and she had hers. With her shoulder bag on her arm, she grabbed her luggage and cosmetic case from the truck.

Perhaps the first thing she needed to do was talk to Wayne and work on a timetable for evaluating the children. The children were her number-one concern. She wouldn't waste time thinking about Harris and wondering if he'd been apprehended.

John McClure could be wrong about Harris. He may indeed be a victim of unfortunate circumstances. What if he hadn't hurt anyone? What then? How she wanted to believe that! If it were true, he certainly wouldn't be the first person to be unjustly accused.

What about the bus? In spite of what the FBI agent had

said, things like this weren't supposed to happened in sleepy New England college towns like Shelly. Amber almost laughed at that absurd thought as she let herself in the side door.

She must remember to take this monstrous problem one small step at a time. One small step, she chanted as she unlocked her apartment door at the top of the stairs.

The overnight bag and makeup case thumped loudly on the floor, narrowly missing her feet as Amber screamed. Her eyes were wide with horror as she read the word BITCH spray painted with bright red letters all over her walls.

Chapter Nineteen

"Lynn, if I haven't said it lately, I'd like to tell you how much I appreciate your help. I honestly don't know what I would have done without you and Ginger this past week." Amber paused for a moment from where she'd been dunking a roller into a tray of fresh paint.

"We're friends! Nothing more needs to be said on that subject." Lynn was seated at the cloth-covered dining room table, busy with a cloth soaked in paint thinner, painstakingly cleaning red paint from the glass and silver antique framed pile of family photographs. The furniture and the carpet were protected by large sheets of plastic.

"I'm beginning to feel as if I'm taking advantage. It's after seven. This is the time you normally spend with your family, especially with Brian and Chad both home from college." Every evening during the past week, the Baldwins had helped Amber restore her home.

"Will you stop? We're glad to help. If Alex didn't have to teach tonight, he'd be here, too."

"Look, girl, I'm trying to express my gratitude. Will you kindly shut up and listen!"

"Nope. Enough has already been said. We're family. In my book that means we're stuck with each other."

"Stuck, you say?"

"Uh-huh. You believed in me from the first. I was so unsure of myself when I came knocking on your door for a job." Lynn grimaced.

"You were perfect for the job. I know a good thing when I see it."

"I was a housewife with no experience at anything but changing diapers and keeping house."

"Girl, you were a pro. If you could manage a household with four males, I knew you could manage the office. So will you please hush and let me get back to shouting your praises."

"Well, I'm just glad one of us had some faith in me, because I sure didn't."

"That was all it took—a little time and faith." Amber went on to say, "Even if you don't care to hear it, I'm glad that you and the boys are here. On my own, it would take me a month to paint and clean up this mess." Amber had been so horrified that Harris had been inside her home that the thought of hiring strangers to do the restoration was equally unpleasant. She felt strongly that everything that needed to be done would be done by loving hands.

"I just hope those three are more help than trouble," Lynn said, listening to the music and the boys laughing in the bedroom. "Even if they won't admit it, they're thrilled to be together again." She smiled when she said, "I can't believe I'm admitting this, but it's wonderful to have the house so lively with their arguing and horsing around, the phone constantly ringing, stereo and television adding background noise along with the refrigerator door opening and closing nonstop."

"What's not to love," Amber teased.

Glancing at Amber from where she was perched on the top rung of the ladder, Lynn said, "This Harris thing really has us all worried." She shuddered to think what could have happened if Amber had been home when Harris decided to pay her a visit. The situation could have been a lot worse.

"I don't even want to hear that man's name. He has caused me nothing but heartache. I wish I'd never given him a chance in the first place. I still can't believe I used such poor judgment in hiring him."

"Poor judgment? We checked every one of his references. What more could we have done?"

"Not we, Lynn." Amber scowled down at her roller. When she lifted her eyes, they were filled with shadows. "Me. I'm the one responsible. I'm the one who hired him."

"Stop being so hard on yourself." Lynn's voice reflected her concern.

"I had an uneasy feeling about him when I first met him. I ignored it."

"Please! Girl, you're not psychic. Stop blaming yourself." In a determined effort to lighten the mood, she said, "Thank heavens, these photographs were all framed and under glass. Otherwise they could have been ruined." Lynn didn't need to be told how much they meant to Amber. They were all that was left of Amber's family, and she treasured every single one of them.

Amber fought the outrage she'd experienced whenever she recalled the heartless act of vandalism she'd walked into on Sunday night.

"Are you sure you want to stay here alone tonight? You're welcome to use our guest room as long as you like."

"Thanks, but no. It's time I put my life back in order. I wouldn't have stayed last night, if I hadn't let you talk me into it. I plan to sleep in my own bed tonight. I won't let that man continue to run me out of my own home." She was angry with herself for staying away as long as she had.

"But—"

"Lynn, I have inconvenienced you and Alex enough. Besides that, you've personally supervised the changing of all my locks, plus put in a full day's work in the office. Enough is enough.''

"Through thick and thin, girlfriend."

Amber blinked back tears. "Thick and thin. I love you, sister-love."

The two women smiled fondly at each other. Neither had a sister of their own, and that fact seemed to strengthen their bond.

"I wonder how the meeting with Ginger and Wayne's attorney has gone? Surely everything is all set for the adoption to go through.''

"I sure hope so. They've waited so long for a baby," Amber said. "Wasn't it great of her to take over driving the van? It's been crazy around here. I don't think the telephone has stopped ringing for one whole minute this entire week.''

"Who you tellin'? Thank heaven's the worst is finally over.''

"Is it? I'm sorry, but I can't share your optimism." Amber sighed wearily. "I'm not looking forward to the meeting with our students' parents. Frankly I can think of a thousand other places I'd rather be tomorrow night than at that meeting. What if Alex and Wayne aren't able to convince them that the situation isn't hopeless? That the children might not have been harmed? I might as well nail a closed sign on the front door. Face it, we're not even sure ourselves.''

"Amber, if you don't stop this negative thinking . . . We're taking this one crisis at a time. Our children's parents are responsible, well-educated folks. Most of them are employed by the university. We're part of a strong and tight-knit black community. Just wait, you'll see. It will be fine tomorrow night. The calls have been running four to one in our favor.''

Amber nodded thoughtfully before she returned her attention to painting.

"Who would have guessed that Brooker Sinclair could have broken the story in the newspaper? I didn't think he had it in him. The most exciting article he's come up with in the last two years was how Anne Barr found her great-great-grandmother's letters in that secret panel in her living room wall. Girl, the man can't find his keys half the time."

Amber chuckled. "He's certainly no ace reporter. I'm beginning to regret reporting the break-in to the sheriff."

"Did you have a choice? He actually got many of the facts right—even managed to spell the name of the school correctly. And that quote he had from the FBI! I for one was impressed."

They broke into giggles like two schoolgirls. When they eventually sobered, Amber said, "Harris hates me."

"Forget him! Let's talk about something else."

"I wish I could forget him. John McClure didn't have any news when I spoke to him today. I just want the whole situation over and behind me. I want our children to be safe. I want my life to go back to the way it was. Then all I had to worry about was coping with the insurance company threatening to triple our rates every few months."

"Right now your nerves are raw, but one day soon this will be behind us. Amber, keep reminding yourself that you did nothing wrong. None of this is your fault. Think of it this way. We haven't had so much excitement since the Johnson brothers fought it out in front of the K-Mart over the Bennett girl." She added, "We lost only two students today."

"And three on Monday. At this rate when we close the school next week for Easter vacation, it might be for good."

"They'll be back. After two weeks of little Roger and Rodney, Janet Campbell will pay us extra the take those twins off her hands." Lynn laughed.

"Those are two very busy little fellows, aren't they? Gosh, I'm going to miss them."

"Amber!"

"I know. It isn't like me to look on the down side of things. I know you're right. But it makes me so mad. I'm not going to let a creep like Harris destroy five long years of hard work." She'd survived the loss of her brother, her baby, and her parents. She would survive this, too ... somehow.

"Go, girl!" Lynn cheered.

Amber smiled, then stood back to survey the freshly painted walls, gleaming from loving care. "I think we both could use a break about now. How about a soft drink? We have orange soda, ginger ale, and cola."

"Cola, please."

"Coming right up."

Amber brooded as she collected the drinks and a bowl of chips. It had been bad enough that that hateful man had violated her private domain, she refused to let him destroy the pleasure and comfort she'd found in her home. She told herself she wouldn't feel uneasy sleeping in the apartment tonight. This was her home, for heaven's sakes.

Lynn had cleared a spot at the table and a chair for Amber, so they could relax for a few minutes. "It's a shame that Ray had to be out of the country on business. Harris wouldn't have had the nerve to try a stunt like this if he had been around. Even a fool can see Ray takes care of his own."

She couldn't possibly detest the separation more than Amber. Although the uncertainty and problems in her professional life had occupied a great deal of Amber's thoughts, Ray remained firmly rooted in her heart. No matter how diligently she had been schooling herself during the day not to think of the danger that was a constant factor in his work, when she was in bed fear often kept her awake late into the night.

Lebanon was not supposed to be such a dangerous place as it had been in the past, yet she couldn't forget he had been shot there once. She comforted herself with prayers for his safe return.

It was the not knowing—if he were safe, hurt, alive or dead that weighted the most on her mind. It should have become a way of life for her after so many years. She told herself not to worry that she had spoken to him only a few times. After each conversation with him, she was so torn up from the loneliness. She wanted him back. She wanted him safe.

The simple truth of the matter was that she could not speak to him often enough to suit her. After all, he was very busy, very focused on what he had to do. Surprisingly her problems with the school helped somewhat to control her fears for him.

The only good that had come out of the entire Harris situation was that it forced them to deal with, and bring into the open, the depth of their feelings for each other. That knowledge was helping her through their separation and this horrible upheaval in her professional life.

"You've been very closemouthed about your trip to Washington. Why all the secrecy?"

"I have not. I told you all about Ray's place. The gallery showing, the hussy that's after him, and the wonderful restaurant where we had dinner."

"You didn't tell me how you feel about him having to go away so unexpectedly. Look, I know how you fear for his safety." Lynn had seen the shadows in her eyes. "If you don't want to discuss it, forget I brought it up."

"Lynn, it's not that I'm trying to keep secrets. It's so hard to talk about this. I'm embarrassed to admit that I wasn't truthful with him. I didn't let him see how much his leaving hurt me," Amber whispered. "He would be furious if he knew the truth. I know he'd insist we go back to being friends. Lynn, I couldn't stand that. I love him too much." Amber wiped away a wayward tear.

Lynn didn't have to be told she could see it and the lingering pain in her friend's troubled eyes.

"The worst was at the airport when we said our good-byes." Amber took Lynn's hand when she went on to say, "When we became lovers, I told him I could handle the constant danger and separation his job requires. It was a lie! It took everything within me not to let him see my unhappiness. I did such a good job of acting, he probably thought I was thrilled to see the back of him."

Lynn gave her hand a reassuring pat. "That I don't believe."

"I kid you not. I was convincing."

"How long can you hide the truth? What will you say the next time he calls?"

"I don't know. When I speak to him, it's either put on a performance or have a real crying fit." She thought of the trembling that had set in when she heard his voice on the telephone. Thank heaven his calls were during the day while she was still at her desk.

She didn't have the heart to tell him what Harris had done to her apartment. Why upset him? What could he do so far away other than worry? She didn't want that. She wanted him to remain alert, focused on the job he had to do. His life depended on it.

"I can see myself on my hands and knees begging him to come home." She hated the dishonesty, but her choices were limited. She didn't want to lose him.

"Don't you think he has a right to know how you really feel?"

"Yes," Amber said hanging her head. "I can't tell him, at least not now. I'm not strong enough. Maybe when he comes home . . ."

"You're stronger than you think."

Amber shook her head. "Not when it comes to Ray. When we finally admitted how we felt about each other, it was so special. I won't risk losing him. I won't!"

Lynn nodded her understanding, giving Amber a hug. "It will work out—just wait and see."

"He is so protective of me. I know he would end our relationship if he even suspected the truth."

"I don't agree. He cares for you. I'm betting that his feelings will not allow him to turn away."

Amber bit her lip in concentration. She realized that she was too scared to even hope for that. She firmly believed that the only thing she had to hold on to was that their intimacy wouldn't let him guess the truth.

"All done in the bedroom," Jason said, smiling from

ear to ear. Honey gold paint covered him from the top of his tight black curls to the grubby Adidas on his feet. "We're ready to start on the kitchen." He was flanked by his two very tall and equally handsome older brothers.

Amber and Lynn burst into laughter at the golden-speckled trio.

Amber closed her apartment door with a weary sigh. The day had started out badly. She'd overslept, then been forced to handle the countless telephone calls from worried parents.

She and Lynn took turns answering the telephone. Fear and frustration were on the rampage through the tiny predominately black university community. Unfortunately there were no real answers to give. They simply didn't know if Harris had molested any of the children. Everyone had been encouraged to attend the upcoming parent meeting that evening.

The meeting had gone very well considering the circumstances. It had been followed by a lengthy and vocal question and answer session. Several times during the heated discussions, Amber had wished to be somewhere else. But she held firm, answering all the questions as concisely and factually as possible. She never lost her cool, although the effort had clearly taken its toll. Thank goodness, she hadn't been alone. She had shared the podium with John McClure, Wayne Adams, and Alex Baldwin.

The concerned parents had been given a list of symptoms to watch for in their children and assured that as soon as the school reopened after the spring break every child on the school's roster would be individually screened and evaluated by the child psychologist. Nothing was to be left to chance. Amber insisted that the evaluations would be of no cost to the families. The school would pay for the service. She felt it was the least she could do under the circumstances.

Afterward, the Baldwins, the Adamses, John McClure,

and Amber had gone out for a late supper. With her shoes in her hand, she padded on bare feet through the dark apartment. She stopped long enough in the kitchen to make herself a cup of tea. She had a monstrous headache. Her neck and shoulders were tight with tension. Aspirin followed by a hot shower and then bed were her focal points as she entered her bedroom.

Placing the mug on the nightstand, Amber shed her clothes in record time. In the shower she stood under the spray, letting the soothing beads of hot water ease the tightness in her muscles.

The telephone was ringing when she emerged. "Who could be calling this late?" She frowned as she absently tied the sash of a thick terry robe before lifting the receiver. "Spencer residence."

"Why?" came the masculine whine. "I did a good job for you."

"Harris?"

"You didn't give me a chance. You're like all the others. You didn't give me a chance. Did you like what I did to your walls? Pretty, huh?" His speech was so slurred, she could hardly understand him.

"Listen to me. You've got to give yourself up. There are people who are willing to help you." She was trembling as she urged, "Tell me where you are, so I can have someone come for you. Please let me help."

He continued as if she hadn't spoken. "For the first time that I can remember, I had a decent place to live. People liked me. Me!"

"Harris, please listen to me."

"You listen to me, bitch! I didn't cause you no trouble. You act like you think I'm stupid. Well, I'm not! I had a real home. Mrs. Kennedy was good to me," he said, referring to his landlady at the rooming house. "Because of you I have no place to go. You sent the cops after me, didn't you? You told them lies about me. I didn't hurt nobody. Didn't touch—" He stopped suddenly.

"Touch who, Harris? Who didn't you touch?"

"Nobody! Don't try to trick me—mix me up!" he slurred.

"Harris, you do have friends here. People who care about you and want to help. Please tell me where—"

"Shut up, bitch! You want them to find me, don't you? You want them to lock me up, again. Never! Stay away from me, or next time I'll hurt more than your damn walls!"

The telephone went dead, but Amber didn't move. She stood staring at it as if she could not quite believe what she had heard. Slowly she replaced it, sinking down on the side of the bed. Her legs were quivering so badly she was afraid to trust them to bear her weight.

There was no doubt in her mind that he was ill . ... very ill. For the first time Amber truly believed Harris had done all the terrible things John McClure had accused him of doing. He had admitted spray painting her walls, defacing her home. She shivered uneasily.

He was fully capable of performing any number of horrible acts. She believed him when he said he had not hurt any of the children in the nursery school. She was also forced to face the possibility that in his twisted way he believed she was the one responsible for his current unhappiness. He truly hated her.

As fear swelled inside of her, Amber suddenly could not remember if she'd locked the side door. Surely she had—hadn't she? For the life of her, Amber could not recall.

Chapter Twenty

"Stay calm . . . stay calm," she chanted aloud. She was letting her imagination run away with her common sense. She told herself over and over again that she had locked that door.

She would not let Harris win. She would not let him scare her. Harris could not get to her. He did not have a key. There was no way he could get in again. She had made it her business to have all the locks at the school changed. Oh, why hadn't she taken Lynn's advice and had the place wired for a security alarm system? For heaven's sakes, now was not exactly a great time to think of it!

Despite her assertion, she made a mad dash through the apartment, turning on lights as she went. She paused in the tiny foyer, listening. There was no unusual sound that she could detect. Ever so slowly she released the dead-bolt lock. Her hands were shaking so badly it took her three tries before she managed to complete the maneuver. Amber stood listening through the door while praying, her heart hammering loudly inside of her chest.

"Calm down, girl. Think!" she repeated over and over to herself as she ever so cautiously opened the door. Darkness enveloped her. She flicked on the light at the top of the landing, her eyes peering into every corner of the L-shaped staircase and the hallway.

"Nothing!" She sighed, hurrying down on winged feet.

"Silly," she whispered aloud but was unable to breathe easily until she tested the locked door. She felt stupid, yet she still turned on all the outside lights.

Amber doubled-checked every window and lock in the school. Her ascent was slower, but nonetheless it was made in record time. She felt as if she had played right into Harris's hands. She'd allowed him to frightened her.

He obviously wanted to get back at her for firing him. He'd done an excellent job! He had her trembling with terror. How could she have let him manipulate her so easily?

The slashed tire and the destruction of her home were his way of dealing with the situation. Not once had he claimed responsibility for his own reckless behavior. Drinking on the job and being unreliable were the reasons she had fired him. She had not even known about his history then. She sighed, realizing she was using logic to understand an irrational mind.

If only she could stop shaking. She gave up trying to be strong and made two calls, one to John McClure, the other to Lynn.

As she replaced the receiver, she accepted that deep down she was furious with Ray. She needed him here with her, not halfway around the globe. How could they have a future? He was never around when she needed him. A single tear trickled down her cheek as she hugged her upraised knees.

"Okay, Amber, tell me what he said, word for word," John McClure asked yet again.

"No! John, it's two fifteen in the morning. Please, can't this wait until morning?" They'd been at it for hours, and she was at the point of screaming.

"Come on, honey," Lynn coaxed, squeezing Amber's shoulder affectionately. "One last time, then the nice man will go home and let us all get some sleep." The last was accompanied by a meaningful glare at the government agent.

"Last time, I promise." He effectively hid a smile.

Amber nodded, wiping impatiently at the unwelcome moisture accumulating in her eyes. "I had just gotten home from dinner—"

"What time was it?"

"Eleven thirty, quarter to twelve. What difference does it make? I've told you this a hundred times. I'm beginning to feel like the criminal here, John." Amber rose from the chair, suddenly feeling hemmed in. She crossed to the mantel, absently fingering a photograph. The grandfather clock was the only sound in the room.

"I'll put on some water for tea," Lynn said to no one in particular.

"No, that's not—" Amber began.

Lynn put in, "It will give me something to do besides hit the nice man over the head." She sent the agent a hard look before heading for the kitchen.

"I know this is hard on you, but please concentrate."

Amber frowned, but her voice was steady when she said, "It was while I was getting ready for bed. The phone was ringing when I came out of the shower. He didn't identify himself. But then he didn't have to. I knew his voice. Harris started telling me how happy he had been here—blaming me for sending the police after him. He said he wanted to pay me back for firing him. He wanted to make sure I knew he was responsible for the paint on my walls. He kept calling me bitch."

"Do you have any idea if the call sounded like it was long-distance?"

"I don't know. How could I tell? I don't understand any of this. I tried to talk to him, reason with him, but that only seemed to make him angrier."

"Did he make any reference to his location? It's important. He may be still in the area."

"Nothing that I can remember. He could have been anywhere."

"Are you sure?"

"Yes!" She raised her voice. "I know you're only doing your job, but you're getting on my last nerve. I'm sorry . . . I didn't mean to say that." She stopped, suddenly more upset with herself than him. He was here to help her.

"Don't worry about hurting my feelings, Amber. But there may be something . . . something seemingly unimportant that may help us find him. We can't afford to overlook anything. He's dangerous. We've got to get him before he goes after another child. What did he say after that?"

"I can't remember."

"Amber, we are almost finished."

"Thank the Lord," Lynn said coming back into the room, carrying a tray.

"Amber, how did he make you feel? Were you frightened? Did he threaten you?"

"Of course I was frightened. Why else would I have called you and Lynn."

"Then he threatened you?"

"No, not really. It wasn't so much what he said, it was how he said it. He was so angry. I remember being so disturbed by the anger in his voice that I couldn't remember if I'd locked the side door. So I ran downstairs and checked all the locks in the building. I didn't calm down until Lynn got here."

John nodded, making another notation in his ever present notebook.

"He mentioned Mrs. Kennedy—said something about not being able to keep his room in her boarding house. I think he was very comfortable there. That's not surprising. Rosa Kennedy is one of the best cooks in town, and she loves having a house full of people."

"She complains between college terms when every room

in her house isn't taken. Mr. Johnson and Mr. Daniels have both lived in her house for years, not to mention Mrs. Abernathy. She's a real mother hen, pampers everyone." Lynn speculated, "That may have been the first real home he's ever had."

"You may have something there. Thanks, ladies. Mrs. Baldwin, you're going to spend what's left of the night here?"

"Yes. I think we'll all sleep better if I do."

"That's not necessary. I had all the locks changed, and the security system will be installed in the morning. I'm perfectly safe, aren't I?" She looked pointedly at the agent.

"For all we know, he could be out of state. To ease your mind, I will have a man stationed outside," he answered.

"No. I don't want someone trailing me everywhere I go. That's guaranteed to make me nervous."

"He'll be here for your protection."

"Amber, be reasonable. Until Harris is caught, you may be in danger."

"So could half the population of Shelly."

"He's made threats against you. You said yourself, he blames you for firing him," Lynn persisted.

"I won't live like a prisoner in my own home." Amber shuddered at the thought.

"You won't know our man is here, Amber. He'll be stationed outside the house, across the road. He will periodically check the grounds during the evening hours. If you have a problem, you have only to signal him from your front window," he explained.

"I don't want to be followed everywhere I go. It will scare the community. They'll think I need a bodyguard to go to the grocery store or to the cleaners. We'll end up losing the students we have left."

"Amber!"

"Lynn, I mean it. I've had enough."

"We'll do it your way. No shadow, okay?"

Amber nodded.

"Just one man outside in an unmarked car."

"Okay."

"If you suddenly remember anything, give me a call. Doesn't matter what time it is. I would like to install a listening device on the telephones. That way if he calls again, we can put a trace on it. Okay?"

"Fine. Thanks for coming."

"It's my job." Lousy timing, John McClure decided with Ray being out of the country. Harris's victims were teenage boys, not beautiful women. Yet there was something about the tone of the call that had him worried.

"I'll see you out," Lynn volunteered before Amber could offer.

"I'll have someone out first thing in the morning to take care of the telephones. Get some sleep."

"Good night," Amber said, trying to smile but failed miserably.

Once they were out of earshot, Lynn asked, "Are you sure she's safe? If necessary, I could try again to persuade her to stay on with us until Harris is behind bars."

"She doesn't want to leave her home. Who can blame her.

"One thing is for sure, she is fortunate to have good friends like you and your husband, as well as Ginger and Wayne Adams," he said as he unlocked the door.

"What if he calls again?"

"He's welcome to call. That way we can track him. Stop worrying. We're not about to give up. I want this guy." He patted her shoulder. "Lynn, rest easy. Help will be as close as the front window."

"That's good to know. Thanks, John."

"Be sure and lock this behind me. Oh, remind her to call if she remembers anything else."

"I will. Good night."

Lynn found Amber in the same spot. She hadn't moved an inch. She sat staring at the photograph she had purchased at the Caldwell Gallery. It graced the wall above the sitting area near the window. Judging from the look on her features, her thoughts weren't exactly pleasant.

"We're locked in as cozy as twin peas in a pod. How does a fresh hot drink sound?" Her eyes went to the untouched tray she'd prepared earlier.

"Lynn, you've done enough."

She shrugged. "A hot drink will help us both sleep."

"No, I wasn't talking about the tea. You don't have to interrupt your life this way. You have a family who needs you. I can't imagine Alex was too happy when you took off in the middle of the night."

"Alex is a very understanding man. That's one of the reasons why I married him. The other is he's sexy as all get out!" Much to her relief that prompted a laugh.

"You've been so good to me," Amber said, going over and giving Lynn a hug.

"Glad you noticed. Why don't you go pop into bed while I fire up the old range."

Amber was just too tired to put up much of an argument. She climbed into bed, trying not to think of how big and empty it seemed. She did not bother to change from the lounging pajamas she had hastily pulled on a couple of hours ago. Hours . . . goodness, it seemed like a couple of years. She pressed her fingers to her temples, her head was pounding.

"What's wrong?" Lynn asked as she came in with a tray.

"Nothing serious. Just a headache."

"Aspirin in the bathroom?" Lynn asked, heading in that direction after handing Amber a steaming mug.

"Mmm . . ." she mumbled, almost too tired to sit up. "Thanks," she said when Lynn dropped two tablets into her palm. "I bet Alex would love to get his hands around my throat. Every time the poor man looks up, I have you off and running."

"Will you stop. Alex happens to be very fond of you," Lynn said, picking up her own mug.

Amber sighed heavily. "Did you find everything you need for tonight? There are extra blankets and towels in the hall linen closet."

"I'm just fine."

"I'm glad you're here. Remember, it's just for one night. Tomorrow I'll get that alarm system installed."

"Amber, our guest bedroom is—"

"I know, always available. I appreciate it," she said, blinking back tears. She was so exhausted, but she doubted she would be able to sleep. "That phone call really threw me. It's not like me to be such a baby about being alone. For heaven's sake, I should be use to it."

"You've been very brave tonight. Now stop being so hard on yourself."

"Oh, Lynn, I just want it to be over," she whispered unable to completely hide her torment.

"It will be, honey. Now try to get a little sleep. The sun will be up soon enough."

"You'll call if you can't find something?"

"Will not . . . Night," she called, crossing to the door.

"Night," Amber echoed. She hadn't expected to sleep, but she did, soundly.

She dreamed that she lay beneath Ray's strong male frame. His lips were a gentle pressure upon hers, as she opened her mouth as sweetly and hungrily as a new plant to the moist warmth of the spring rain. He groaned, huskily, his tongue stroking hers. The pleasure—oh, the sweet magic.

"Ray," she whispered his name softly in her sleep, curling her arms around the cushiony softness of the pillow. She sighed again as his lips journeyed along her throat. His lean strong hands were incredibly gentle as they encircled her throat, his thumb meeting in the hollow, caressing the scented place. Suddenly, strong fingers tightened, pressing down into her windpipe. She tried to scream, but no sound emerged.

Amber's eyes flew open, her entire body stiffened in alarm as she realized the hands that had tightened around her throat were thin, but nonetheless strong. The face above hers hadn't been Ray's but Harris's. Her whole body shook.

"A dream," she soothed herself, blinking rapidly, forcing herself awake—concentrating on her breathing, slowing it until it returned to normal. Her eyes traveled around the room, lingering on the familiar furnishings in her bedroom.

"Only a dream," she repeated, hugging her empty arms. "Ray . . . oh, Ray—I need you." Tears that burned her eyes didn't fall no matter how much she ached for their release. The sun was creeping toward the horizon when she finally managed to fall back to sleep.

Chapter Twenty-One

"Your turn," Jason and Amber said simultaneously at the sound of the telephone.

They were in the art center—washing down, relining shelves, and stocking supplies. They'd been at it for hours, having taken time out for lunch at the local fast-food restaurant.

"I went the last time." Jason smiled, yanking open yet another carton of assorted colors of construction paper.

Amber, busy measuring shelf paper, teased, "But it's your mother."

"Probably." His smile widened before he dashed down the hall toward the office.

"Tell her she's supposed to be on vacation," Amber called after him.

The first three days of spring vacation had been devoted to paperwork. It had taken that long to clear her desk. She still had some files to update on the computer, but she decided it could wait. She preferred the demands of physical labor—it tired her out so that she was able to sleep at night.

With Jason's help, they'd been unpacking and sorting supplies. They still had the Wendy House, the music room, and infants' rooms to get through.

"Miss Spencer," Jason called down the hall.

"Huh?" Amber said, going to the door.

"Mom wants to know if you can come home with me for dinner. She says it's only pot roast but German chocolate cake from scratch."

Amber chuckled, thinking Lynn has been a busy little bee today. "Thank her for me, Jason, and tell her I want to finish in here while I'm in the mood. Perhaps tomorrow night at my place. Everyone is invited."

"Okay. Be right back," Jason called before disappearing inside the office.

Humming to an old Motown tune on the radio, Amber went back to work, not even looking up when Jason returned.

"I'll bring those other two boxes of construction paper up from the basement. Shall I take these empty cartons to the shed out back?"

"Please," Amber said absently. "You know, you don't have to spend your whole day working. Wouldn't you rather be out with your friends? This is your vacation, too."

Jason shook his head. "Naw, I can hang out with the fellows anytime. This is more important, earning extra money."

Amber hid a smile, thinking not for the first time what a great kid Jason was. Lynn and Alex had good reason to be proud of him.

"I bet you miss your older brothers."

"It was great having them home again. Although I got tired of never getting any food. Those guys go through cases of chips and ice cream and cookies like you wouldn't believe. The telephone was constantly ringing ... girls, girls, girls. That is all they think about ... talk about. I don't know how they keep all those girls straight."

Amber laughed. "In another year or two I bet you will

be just like them. I must admit I do admire your attitude.
You're willing to work for what you want."

"Thanks. I probably would have given up last month if
it hadn't been for your friend, Ray."

"Ray? What does he have to do with this?"

"He's an all-right guy. I really liked him. He didn't treat
me like a kid. Did you know he was kinda small like me
when he was a kid?"

"No, I don't think I did," Amber said, effectively hiding
a smile.

"Yeah, anyway, he said that if I keep at it, by the time
school started in September I probably not only would be
bigger but would have all the money I needed. Good
advice, huh?"

"Sounds like it." Amber felt her heart swell, not that
she needed reminding that Ray was a good man. It was a
treat to hear that others also appreciated his finer points.
Generally he was such a self-contained, private person that
most people found him just plain cold. With Jason and
her friends here in Vermont, Ray had allowed them a
glimpse of the man she loved.

"Be right back." Jason dashed out with a burst of youth-
ful energy.

Amber sighed, knowing it was too soon to even speculate
on the future. She knew she wanted a lifetime of love and
commitment with Ray. She needed to be a part of his life.

She found herself wondering what it would be like to
live each day knowing it would be shared with him . . . to
wake up each morning in his arms. Unfortunately their
situation was not that simple. They spent more time apart
than they did together.

"Get busy," she told herself aloud. Thoughts of Ray
seemed only to intensify her worries for his safety. They
never really went away. How long could she go on pretending to him that she could handle the danger? She had
not spoken to him recently. She knew he was working, but
each day without word seemed—

"Miss Spencer?"

Amber forced a smile. "Yes?"

"I remember putting the padlock back on the door of the shed when I put the lawn mower away on Monday. The shed is open. Have you been out there?"

"No." Amber frowned, her mind instantly going to Harris. "Did you notice anything else that was unusual?"

"Like what?"

"Anything out of place."

"No—why do you ask?"

"No special reason," Amber said evenly, trying to appear unconcerned. "I just want to make sure there hasn't been any vandalism." Surely Harris couldn't still be in the area, especially with the police watching the house. It had been over a week since his telephone call.

"Nothing was messed up. Does this have something to do with Mr. Harris?" Jason asked.

"What made you think of him?" Amber worked to keep her features casual.

"Not you, too, Miss Spencer. I'm tired of everyone treating me like a baby. I will be thirteen next month! Whenever I come into a room, Mom and Dad stop talking about him and change the subject. I'm no dummy. I know something is going on. The kids were talking about him in school last week. They say he's some kind of nut."

"I'm sorry, Jason. I didn't mean to talk down to you. I had to fire Mr. Harris. He was very angry because of that. That was his reason for spray painting my walls." She suppressed a shudder. "I don't know if the other stories about him are true. I only hope he's a long way from Shelly by now."

"Thanks for not treating me like a kid." Using his knee for leverage, he ripped open another carton.

"Telephone," they both groaned aloud a few minutes later.

"I'll get it this time," Amber volunteered, getting to her feet. She massaged the taut muscles in the small of her back as she went.

Amber grinned when she returned. "Guess who?"

"Mom." He laughed. "She wants to talk to me."

"Just a reminder to pick up milk from the market on your way home."

"Will do."

"It's after five, maybe you should get a move on."

"I can stay if you need me. All I have to do is call my mom."

They both laughed at that. "I mean—"

"I know what you mean. Thanks, you've done enough for today. You've earned yourself another ten dollars."

"All right! Thanks, Miss Spencer. I'll be over around eight tomorrow morning." He pocketed the money, quite pleased with himself.

"Make that nine. This is vacation week, remember. You know you don't really have to spend your free time here."

"I like to. Besides, I have a goal." He beamed.

Amber shook her head. "Okay, you'll get no argument from me. Give your mother my love. Bye."

"See ya." With a wave he was gone.

Amber went back to work. When the telephone rang thirty minutes later, she groaned. Mumbling to herself, she raced for the office—she really should do something about getting a wall extension in the main hallway.

"Hello, Lynn," she answered automatically.

"Hello, Lynn, yourself. This is Ginger. How you doin'?"

"Hi. Sorry about that. Jason has been helping me all day, and you know Lynn. She is dying to get back here. I'm insisting she take some time off. What are you doing calling? I thought you had better things to do, like organizing the baby's room."

"I have been, but you still haven't answered my question. How are you?"

"Tired but it's a good tired. I've been busy here taking care of all those things we never get time for when the school is open."

"Working! Shame on you. Come over for dinner tonight. I've got steak, scalloped potatoes, and homemade apple pie."

Amber laughed. "What is it with all the cooking? You and Lynn own stock in a cattle ranch or something?"

"Huh?"

"Never mind. Thank you, dear friend, but I have too much to do here. I hope to have the Baldwins over soon. I'm hoping you and Wayne can join us."

"Great. Now tell me more about this baby shower you two are planning. Need any help?"

"Not from you, lady. Oh, so that's what this call is about. You're pumping me for information! We want a few surprises."

"Okay, I'll behave. Listen, Wayne is due in soon. I better get back to the stove—wouldn't want to burn his first home-cooked meal in months. Don't work so hard. It will be there when school reopens."

Amber was just finishing up in the art room when there was a knock on the side door. She found herself hesitating for a second. She hurried forward when she heard Lynn calling her name.

"Hi." She smiled, throwing the door wide. "Don't tell me, you can't take no for an answer. I must owe you and Alex at least a half dozen meals within the last two weeks alone," she said waving Lynn inside, then shutting the door behind her.

"Amber Spencer, what are you talking about?"

"Didn't you come to offer a personal invitation that I couldn't refuse?"

"Now that you mention it," Lynn teased. "No, really, I came to yell at my son. I expected him over an hour ago. I suppose earning a few extra dollars has more appeal. Where is he?"

"I don't know."

"What?"

"He left almost two hours ago."

Both women read the rising apprehension in the other's eyes.

"You don't think—" Lynn began.

"No, I don't think anything is wrong. There is a logical

explanation, and we are about to find it. We aren't going to panic. Understand?''

Lynn was shaking so badly she could only nod.

"Come on. We're going to your house. I bet he will be home by the time we get there. He probably stopped to talk to a friend on his way. Give me a second to find my keys and purse, and I'll follow you in my car."

They drove slowly, scanning the streets for any sign of him. The only stop they made was at the market. Neither Mrs. Moore, the owner, or her nephew, Joey, had seen Jason that day.

Amber had barely brought her car to a stop in the drive of the Baldwins' rambling brick home when Lynn raced inside. Lynn had just emerged from the kitchen when Amber entered.

"Is he here?"

Amber judged by the stricken look on her friend's face that the answer was no. Jason wasn't home.

"Where could he be?" Lynn whispered.

"Let's sit," Amber ordered, moving toward one of cane-backed chairs at the oak dining table in front of the window alcove. "We are going to put our heads together. Between the two of us, we're going to handle this calmly and rationally. Where does Jason keep his address book with all his friends' phone numbers?"

"In the desk in his room."

"I'll get it."

Tears filled Lynn's large dark eyes. "My baby . . ." She couldn't go on. Her dark eyes seemed to shimmer in the fading light coming in through the lace curtains. They were filled with fear. "I need to call Alex," she mumbled almost to herself.

Amber held her hands, communicating a shared sense of fear and grief neither was able to put into words. Lynn was the sister she hadn't been fortunate enough to have.

"As far as we know, nothing has happened to Jason. He's merely late. We won't think the worst . . . we won't." She gave Lynn a quick hug before handing her the telephone. Amber swallowed the tears rising in her own throat. "Call Alex. Maybe Jason has called him."

Amber hurried toward the wide staircase leading up to the bedrooms. "Anything?" Amber asked when she returned a short time later with the address book in hand.

"No, Alex hasn't heard from him. I also called Ginger, she hasn't heard from him, either. They both will be here soon. Oh, Amber," she said, taking her hand. "You're right. There has to be a simple explanation. And when I get my hands on that boy—" Lynn made a valiant attempt to smile.

"That's the Lynn I know and love. Are they having anything over at the junior high school for the kids? What about Jenny's Sweet Shop? He could have met one of his buddies there for a banana split."

"Jason is such a responsible kid. He wouldn't just go off without calling me first. He knows how I worry. He also knows I was expecting him with that milk for the potatoes I never got around to mashing for dinner." Lynn motioned her hand to the range top and the diced vegetables on the butcher block work island in the center of the room. "Where could he be?"

"He's dependable. But he's still a kid. Sometimes they do foolish things. You know that," Amber said, trying not to ring her own hands in hopeless frustration. She had to stay calm for Lynn's sake. She wouldn't be much help to anyone if she broke into hysterics.

"I'm so glad you're here. I'm just not thinking straight. Let's start calling his friends. We're bound to find him."

Jason wasn't with any of the half dozen friends he had listed. Nor had Jason arrived by the time his father, Alex, got there or Ginger and Wayne at seven thirty.

Between the two of them, Amber and Ginger managed to get the meal together for all of them—not that anyone seemed inclined toward eating it.

John McClure had come and gone questioning each of

them, Amber more intensely than the others. The hours seemed to drag. Unfortunately when telephone did ring, it was one of the Baldwins' friends eager for news.

Although no one voiced the thought, they all feared that Harris was connected to Jason's disappearance. There was no ransom demand—nothing to give a clue to the boy's whereabouts or the reason for his disappearance, other than the most dreaded one—that Harris had taken him.

Alex paced the den while Ginger and Amber did what they could to support and reassure Lynn. Wayne manned the phone, fielding the calls. It was a long, long night.

Amber wrestled with her own sense of responsibility and regret. She couldn't stop thinking that it could have been prevented. If she hadn't been so self-absorbed, if she'd agreed to have dinner with the Baldwins, then she would have driven him home. Jason would be in his own room right now, probably playing his music at full volume, much to his parents' chagrin. Harris could not have gotten to him.

Common sense dictated that if Harris was responsible for the boy's disappearance, one failed attempt would not stop him, probably only lead to another try. Logic and reason were not keen parts of her thought patterns this night. She was functioning on pure emotion, and she couldn't seem to control her mounting fears.

Wayne and Ginger went home around two thirty in the morning, leaving only after the Baldwins promised to call if there was news.

Amber stayed the night, preferring to be on hand given the off-chance that she was needed. She would gladly do whatever was needed to help Lynn and Alex through this horrible time. Lynn had been there for her during the rough times from establishing the nursery school and through to the worst of Harris's scare. She had never lost faith in Amber or blamed her for hiring the man in the first place.

Amber could not stop wondering if she would have been

quite so generous if the circumstances were reversed. A crisis like this forced her to realize what her friendship with the Baldwins had come to mean to her. She valued them both. They were good people. They certainly didn't deserve this kind of heartache. From the first, Alex Baldwin had volunteered his professional services to the nursery school with no thought to his own demanding schedule at the university. Their entire family helped Amber put her home back together after the vandalism.

In the guest bedroom Amber woke warily. She hoped the others had managed to get some sleep. None of them had gone to bed until after four. With barely four hours sleep, she pushed the velvet coverlet back and padded into the connecting bathroom. She showered but was forced to dress in the same jeans and sweatshirt she'd worn the day before.

"Something smells good. Mornin'," Lynn said when she entered the sun-brightened kitchen. Her smile didn't reach her dark brown eyes.

"Coffee's ready. Sit, I'll get you a cup."

"Amber, you don't have to ..." She gestured to the delicious smells coming from the covered warmer.

"I know I didn't have to, but I wanted to do something. Bacon, french toast, scrambled eggs are ready." Amber encouraged as she poured coffee into a yellow flowered mug.

"Just coffee, I don't think I can eat. I'm glad you stayed last night." Lynn made herself comfortable at the kitchen table.

Amber filled two plates, certain she wouldn't be able to eat anymore than her friend but determined to try. "Here we go. Did you get any sleep?"

Lynn shrugged, taking no notice of the plate Amber placed on the placemat in front of her when she joined her at the table. "A few hours. How about you?"

"Same. How's Alex? Did he manage to get some sleep?"

"A little, thank goodness. I think he is taking this harder than I am. Jason is our baby. Every time I closed my eyes,

I saw him. Hungry . . . hurt—" Lynn broke off with a sob. "Sorry," she said, reaching into her pocket for a Kleenex.

Amber's eyes were also brimming with tears that she had been struggling not to let fall. She had to remain strong for Lynn's sake.

The two looked at each other through watery eyes. Suddenly they were holding each other and giving vent to all the fear welling up inside of them. Tears rushed down their cheeks while they rocked and sobbed.

"He'll be fine. He just has to be," Amber reassured, drying her face on a paper napkin.

"I keep telling myself that. If only there were something we could do. We called Jason's brothers this morning. It was so hard, so hard. But we can't keep this from them."

"I wish I could do something to help . . . anything." Every time she thought of him as he was during the day yesterday, her heart ached.

Lynn shook her head. "All we can do is pray."

Amber nodded, impatient with the long wait . . . the waiting was driving them all crazy.

They ran out of tissues and napkins before they ran out of tears. They laughed when they realized they were mopping their faces on one of Lynn's yellow dishtowels.

Lynn surprised Amber when she gave her a hard squeeze. She lifted a fork with a determined glint in her eyes. "Eat."

They'd barely started when Lynn said, "Amber, I want you to stop blaming yourself. None of this is your doing."

"How?"

"How did I know?"

"Yes. Have you started reading tea leaves?"

"I know you. You feel responsible. You're not. That horrible man is the only one to blame for this. I feel it in my bones. I just know he has my son. This was such a nice, peaceful little college town. Small, secure, a wonderful place to raise children. Ever since he showed up, it has been one problem after another."

"If only we'd known . . . something—" Amber stopped abruptly and started eating.

"Amber, I'm not made of cotton candy. Speak your mind, girl."

She chose to change the subject instead. "Are the boys coming home?"

"Alex and I haven't decided. To tell you the truth, Amber, I couldn't deal with the anxiety of having either one of them in an airplane. I want them to stay where they are . . . safe. I know its illogical, but that doesn't change how I feel."

"I can understand your feelings."

"Oh, Amber, I can't stand the thought that that hateful man might be . . . He's so young, too young to even understand any of this. I'm thirty-nine, and I don't understand it!"

"Oh, honey, don't. Please, don't torment yourself this way. We really don't know if Harris has him."

"Morning," Alex said, reaching for the coffee mug with one hand and the percolator with the other.

Amber did not need to ask how he was. One look at his haggard bronze features was answer enough.

"Sit. I'll get his breakfast." Lynn pressed Amber back down into the chair. "It will give me something to do."

They had barely finished breakfast when the doorbell and telephone both started ringing. It was the beginning of another long day. Time passed slowly with no real news of Jason or Harris. It was as if the two of them had disappeared off the face of the earth. John McClure sent several agents over. They went through the house, asking question after question while others manned the telephone and monitored the area. None of them seemed able to supply any new information.

Ginger and Wayne came in the early evening with a meal and plans to spend the night. A tired and disheartened Amber left for home with the promise that she would return in the morning.

It was after ten when she turned into her own drive,

waving at the man parked across from the house. As was her custom, she parked in the garage. The old rambling house was completely dark. The wind whipped briskly from off the lake, as if a storm might make an appearance before dawn.

Amber was too tired to pay much attention as she pulled the collar of her jacket close to her neck. It was such a dismal night. Probably downright frightening to the young boy out there somewhere. Amber shuddered with ever increasing dread.

"Please, dear God, let him be unharmed," she prayed softly, disengaging the alarm system before she let herself inside. She stepped on something underfoot, then flicked on the hall light before stooping to retrieve an envelope.

She had hung her jacket in the foyer before she opened the envelope. After reading the single handwritten sheet through, she was shaking so badly that she had to lean against the door for support.

> *Boss Lady,*
> *He's safe for now. Be at the*
> *telephone booth in front of Anderson's*
> *Drugstore, if you want to keep the boy*
> *that way. Ten thirty! No cops!*

Chapter Twenty-Two

The note was not signed, but Amber had no trouble recognizing the handwriting. Impulsively she shoved it into her purse and grabbed her coat. She ran back down the stairs and out the door.

Her only thought was for Jason and his well-being. She had less than twenty minutes to reach the drugstore in town. The boy's life might depend on her! He had said no cops. She didn't even consider disobeying. She trusted Harris about as far as she could throw him. What she did believe was that he would not hesitate to hurt Jason if she didn't do exactly what he said.

As she backed out of the drive, she gave silent thanks that the FBI was watching the house and not her. With any luck he would think she had run out of bread or something.

She broke the speed limit getting from the nursery school to Main Street. Luckily for her, the sheriff was busy at the police station, working with the FBI rather than on the road. She was out of breath by the time she parked the car and then raced to the telephone booth. She grabbed the telephone before it could complete its inital ring.

"Hello?"

"Where have you been spending your nights, boss lady? Got a new boyfriend?"

"Do you have Jason? How is he?" she blurted out, her heart racing with fear.

"Not so fast. I talk, you listen."

"Is Jason there with you?"

"Yeah, I've got the kid."

"Please, let me talk to him."

"Ain't we polite," he said with a jeer. "No, you can't talk to him. I give the orders. I'm not taking them from you anymore. Understand?"

"Yes," she said, taking deep breaths in an effort to calm herself. She must remember everything. She had to concentrate. Jason's life might depend on it. It was difficult because his words where slurred as if he had been drinking.

"You got your phone wired, didn't you. I saw the cop out front. But I can still get to you, can't I." He apparently found the idea funny because he laughed uproariously.

"Please, may I speak to Jason?"

"I like it when you beg, boss lady." He chuckled.

Amber was having difficulty swallowing. "Please, let me speak to him."

"I need money. Big money. I want you to get it for me."

Amber didn't make a sound. She waited with baited breath for him to go on, her thoughts racing.

"Did you hear me?"

"Yes, I heard. But why are you asking me?"

"You're the one I hate. If you want to see him alive, you'll do what I say."

Amber had no trouble understanding his reasoning. She was the one to blame because she had hired and fired him. This whole thing had apparently been designed to get back at her, not the Baldwins.

"I want fifty thousand dollars in cash by tomorrow morning."

Amber didn't even bother to pretend she did not have access to that kind of money. It was a waste of precious time. Just after he started at the school, there had been an article in the newspaper about her background and her family. Everyone in Shelly knew she came from money. The tender hold she had on her emotions snapped, and she said angrily, "I won't help you if you hurt Jason. I won't!"

"Shut up! I'm the one making the decisions. You ain't the one in charge this time. Listen good"—he paused— "I need that money. You have less than twelve hours to get it for me and be back on this line tomorrow at ten. Then I'll tell you where to bring the money."

"No! Now you listen to me. I won't do it. If you don't let me speak to Jason, I won't give you a dime. I'll be the one hanging up this phone and calling the police!"

"Don't you dare threaten me. Have you forgotten what you've done to me? Have you!"

"I won't give you the time of day unless you let me speak to Jason. If you've even touched him, hurt him in any way, I won't give you a nickel!"

Amber forced down the terror. She ignored the quivering in her limbs. Jason was all that was important. She loved Jason, and she knew his parents were counting on her to keep him safe.

"Okay." There was whispering, muffled sound then finally Jason's terrified voice came over the line.

"Hello?"

"Jason! Oh, honey, are you all right? Has he hurt you?"

"Miss Spencer? Is that you?" He started sobbing.

"Jason, are you hurt?"

"Enough!" Harris said, taking over the telephone. "Now let's talk dollar bills."

"I'm warning you. You better not hurt him," she said, fighting tears.

"Ten o'clock with the money."

"The banks don't open until nine thirty!"

"I suggest you set your clock. Get the money. Then wait

for my call. I'll tell you what to do next. No FBI . . . no cops. Understand?"

"Yes."

The buzzing in her ear signaled the connection had been broken. Amber stayed where she was for some time, too shaken up to move. In fact, she did not stop shaking until she was inside her apartment . . . the security alarm on, all the doors and windows locked.

She lost count of the times she reached for the telephone, only to pull back at the last second. She desperately wanted to call the Baldwins. But what could she say? And she certainly did not dare call John McClure.

She lay in bed, wide awake, promising herself that she would do whatever had to be done in order to ensure Jason's safety. She owed it to Lynn and Alex Baldwin. She owed it to herself, and she owed it to Jason. She would follow Harris's instructions except for one small detail. She wouldn't hand over the money until she had Jason back. With any luck, tomorrow night the boy would be at home with his family where he belonged.

"Oh, Ray," she whispered aloud. If only he would call. If only he were here. He would know what to do. He would know how to go about getting the boy back.

Was she wrong in not calling the FBI? What if she were making a huge mistake? No—she could not even let herself think that way.

Was this how it was always going to be, with her man thousands of miles away when she needed him the most? Tears of anxiety and loneliness soaked her pillow before exhaustion claimed her, and Amber finally slept.

"Good mornin', Miss Spencer. Decided to get an early start?" The aging security guard grinned, having unlocked the door to the bank.

"Morning, Mr. Williams. How's your wife today? I heard about that fall she took down the back stairs." Amber smiled, trying to act as if her stomach was not twisted with anxiety.

"Much better since Doc gave her that new medicine." His brown face creased with laughter when he said, "But her disposition ain't improved much since she cain't get out there to get the garden started like she wants. Be another couple of weeks before that."

"Tell her I said hello." Although impatient to get her own business taken care of and be out the door within the time limit Harris had set, Amber concentrated on appearing unhurried. She could not risk doing anything that might draw undue attention to herself.

"Yup. That little granbaby of mine sure does miss that school bein' open. She don't have no time for spring vacations when there are baby dolls to play with and pictures needin' paintin'." His hearty laughter ended in a burst of coughing. "Yes, sir. The Missus was sayin' just the other night how good your place been for the little one." He leaned forward, whispered, "Don't let these busybodies in this here town run you away from here, gal."

"Thanks, Mr. Williams, I'll remember that. Good day to you."

She was off across the lobby. The warmth and interest in others was one of the things she liked most about small-town life. Unfortunately this morning that charm was about to drive her nuts. She was stopped twice with inquiries about Jason. Word had somehow leaked out.

"Good morning, Amber," Jan Erickson, the assistant manager, said with a smile. "My, you are out bright and early this morning. If I was lucky enough to be on vacation, I wouldn't be up a second before noon. Better still, I might be on some romantic cruise in the Caribbean." She had a dreamy look in her eyes. "How are Lynn and Alex?"

"Doing as well as you can expect."

"It's a crying shame about Jason's disappearing. Well, what can I do for you today?"

As Amber prayed that her features didn't appear as fragmented as her thoughts, she suddenly recalled a bit of local gossip. Jan Erickson was supposed to be dating Sheriff Matthew Brown, Shelly's finest. The stylish black divorcee's love life was the focus of much speculation. Her two-year-old daughter, Anita, was enrolled in the nursery school. All Amber needed was for Jan to casually mention over lunch to the lovesick sheriff that Ms. Spencer had needed to get in her safety deposit box. How long would it be before he figured out that what she needed was money? Money to free Jason.

Surely there was some law about confidentiality in the banking system? In Shelly? Amber would have laughed aloud if she weren't so busy hiding her trembling hands in the pockets of her dark blue linen slacks while she waited for Jan to lead her through the maze of locked doors in order to reach her box.

Jan hesitated before leaving saying, "I hope you're not thinking about closing the school. We working moms need you desperately. I know what some folks are saying. But I for one don't believe it for a second. I had a good talk with my baby girl, and she is fine. I even took her to her doctor to have her checked."

Amber fully understood Jan's parental concerns, but she was so shaken by the time constraints that she was under that she barely got out. "That's wonderful. I'm so glad Anita is fine."

"Well, are you?" At Amber's blank look, she repeated, "Going to close the school?"

"No. I'm just in kind of a hurry. I need to sort through some insurance papers this morning."

"Well, I am so glad. I was telling Matthew, only last night, that I didn't believe a word of what they've been saying about that Harris person. You would not let a soul hurt any one of those precious children. They are so well cared for at your school. Brooker Sinclair ought to be ashamed of himself for printing that awful story."

Amber's worst fears were confirmed. Jan was dating the sheriff. Now what? She could not very well ask the woman not to mention having seen her this morning.

"I appreciate that wonderful vote of confidence you have given the school. We need more parents like you, Jan. Now if you will excuse me, please."

The woman beamed at the compliment, then finally excused herself.

Amber nearly sagged to the floor with relief, thankful that she kept a considerable amount of ready cash in her safety deposit box for emergency purposes.

Amber knew she was over reacting. Jan would not be on the telephone the instant she walked out of the bank, calling the sheriff, who would not be calling the FBI. Jan had no reason not to believe the story about insurance papers.

She hurriedly placed the money in the navy tote bag she'd brought for that purpose. Half a dozen times this morning, she'd reached for the telephone only to take her hand away at the last minute. She had even gone so far as to punch out most of the Baldwins' telephone number. On the last digit she had made herself slam down the receiver. The line was being monitored by federal agents.

What was she thinking? Harris had been very clear . . . no police. How could she tell Lynn what she was up to without involving them?

Harris had placed her in an terrible predicament. All morning she had been constantly fretting that she might not be doing the right thing, while at the same time believing she had no other choice. No matter how many times she reaffirmed the wisdom of her actions, she could not stop worrying. If she could just talk to Lynn. But what purpose would it serve, other than to relieve Amber's doubts and scare her friend half to death?

Fear was a primary concern—fear for Jason's safety. There was no doubt in her mind that Harris would carry out his threats. He could not be trusted. Amber was going to do whatever was necessary to prevent that. Somehow she would get Jason away from that horrible man, even if it meant risk to herself.

"I won't let you hurt him," she whispered over and over to herself as she rushed out of the bank.

Amber couldn't breathe a sigh of relief until she reached the car. She dropped her keys four times before she managed to unlock the door and get inside. "Girl, will you calm down before you do something really silly," she mumbled to herself. She had to keep her wits about her. She carefully drove the three and half blocks to the designated telephone booth outside Anderson's Drugstore.

She heard the phone ringing as she closed the car door. Snatching up the receiver from the cradle, she said, "Hello?"

"Where have you been?"

"Where do you think?"

"Look, boss lady, I'm not taking orders from you anymore. Did you get it?"

"How is Jason?"

"The kid is fine. Did you get the money?"

"Yes."

"Good. Now listen. I want you to take a little drive into the countryside. Nice day for a drive, don't you think?" He laughed as if he'd made a joke. He apparently did not expect an answer and didn't receive one. Amber was straining to remember every detail. "Take the old River Road, pass your place, drive down to the turnoff. Are you with me so far?"

"Yes."

"Take the turn to the right, drive all the way to the dead end. Leave the money at the big oak in a red garbage bag."

"Red? Where am I supposed to find a red garbage bag?"

"Just do it! Make sure every penny is inside. Leave it, then drive back to town. If you want the kid unharmed, you won't contact the authorities, understand?"

"Wait! What about Jason?"

"What about him?"

"Where will he be? You are going to release him at the same time, aren't you?"

"Who said anything about releasing him? I said I won't hurt him. That was the only deal I made."

"Are you crazy?" she screeched into the telephone, losing control of the precious hold she had on her temper.

"Don't call me that! You just get the money here by eleven. One hour, boss lady!"

"Forget it! I'm not paying you one stinking penny, if you don't let that child go free. Do you hear me?"

"You're forgetting one important detail. I'm running this deal, not you."

"I'm going to hang up this phone right now and call the FBI. They'll know what to do a with creep like you." Amber's knees were shaking so badly she had to hold on to the ledge inside the booth to keep from falling.

"Do that and the kid is dead!"

When this was followed by prolonged silence, tears burned her eyes, but she did not make a sound. In fact she bit her lips, forcing back a moan of surging despair.

"You have one hour. Get moving."

"You have to promise me that you won't hurt him." Now was not the time to show even a hint of weakness. "I won't let you play with that child's life."

"The kid is fine . . . for now." The telephone went dead in her ear.

Amber did something she knew she should not, but she could not help herself. She dropped another quarter into the slot and punched out the Baldwins' telephone number.

"Hello?" Lynn answered.

"You wouldn't happen to have any red garbage bags, do you?"

"Yes, I used them for a Christmas craft project. Why?"

"I'll be there in a few minutes. Meet me out front." Amber prayed that Lynn would not draw the interest of the officers inside her house.

When she drove up to the house, Lynn had just stepped outside, bag in hand. Amber met her at the center of the drive.

She gave her a quick hug and said, "Please don't ask

any questions. Promise you won't tell anyone, not even
Alex. Promise?"

"What's going on?

"Promise!"

"Okay."

Amber quickly explained what had happened and what
she was about to do, leaving out the drop-off point. She
ended with, "This is not open for discussion. If you haven't
heard from me by nightfall, tell Alex and John McClure."

"Amber, please, don't do this." Lynn grabbed her arm
as if to hold her.

"I have to. Love you," Amber said, getting inside the
car.

Tears filled Lynn's eyes as she waved, "Be careful.
Thanks."

Amber didn't have time to worry about what explanation
Lynn would come up with for their brief meeting, nor did
she have time to wonder if she was handling this situation
correctly. She'd agreed that she would not tell the authorities. Harris had not said anything about Lynn. Her child
was involved, but Lynn would keep her word. By nightfall,
if Harris had not released the boy, the FBI would be out
hunting for him.

Amber was not about to take any chances with Jason's
life. Harris might get the money, but she intended to be
on his behind, making certain that Jason remained
unharmed. With any luck Harris would lead her right to
Jason.

Once she had passed the city limits, she pulled over to
the side of the road. Amber stopped long enough to
recover the small gun from the glove compartment. Pocketing it in her windbreaker, she returned both hands to
the steering column and pressed down hard on the accelerator. Thanks to Ray, she not only owned a gun but she
knew how to use it. Unfortunately she had never overcome
her revulsion for the deadly thing.

There was nothing for her to be afraid of, she told herself
purposefully ignoring the speedometer as the numbers

flew pass eighty. She would do what had to be done. There was no time for panic or fear.

The money had never been important to her. She had received a trust fund on her twenty-first birthday. Her grandmother had been the first female and first African American to become a partner in a very lucrative Boston law firm.

The amount Harris was asking did not even come close to the settlement she had received after her parents died. Amber blinked back tears. Money could never make up for the loss of her family. Mom, Dad, Brad, and her baby—all gone. But she knew she was lucky. She had Ray and good friends like Lynn and Alex.

"I'll get him back for you, Lynn. I promise. I'll get him back."

Chapter Twenty-Three

Amber had not chewed a fingernail in sixteen years. She had bitten off three before she realized what she was about. It was either that or pull her hair out by the roots. Right now it didn't seem like such a bad idea, considering the way it was constantly clinging to her damp forehead and neck. Searching her pockets, she found the silk scarf Ray had given her on one of his trips to Paris. She used it to tie back her hair.

She'd dropped the money at the assigned spot twenty minutes earlier, then walked back to the car and drove off. She'd parked just around the bend and ran back to hide behind bushy scrubs.

Nothing was moving except the wind. The money was still where she had left it. Where was Harris?

Amber had bitten two more nails before she heard the snap of twigs and rustle of a nylon windbreaker. She sat without moving, barely breathing.

Harris's tall lanky frame passed within inches of where she was hidden. He moved cautiously, scanning the area before approaching the bag propped against the lone tree at the end of the dead-end gravel road. He stepped out into the road, circled the tree, then grabbed the bag. Tucking it under his arm, he took off at a run across a hill in the opposite direction from where he approached. Harris darted to the left, passing several boarded-up summer homes.

Amber was several yards behind him. Suddenly she was grateful for the aerobic classes Ginger and Lynn had dragged her to at the university's health center.

Unfortunately Harris was faster with those long legs. The fact that it had rained the night before didn't help, either. The grass was slick, tough going as they moved through the wooded area bordering the lake. The ground was soggy and uneven in places, causing mud to soak into her athletic shoes. Why hadn't she thought to wear boots?

Amber was forced to duck behind a tree when he stopped to search the terrain. She didn't so much as blink until he seemed satisfied and started off again at a brisk pace. All too soon for her peace of mind, he left the relative protection of the woods and was racing across a overgrown field of weeds and decayed cornstalks.

Amber knew better than to move into the open. She waited until he disappeared from view, then ran to catch up. She was out of breath when she spotted him again, heading for the fence bordering the field. She dropped down flat on the ground, burying her face in her arm when he searched the area before jumping the fence and continuing on.

Ignoring her mud-caked knees and hands, it took her a few precious minutes to climb the fence, but she managed. A piece of cake, she congratulated herself with a smug smile of satisfaction on her lips. She'd gotten quite a bit of practice in the old days when she was forced to keep up with Brad and Ray or be left behind.

From behind a nearby oak tree, she watched Harris slow, look behind him, then disappear inside an isolated cottage.

"But of course!" she whispered. The cottage belonged to Mrs. Kennedy, the owner of the rooming house where Harris had lived. The elderly woman had no use for it anymore, but often rented it out during the summer months. Mrs. Kennedy must have inadvertently told him about this place.

Amber was halfway to her car when she stopped suddenly. Was she wasting valuable time by going back to the car to use the telephone to call John McClure and tell him where Harris was hiding? What if he didn't still have Jason? What if it was all some elaborate hoax? Harris had the money. There was nothing to prevent him from taking off. He could go anywhere he wanted with that kind of money.

No, she had to go back and find out for sure that he had Jason. Where was her head? Why had she remembered the gun but had forgotten to bring the cellular phone with her? Where was her mind?

If she were lucky and there was a back door, or even a window, she might be able to reach Jason and get him away before Harris discovered he was gone. At the moment she was all the protection Jason had.

In the next instant all the horrible things John McClure had said about Harris flashed through her mind. Chilling fingers of terror raced through her system as she quickly retraced her steps. Ignoring the stitch in her side, Amber made it back to the cottage in record time.

After a careful study of the grounds, she quickly moved out into the open before pressing herself against the cottage's rear wall. Moving on tiptoes, she inched her way around to the side wall, taking care to stay as low to the ground as she could, even though both windows were covered with wooden boards.

Creeping forward, she stumbled over a loose board in the porch and barely managed to catch herself to keep from falling. Her heart was pounding so wildly that she had to take deep calming breaths. She stood absolutely still, listening. There was nothing. No movement from behind the windows. She strained to take in every sound no matter how small.

Satisfied that all was well, Amber eased over to the first window. She cautiously peered in though the slats of the nailed boards, squinting until her eyes adjusted to the gloomy interior.

A hard-backed chair and bureau shared one wall. The adjacent bed was unmade and appeared to have been used recently, although the room was dusty and dirty. There was no sign of Jason.

Refusing to give in to the disappointment fighting to gain control of her emotions, Amber moved on to the next window and looked inside. As her eyes shifted methodically around this smaller but no less neglected bedroom, a sudden creak of bedsprings made her jump back with a start. Her stomach had balled into such a tight knot of tension that she had to press her palms against it in hopes of calming herself.

It took her a few more moments to talk herself into returning for a closer look. Beneath the window was a narrow bed, and Jason Baldwin's hands and feet were tied to wrought-iron head-and footboards.

Amber bit her lips to contain the wealth of emotions struggling for release. She felt a combination of heartfelt relief and crushing horror. She could hear Jason shift, then moan as if he were in pain.

She told herself that she had to get to the telephone, now. She had to get help for Jason. It shouldn't take long to reach the car. As she turned to leave, whipcord thin but strong arms grabbed her from behind, pressing hard against her rib cage, making it almost impossible for her to breath.

"Couldn't leave me alone, could you?" Harris hissed, shaking her.

Amber screamed and frantically fought to gain her freedom. If she could only reach the gun in her windbreaker. He was incredibly strong for such a slender man. He held her fast, her arms pinned to her sides. "Let me go!" she said in a wild attempt to throw herself to the side and tip him off balance.

Harris shook her as if she weighed next to nothing.

"Take your hands off me!"

"Go ahead, scream your head off. Nobody's around to hear you."

"Let me go! Let me go!" She fought on, although she was rapidly losing what strength she had.

The man only laughed, tightened his hold on her, squeezing until she could barely catch her breath, let alone fight him. "You wanted to see what's inside, huh, boss lady?" He reeked of liquor, but he was steady on his feet. He seemed confident, almost to the point of being cocky. In spite of his slight build, he outweighed her by a good forty pounds. His fingers bit painfully into her flesh. "Yeah, I'll be glad to let you look." He chuckled as if he were thoroughly entertained.

Amber had never been so frightened in her life. Yet she kicked and strained with renewed vigor against the physical restraint placed on her as he dragged and half carried her around to the front of the cottage.

Once he had her inside, they crossed a large room that was a combined kitchen-dining-living area.

As tired and bruised as she was when he tossed her into one of the high-backed kitchen chairs positioned around a large oak table, Amber would have continued to fight him if the gun had not fallen from her pocket and skidded along the planks of the hardwood floor until it came to rest beside Harris's booted foot. She sat frozen in place as she watched him stoop to get it.

"Nice . . . really nice. Thank you." He grinned at her as if she had given him a present. "But I prefer this," he said, pocketing the gun, then slowly pulled out a thin steel blade from his boot. "It does wonders with tires. Don't you agree?"

"So it *was* you," Amber whispered, recalling the blowout on the bus that had nearly cost Ray his life.

Harris's grin widened. "What's wrong, boss lady? Don't like it when you're no longer in control? Why did you follow me—I told you the kid was safe." His eyes burned with hatred as he bridged the space separating them.

Much too frightened to move, almost too scared to swallow the lump threatening to choke her, Amber did not so much as blink an eyelid. She was painfully aware that she had made the wrong decision in not going for help. Her mistake might very well cost them their lives.

Harris stared at her for a time. Then he moved past her to the kitchen counter. From a nearly empty bottle of whiskey, with his eyes on her, he downed the contents. "Why couldn't you follow orders?"

Refusing to show her fear, she said, "I had to see for myself that Jason wasn't harmed. May I see him, please?" She heard Jason's sobs coming from the back bedroom.

"Shut the hell up, kid!" he roared. "I'm the boss here, understand!" He glared at Amber. Then as if suddenly realizing something, he asked, "Did you come alone?" Grabbing her by her jacket lapels, Harris hauled her up to her feet. With an arm across her throat, the cool steel of his knife pressed against her soft cheek, he asked, "Did you call the cops?"

Amber clawed at the arm cutting off her air.

"Answer me, damn it!"

"No," she gasped, "Now let me go!" Despite her fear, she fought against the arm threatening her supply of air.

"You'd better not be lying to me."

She shuddered. She was trembling so badly, she would have fallen if he hadn't been holding her. Abruptly he released her, shoving her back into the chair.

He went over to the window, flicking the curtain back, apparently unconcerned about her since he was between her and the door. He scanned the yard.

Struggling to control her hysteria, she concentrated on slowing her breathing in a thin hope of soothing herself so that she could think rationally. She could not do herself or Jason any good if she broke down now.

"Even though you're black, you look like her," he said so softly that she wondered if he were speaking to her.

"What?"

"You look like her—same smile, same color eyes," he said as if he had given her a perfectly reasonable explanation. "She would come home from work, fix herself up. Then she'd go out with some man. She was never without a man. Pretty, so pretty. Sometimes she was gone all night. Sometimes she didn't come back for days. Lying whore! She always left me . . . always left me with Ben."

Amber shuddered at the cold fury in his eyes. It was as if he'd forgotten she was there. She didn't dare comment. She didn't move.

"I never called her Mama. She wouldn't let me . . . had to call her Lisa. Such a pretty name." He lifted a liquor bottle to his mouth and drank deeply.

"You don't have to tell me," Amber whispered, hoping to keep him calm.

He continued talking as if she hadn't spoken. "See this?" He held up the hand with the missing digit. "It was his doing. I even told her how he hurt me . . . the things he made me do while she was gone. I got this for telling."

He laughed bitterly at her horror. "That's right." He started laughing so hard, for a moment Amber considered trying to make a mad dash for the door. Unfortunately he recovered before she could gain the nerve to try. "One day she left and never came back. I had to stop him . . . had to . . . I couldn't let him do it no more. Couldn't let him hurt me!" He looked at her as if he were pleading with her to understand. "They said it was murder. It wasn't—it was self-defense!"

Amber bit her lip as waves of nauseating fear rose inside of her. Everything John McClure said about Harris was true. The man was a killer. And she and Jason were at his mercy.

How could she have been so foolish? Why hadn't she let the professionals handle this? Thank God, she'd had the foresight to contact Lynn. If they weren't back, Lynn was bound to let the authorities know what had happened. Help would be only a few hours away.

There was no need to remind herself that the others had not one clue as to their whereabouts. How could she forget even for an instant? That shouldn't matter! John McClure was a trained professional, he was bound to find her car. It would not be long before he found them.

Even though she was terrified and angry with herself, she recognized the need for a level head. Yet she found herself wishing for the impossible. Wishing for Ray. If only he were close by, then she wouldn't be so afraid. Unfortunately Ray wasn't anywhere near Vermont. He wasn't even in the country. He was where he always was—he was out in the field, working.

Amber blinked away tears, suppressing a disheartened sigh. Why hadn't she listened to him? He had warned her to be careful. He'd been convinced that Harris was a dangerous man. And he was so right. Just watching Harris drink from a freshly opened pint bottle of whiskey while he sat mumbling to himself was terrifying. He seemed capable of anything.

"What now?" Harris was muttering beneath his breath. He raked his hand through his hair, glaring at her. "Why couldn't you stay the hell out of it? All I wanted from you was the money!"

Amber could see that he was almost as shaken as she was. Her eyes widened as he steadily drained the bottle. She was amazed by the amount of alcohol he consumed and still remained on his feet.

Feeling her disbelief, he laughed, wiping his mouth with the back of his hand. "Want some?" he said, speech badly slurred.

She shook her head before saying, "Please, can I see Jason? I promise I won't try anything."

"I told you the kid was okay. Why couldn't you take my word for it? What the hell am I suppose to do with you? I never killed a woman—" The last apparently wasn't meant for her ears because he swore heatedly, then lifted the liquor bottle only to find it empty. Flinging it across the room to a pile of trash in the corner, he paced the length of the table.

"I want to see Jason, *now,*" she said, lifting her chin as regally as an ancient Nubian queen.

He ignored her, moving over to the dirty refrigerator. "Nothing but beer," he complained, yet pulled out an eight-pack. "Should have told you to bring more. Can't get a decent buzz with this stuff. Nothin' is going as I planned," he grumbled to himself, then suddenly he turned on Amber. "It's all your fault. Your fault. You sent the cops after me. Told them I was the one, didn't you? Nobody knew it was me." With eyes boring into hers, he insisted, "Never meant to hurt the others."

"I don't know what you're talking about."

He frowned at her as if he didn't recognize her. "I was doing okay. I was working so hard, getting a regular paycheck. Then the dreams started." His voice dropped to a whisper as if he were revealing a secret. "Dreams about Ben. They came every night. I couldn't get any sleep . . . any peace. That's when I started drinking again. That's the only reason."

Amber nodded when she realized he expected her to sympathize, even though he was clearly rambling. She had to use her head. She couldn't let her fear control her actions. She didn't have just herself to think about, she had Jason as well.

He opened a tall beer can. He didn't speak again until he had down a good measure of it. "Tell me, did ya like the way I decorated your walls. Did ya?"

"Can I see Jason?"

He took another deep drag before he shrugged indifferently. "Yeah. Might as well tie you two together until I figure out what I'm going to do with you."

When she attempted to stand, Harris grabbed her arm, twisting it behind her back.

"What are you doing?" she cried out in pain. Despite the alcohol, he was relatively steady on his feet, and his grip almost brutal.

"Make one wrong move and I'll put this knife in your back. Understand, boss lady?" He yanked hard on her hair.

"Yes," Amber gasped out.

He pushed her ahead of him, along the narrow hallway, past a bathroom and on to the back bedroom. He shoved her inside.

Chapter Twenty-Four

Amber barely recovered her balance when she spotted Jason. She didn't hesitate, she ran to him before Harris could stop her.

"Jason!" she cried. "Thank God!" Her eyes filled as she hugged him. She managed to run her hands over his arms and legs. "You're okay, aren't you?"

"Yeah . . ." His dark brown eyes reflected the relief he was feeling, while his bound hands and feet prevented him from reaching out to her.

"Not so fast!" Harris grabbed her, pulling her off the bed, and pushed her away from the boy.

"No! I just want to make sure he isn't hurt."

"Shut up!" Harris said, breathing heavily from the effort to contain her. He raised his hand as if to strike her. Jason yelled no, begging him not to hurt her. "You shut up too, kid!"

"Shush, Jason. I'm fine, really I am," she said quickly. Harris was not only unpredictable but dangerous. She certainly didn't want to antagonize him. Amber sat absolutely still while he bound her hands and feet to a straight-backed chair.

Jason quieted, but his eyes never left the man.

"I don't want to hear any racket out of either one of you. If I do, I'll be forced to do something about it. Understand?"

Both nodded wordlessly, never taking their eyes from him until he walked out of the room.

"Oh, Jason, I'm so glad to see you. Did he hurt you?" Amber said in an urgent whisper, her anxious gaze meeting his.

"It's good to see you, too. Are you, okay?"

"Yes, but what about you?" She repeated the earlier question.

"How did you find me? Did you come alone?"

"After I placed the money by the tree, I hid. Then I followed him back here. He caught me when I peeked into the window, looking to see if you were inside."

"You came alone?"

Amber nodded wearily. "Jason, is there a telephone in the cottage?"

"Yes, it's a cellular phone. He used it last night to call you. Are the police looking for us?"

"For you, yes. No one knows that I've come looking for you except your mom. I told her to tell them everything if I'm not back by nightfall. The trouble is, I couldn't tell her exactly where I was going."

"I guess my folks are really worried, huh?"

"Yes, we all were. Jason, please tell me the truth. Has he tried to hurt you?"

Jason didn't seem to have any trouble understanding what she meant. His answer came readily. "He hit me a few times because I wouldn't do what he asked. But he has been so drunk that last night, like the one before that, he passed out in the chair. I've tried and tried to free myself. Nothing worked."

"I'm sorry, but I had to ask. I was so scared he'd hurt you."

"Miss Spencer, I know what you're talking about. My brothers told me about guys like him and what to watch out for.'' Suddenly tears filled his dark eyes and rolled down his brown cheeks. He turned his face away, flushed with embarrassment that he'd broken down in front of Amber.

Amber was so relieved she nearly cried herself. This was like some horrible, horrible nightmare. "We've got to find a way to get out of here and away from him.''

She didn't say before Harris seriously hurt one or both of them, but that was what she was thinking. How much time did they have before he came back? How could she protect Jason like this? They both were helpless as pawns on a chessboard.

"I want to go home, Miss Spencer.''

"I know, honey. I know. But for now we both have to be strong for each other. We can't give up hope that they'll find us soon.''

Time dragged at a snail's pace as the afternoon disappeared into the evening. Amber and Jason whispered together in a valiant attempt to keep their spirits up. Harris untied each one of them in turn, only long enough to use the bathroom. It was quite late when he brought them dinner, if one could call a sandwich and a cup of water a meal.

Amber was a nervous wreck the short time while Jason was out of the room and alone with Harris. She was terrified that he would hurt him. She had never felt more powerless in her entire life. If only there was some way she could prevent him from harming the boy. After they'd eaten, Harris tied her to the opposite end of the double bed so that she could sleep.

As the room darkened, her fears intensified accordingly. She forced herself to stay awake so that if he came back she would be prepared. She had no choice but to try to outwit him. She had no weapon to use against him. If she could keep him talking . . . keep him away from Jason . . . The rough rope bit into her soft skin as she tried time and time again to pull free. He didn't return, and she eventually slept.

The next day moved along the same lines as the one before—the highlight of which was when Harris paced from the small bedroom to the front window and back again, talking and swearing to himself. By late afternoon he was drinking again, listening to a small portable radio.

The evening shadows spilled across the floor when Jason whispered, "If only he would leave behind that knife, so that when he passes out we could get loose."

"Too convenient." She had barely finished speaking when Harris came crashing through the door.

"We've got to get out of here! Got to leave now!" He weaved his way across the room.

Amber and Jason exchanged a look before hastily looking away. Now was their chance. Whichever one of them he untied first would make a run for it while he was busy untying the other. Surely he couldn't watch them both at the same time. The one who was free would keep going until they reached Amber's car and the cellular phone.

"What are you talking about?" Amber challenged.

"We can't stay here. We've got to leave here . . . tonight. They are looking for you. Should have left, yesterday!" Harris glared at her, obviously in a rage. When he went to lift his hand as if to strike her, Jason yelled, "We'd better hurry."

Amber let out a breath, shaken by his mood swings. He was clearly out of control.

Harris sliced through the rope at Jason's ankles. She and Jason watched as he untied one of his hands only to tie them together in front of him. When Jason tried to move away, he grabbed him. "Be still." He threatened by pressing the knife against his throat.

Jason swung frustrated eyes to Amber, causing her heart to wrench.

"What are you doing?" she demanded, when he made no effort to release her.

"What does it look like? I'm taking the kid and the money and leaving you here. Where did you leave your car?"

"How can you drive and watch Jason at the same time?" Amber asked. "What if you're stopped? How are you going to explain what you're doing with a black kid? It would be best if you took us both. That way no one would question an interracial couple and their child traveling together. I'll drive so you can keep an eye out for trouble." Amber was talking so fast she stumbled over words in her haste to persuade him.

"Where's that car? I've wasted enough time."

"I'll show you, if you promise to take me along."

Harris sneered. "Make one wrong move, and I promise I will kill you. Understand?"

Amber nodded. He reached behind him and pulled out the revolver. With the gun trained on Jason, he quickly knelt behind Amber and sliced through the rope. His knife narrowly missed her soft skin.

"Undo your feet," he ordered, careful to keep Jason in front of him. "Hurry up! We haven't got all night. I want to be on the road by the first cover of darkness."

The knots were stubborn, and it took her trembling fingers several seconds to loosen the rope. He motioned with the gun for them to precede him down the hall, the gun trained on their backs.

It was hard to see, without so much as a porch light to guide them. In a couple of weeks the summer cottages would be filled to capacity as their seasonal residents returned. For now the choice lakefront properties were isolated and deserted. A sharp wind ripped at their clothes.

Jason stumbled over an exposed root. Amber raced to him. Harris was a step behind them, a loaded gun in one hand, the canvas bag of money in the other.

"Get up!"

Jason sobbed in frustration as his soft-soled sneakers slipped from under him on the rain-slick grass. He stopped himself from going facedown in the mud with his bound wrist.

"Let me help you," Amber whispered, using her slender frame to shield the boy. "Don't!" she screamed when

Harris took a menacing stop toward Jason. "Can't you see, he's trying to get up!" She was close to hysteria herself.

"Shut up!" He swung his arm, hitting her across the face, splitting her lip.

"Leave her alone!" Jason cried, intent on rushing him.

Amber caught the furious child just in time. "No! I'm fine," she insisted, trying her best not to cry.

"I've had about all I can take from you. If I didn't need that car and money, I'd have killed you on the spot. You're the reason we have to leave. Jason and I were doing fine until you stuck your nose in our business." He waved the gun in her direction.

"No!" Jason cried, "Don't hurt her!" He used his small body to block hers as best he could.

Harris swore, out of patience with both of them. "Just get moving. Both of you."

There was no reasoning with him. They listened to his continued grumbling as they moved through the thick foliage.

"Where is the damn car!"

"A little farther," Amber mumbled, trying to ignore the sting of her badly swollen mouth. It was all such a mess. She kept hoping that the FBI would have found the car by now. If she could just keep him talking, keep him calm, maybe they would be safe. "What do you hope to gain by this? If you only want money, you can take it and leave Jason and me out of this."

"Shut up!"

"It's kidnapping, you know? You could go to jail for this!"

"I said shut up."

Although Amber was scared, she knew she had to do whatever she could to discourage Harris from taking them. "You're angry with me, and I can understand that. What did Jason do? He hasn't done anything to you. Let him go."

Harris pressed the gun into the small of her back. "One more word and it will be your last."

"Amber, stop . . ." Jason sobbed. "Do what he says."

Amber's shoulders drooped, suddenly too tired and too afraid to continue trying to reason with the man. She concentrated on placing one foot in front of the other and not getting lost.

"It will be all right," Jason whispered beside her, his young voice weary, but his small chin lifted determinedly.

Amber's heart swelled with pride. "Thanks, I forgot for a minute there. You've been very brave. Your parents have every reason to be proud of you."

"Will you two shut up!"

They were numb from the cold by the time they approached the car on the deserted back road. Harris pushed Jason into the backseat. With his hands bound in front of him and his seatbelt on, he was effectively locked in place. He motioned for Amber to drive.

She could have screamed in frustration. There were no police, no FBI, nothing but a long, dark road ahead.

They took the back roads until they reached the interstate, leaving the small college town behind.

Chapter Twenty-Five

Ray was beat by the time his plane touched down in Burlington. Although he had been tempted by the line of telephones in the airport, especially when his plane touched down in Dulles, he had not called Amber. Hearing her voice was not good enough.

He needed more, much more. He had a king-sized ache to look into her golden eyes, to hold her against his heart. Amber . . . She was his heart, his world. Without her he had no life.

He closed his eyes and leaned back in his seat. He was getting conventional in his old age. Hearth and home were looking mighty good these days. He wanted them . . . he wanted it with her. Day after day, week after week, month after month, and year after year of loving each other—a lifetime together was what he'd been longing for. He didn't want there to be doubts in anyone's mind that they belonged to each other.

How long would it take him to convince her to marry him? If it took a lifetime, it would be worth the effort to have Amber as his wife.

It had been a rough few weeks. He had worked like a

dog in order to complete his assignment and get back to her. He found no pleasure in being separated from her. For the first time, he had not even found fulfillment in the work. He did what he had to do. The photographs, the articles, and later the book would all have his unique style and insight. Yet they were not what had captured his thoughts and wouldn't let go. Amber alone had that distinction.

He knew he had some thinking to do concerning his career. Perhaps he'd reached the end. Perhaps it was time to do something else. The demands to oversee the children's charities he had established were increasing with each passing day. Giving away money was easy, making sure that as much as possible went where it was intended to go was the real challenge. How much longer could he leave that critical job to others?

He felt about a hundred and two when he reached the car rental booth. A good night's rest on Amber's sweet-smelling sheets, with her pressed against him, her soft limbs tangled with his—he would feel like a new man in the morning.

Ray rolled down his window, preferring the crisp breeze. Spring had finally made it to New England. The lush greens along the roadside were appealing. He congratulated himself on making good time. Ray smiled, thinking how surprised she would be when he appeared on her doorstep without warning. Amber could not be nearly as pleased as he would be. Just the prospect to being near her again had his pulse racing.

He would let her spoil him. A hot meal, a long soak in the tub sounded so good. He would make himself comfortable in front of the fireplace. He smiled as he made his plans to enjoy every second of her loving attention.

He would not rush her into the bedroom, although the thought of her sweet body open to him had him hard and aching, ready to bury himself deep inside her. His body was growing heavy with a familiar unmistakable need.

Amber . . . sweet Amber. She was all woman, soft, as

delicious as honey but feisty as the devil when she was angry. She knew her own mind, and she went after what she wanted. He loved to see her golden brown eyes sparkle with laughter or even flash with temper. She knew how to keep this man coming back for more of the same. He chuckled, laughing at himself as he recalled that he'd been aroused the instant the plane rolled to a stop in Vermont.

He couldn't wait to see her lovely eyes darken to rich molasses as they sizzled with sexual desire. He planned to take his time making love to her. He would not stop until her soft sweet mouth was puffy from his kisses—only then would he love her.

He planned to tantalize her with deep slow strokes . . . just enough hard friction to take her to the very edge of fulfillment, but not beyond . . . not until she screamed his name and dug her nails into his back, her entire sweet body begging for release. Then, only then, would he give her the raw, relentlessly satisfying thrusts they both craved. Ray shivered from the power of his own need.

He floored the accelerator and the car shot forward. When he realized what he was doing, he eased his foot off the pedal. Ray grinned at his impatience, nearly missing the turnoff. Within minutes he saw the sign, THE THREE BEARS NURSERY SCHOOL, and turned into the drive.

His thoughts slid backward to that bitter cold March day when he'd come to her wanting nothing more than to see her, perhaps spend a few days with her. Maybe even lose himself in her sweetness, in her warmth, and somehow ease his pain and loneliness through her gentleness. So much had changed since then. So much had changed between them.

This time he came with the assurance that they belonged together . . . were in love with each other. Nothing nor anyone could alter how they felt about each other. They belonged together. Not even the danger and constant separation connected to his job was reason enough for them not to make a commitment to each other.

His time away from her had allowed him to really think

about their situation, to consider what they both wanted and needed for happiness. They had wasted so much time already. His brush with death had forced him to accept a hard reality. Life was painfully short.

Ray was finally convinced that Amber meant all that she had said. He believed that she was able to cope with the uncertainty and inherent danger involved in his work. She had not made even a single protest when he told her he had to leave so unexpectedly this time. She had taken it much better, in fact, than he had. She had accepted their separation with a smile and tender understanding. There had been no tears at the airport when they had said their goodbyes. Nor had she clung to him, begging him not to go.

Ray smiled with the assurance that there wasn't a doubt in his mind concerning their feelings for each other. Their love would only grow with time. If he was lucky, they could be married without delay. Was a week long enough to plan a wedding?

Although every muscle in his body ached with fatigue, Ray's heart pounded with excitement. He loved her . . . wanted her . . . needed to hear her say that she felt the same, he decided as he slammed the car door and mounted the front stairs two at a time. The brass doorknob didn't move in his hand. It was locked.

It was a little after six—surely too early for Amber to close for the day. But of course, the holidays! Inhaling deeply, he relished the rich pine scent in the air. It was beautiful here, he had not realized at the time. It was during the time he was away that he had missed the tranquility and rich beauty of the countryside. Ray whistled softly as he rounded the house and started up the drive to the rear of the property. When no answer was forthcoming, he crossed to the garage and peered inside. The school bus was inside, but Amber's car was gone.

Determined not to focus on his own disappointment, he mumbled to himself that it was his own damn fault for not calling. One quick telephone call and she could have been waiting for him at the airport. But he had not wanted her to make that long trip into Burlington. He'd wanted to surprise her, see her beautiful golden eyes light up with pleasure and welcome.

"She could be anywhere," he grumbled to himself—out shopping, visiting with Lynn or Ginger. He crushed the cigarette under his booted foot, realizing he might as well drive over to the Baldwins. Lynn was bound to know what Amber's plans were for the day.

"Hi, Lynn," Ray greeted. "What are all those reporters doing camped out on your front lawn?" He had seen some familiar faces, but he hadn't taken time to linger.

It took her a full second to find her voice, then all she could seem to say was, "Ray!"

Something was definitely wrong, he could feel it. Yet his voice didn't waver when he said, "As you probably guessed, I'm looking for Amber. Is she here?"

"Come in . . . come in—"

"What's wrong?"

"It's good to have you back." Lynn linked her arm with his. "There's coffee going in the kitchen. Bet you could use a cup. You've just missed Alex. He went down to his office for an hour or so."

"Lynn, talk to me. You're shaking like a leaf." Ray disengaged himself and clasped her hands in his own large steady ones. "Tell me."

Her dark eyes filled with tears, and she bit her lip to keep from screaming out the fear and frustration. "So much has happened since you've been away. I can't think."

"You can start by telling me if something has happened to Amber." There was so much pain in Lynn's eyes. As he watched her struggle for the words, a chilling sense of alarm went off like a rocket blast inside his head. His hands slid to her shoulder pads and tightened automatically.

"That's it—both Jason and Amber have disappeared, Harris—" Lynn was crying in earnest now.

"Harris has them?"

Lynn could only nod, trying to speak but choking on the sobs locked in her throat.

Ray placed a comforting arm on her shoulders, while rage along with fear mounted at an alarming rate deep inside of him. Amber was at the mercy of a killer.

"I'm sorry . . . so sorry," Lynn sobbed.

"There is no need to apologize," he said, offering his handkerchief. "Come on, let's get that coffee."

Once they were seated at the table in the kitchen alcove, Ray spoke quietly even though his stomach was in knots. Years of training in knowing how to handle himself in stressful situations came into focus. "I know this is difficult, but I need to know what happened."

"We were closed for spring break. Jason had been helping Amber work at the school. He was on his way home, but he had one stop to make—the market for milk." Tears trickled down her cheeks.

Ray knew what she was going to say even before the words left her mouth.

"He never came home that night."

Ray controlled his urge to smash his fist through something, anything. Instead he listened without interruption.

Lynn went on speaking, but so quietly that he had to lean toward her in order to hear. "I went over to the school to see what was keeping him—never suspecting anything was wrong. Amber came back with me. In fact, she stayed that first night here with us. She didn't go home until late that next evening. She stopped by the day after that to tell me that Harris had left a ransom note, and she was taking the money to him." When Lynn ended, she was crying in earnest. "She told me to tell the FBI everything if she was not back later that evening. She didn't come—" Lynn was sobbing so hard she could not finish.

With each breath he took, rage simmered inside of him, but his voice was steady when he asked, "Why would she be taking him money? Why didn't McClure stop her?"

"She made me promise not to tell anyone until that

evening, not even Alex. She thought if she took the money, she could find out where he was keeping Jason—"

"Damn!" He banged his fist against the table. "Where is McClure now?" Ray bit out, barely able to control his furor and increasing fear.

"There is an agent in the living room manning the phone, but John and his men are set up at the sheriff's office, except for the man watching the house."

Ray was outraged. "What did she think she was doing! I told her before I left that Harris was dangerous." He was livid. Yet Ray knew he wasn't really angry with Amber. He was furious with himself for not being there when she needed him. If he had been here, there was no way he would have let her put herself in danger. "Why would Harris ask Amber for money?"

"I'm not sure, but I suspect he blames her for losing his job. Ray, I didn't want her to do it. I tried to talk her out of it."

Ray nodded, patting her hand absently. "Has anyone been over to Amber's place?"

"We were there last night. I have the key. The only thing we found was a crumpled note with directions for Amber to go to the phone booth in town and wait for a call if she wanted to see Jason alive." Her voice caught. "I know she did it to protect Jason. Now he has them both."

Deep in thought, Ray eventually asked, "Have you seen or spoken to John today?"

"Yes, he stopped by earlier. There hasn't been any news. They're searching the countryside, looking for her car."

"Apparently they still think he is in the area," Ray surmised.

"It's the not knowing that's driving me nuts."

"We'll get them back," he said quietly, his voice laced with steel.

"I was so hopeful in the beginning. Now I'm just plain scared. Jason is my baby, and Amber is my best friend. I can't bear the thought of losing either one of them."

Ray refused to even consider the possibility of losing

Amber. She was his woman, his life. He wanted the future he'd been dreaming about, wanted to share it with her "We'll get them back—remember that." He was on his feet now, impatient to be gone.

Lynn smiled for the first time, needing to believe.

When Ray left John McClure at the sheriff's office, he was livid. He ground his teeth together in acute frustration. Impatience and fear seeped from every pore, combined with pure rage that steadfastly colored his thoughts and clouded his vision.

He didn't slow his pace when he reached his rented car but walked right on by it. He passed the drugstore, the florist shop, and the cleaners. The sky was shrouded with clouds, the moon barely a sliver in the gloomy night. The wind had picked up and pulled at his clothes. He walked on with purposeful strides, following Main Street until he reached Vine, then turned right at the corner en route to Mrs. Kennedy's rooming house.

John had warned him the trip was a wasted effort. Ray knew better. Ray lifted the collar on his navy leather jacket against the sting of the wind. His deep shudder had nothing to do with the drop in temperature. He had damn near attacked a close friend as detail after deadly detail of the kind of danger his woman faced was revealed. Ray had come close to strangling McClure. The ransom note was merely the tip of a hideous iceberg. Spray painting her walls, defacing her home, late night phoned threats—and they had not caught the bastard! It had taken all his willpower to hold on to his temper. He had walked out the door without uttering another word.

Amber was his, and he intended to find her. If Harris had hurt her, he would kill him with his bare hands. Ray knew he was close to completely losing his self-control. He was hanging on to it by a fingernail. He had been wrong to trust another man to keep his lady safe. That was Ray's job. And he had failed. That realization ate at his insides.

He'd done it again, put another assignment ahead of her needs. He knew the possible danger she faced when he boarded the plane for Lebanon. If he lost her, there would be no one to blame but himself.

"Amber . . ." he whispered her name, forcing back tears that burned his eyes. She was out there somewhere at the mercy of an animal like Foster Harris. Ray should have hunted him down after the fool had slit Amber's tire. If he had, then Harris would not have been a threat to anyone. Jason was a good kid, he did not deserve to have his whole life messed up. Damn Harris! Did he have any idea who he was messin' with? Amber belonged to Ray, and he protected what was his.

Fear was not new to Ray. Long ago he had learned how to live with it. He faced it on every assignment and used it to keep himself alert and his senses sharp. What he was experiencing now was different. It was a stark terror of the worse kind.

It was fully dark by the time he'd cooled down enough to know he would be using his head rather than his heart. It was so much easier to blame John than face the truth. If Ray were a different kind of man, with a ordinary job, Amber would not have been left alone. They would be married by now. He would come home to her and spend each and every night in her loving arms. No way could Harris have gotten close to her. No way.

"I'll find you, angel. We'll make a life together," Ray whispered as he paused in front of the large two-story white colonial on the edge of the university.

Ray's eyes twinkled with unexpected humor as he imagined her turning down John. It was just like her to stubbornly refuse protection. She would not ever consider living like a prisoner in her own home. He pictured how her small chin would lift with determination. She was so wonderful to look at, but she was much, much more. Her beauty went beyond the surface. She cared so deeply about others.

How often had he warned her to be careful? She was

too independent for her own good. McClure might have a hard time understanding why she'd done what she did, but then he didn't know Ray's woman.

The money would be the least of her concerns. It would not have been a sacrifice to Amber because she loved Jason and Lynn. Even at risk to herself, she would not back down. His stubborn little angel probably blamed herself for Jason's disappearance because she had been the one to hire the man.

Ray recalled how her eyes had glinted with fierce amber light the night she told him she wanted to be his woman . . . emphasized that she was not a child in need of his protection. Damn it to hell, he wanted her back! In spite of his exhaustion, he knew he could not rest until she was safe.

For years he had considered the most difficult time for them was during the years they were estranged. He had not been able to see her or even talk to her. Now he accepted that it had not been the worst torment imaginable because at least then he had known that she was safe, building a new life for herself as she worked toward her goals.

"I'll find you, my love—I will," Ray vowed as he pressed the doorbell.

Chapter Twenty-Six

"Hey, what are you doin'?" Harris yelled from the back-seat as she jerked hard on the steering wheel. They were riding the shoulder of the road as she struggled to gain control of the car.

Amber felt the pressure of the hard metal gun as he pressed it to the back of her neck, but she did not answer. She focused on her driving until they were back on the road and she could breathe again.

"I asked you a question."

She quivered involuntarily, although it was a true struggle to keep fear out of her voice. She refused to give him the satisfaction. "I'm tired. I can hardly keep my eyes open. If we don't stop soon, you're not going to need that gun. I will have run into one of these deep ditches. Why can't we use the main highway?"

"You have an awfully smart mouth for a broad with a gun in her back. You think I'm afraid to use it?"

Amber bit her lips to hold back a whimper. She rolled down her window a bit, grateful for the cool breeze blowing on her face. She was nauseous from the liquor fumes coming from behind her. She did not have to glance in the rearview mirror to know that Jason was as mentally and physically exhausted as she was and just plain scared.

Harris scanned the badly rutted two-lane road. "Just keep drivin'."

Amber was too weary to reply. She had been driving for half the night, with no idea of where they were headed. They'd crossed the state line about thirty miles back.

Every time she tried to slow down, Harris would start swearing and waving that gun around. For a while there, she thought he might pass out the way his head drooped occasionally, but the instant she let the car coast he jerked up wide awake and was as mean as a snake.

"We're almost out of gas," Amber reluctantly told him, deciding they were better off at a gas station, where there might be some possibility of help, rather than being stranded in the middle of nowhere with Harris. She keep telling herself that sooner or later they had to stop.

He leaned forward in order to study the fuel gauge. "We've got almost a fourth of tank—plenty to get where we're goin'. Now shut up, I'm sick of your complaining."

Amber did not open her mouth until the needle was pointing at the empty mark. "We have to stop soon. I have to use the bathroom, and I sure Jason has to go, too. We haven't eaten in hours."

"Yeah!" Jason echoed.

"Okay . . . okay. There is the turnoff up ahead. See it— take it!"

Amber's heart hammered in her chest. With a little luck they might find someone willing to help. If only he would leave them alone, even for a few minutes, she might be able to call Lynn. She'd carefully watched for road signs. They were in Franklin County, heading north toward the Canadian border. If only he would leave her alone long enough for her to use the celluar phone in her glove compartment.

Judging from the way Jason slumped in his seat, he was every bit as weary as she. She was proud of him. He had been so brave throughout this whole horrible ordeal. She

did not even want to think of the mental anguish he had
endured alone with Harris. How much longer could the
child hold on—how much more could she?

"There is nothing here," she said dejectedly, nothing
but trees alongside an almost deserted roadway. She
rubbed tired bloodshot eyes when she stopped at a stop
sign.

"Make a right and keep going until I tell you to stop."

Amber flicked on the turn indicator, then slowly eased
her foot off the brake. Her hands where so unsteady that
she had to practically lock her fingers around the steering
wheel.

She was so tired. She longed to put down her head and
cry out her fear and frustration. Fatigue was no excuse for
not using a little common sense. Her father had always
said she had more nerve than sense. She could not remember what she had done to upset him. Oh, yes, she had
jumped into the deep end of the pool to save a stray dog
that had turned out to be a much better swimmer than
she was. How old had she been—ten, eleven?

What made her think of that long-forgotten incident?
Her dad had always accepted her the way she was: quick
tempered, softhearted, and stubborn. He did not try to
change her.

"Here, turn here!" Harris barked.

Amber had nearly missed the turn and had to cut the
wheel sharply. In the process they nearly sideswiped a
guardrail before bouncing back onto the road. Her forehead was beaded with perspiration by the time she had
the car under control.

"Watch what you're doin'."

After a time she hazarded a quick glance at Jason. She
was relieved to see he was asleep. He needed the rest, he'd
been through so much.

Amber did not bother to look at Harris. She did not
need to in order to know he still held the gun on his thigh,
the shaft pointed toward her.

She needed to think of pleasant thoughts, needed to

get her mind off the man behind her. Ray . . . She smiled remembering what it felt like to be in his arms with her cheek pressed over his heart. She longed for the security and comfort of his strong male length.

"There's a gas station up ahead. See it?"

"Yes," she said barely above a whisper, with her heart starting to hammer with excitement.

The station was a few yards away from a convenience store. A telephone booth was at the end of the parking lot. She brushed impatiently at the moisture filling her eyes. Could she do it? How? How could she get to the telephone without his knowledge?

"Here!"

He pushed a hundred dollar bill into her hand. "You have fifteen minutes to get everything we need—bread, meat, liquor." He gestured toward the food store. "The kid stays with me."

"How do I know you won't just leave me here?" she asked, suddenly petrified that he would take off with Jason. She was the boy's only protection against the man.

"I'd like to leave you, that's for sure. But I need you for cover. That's about all you're worth to me. You got fifteen minutes. I'll be watching through the glass. Don't say one word . . . not one word to anyone. Don't forget the liquor. If they don't have any, get a couple of eight-packs."

Amber reluctantly got out of the car, her leg muscles sore and stiff after long hours in the car. Pinpricks shot through her numb feet as her circulation returned in a rush. She ignored the discomfort. All she had was fifteen minutes to find a way of getting help for them. Their lives depended on her resourcefulness.

The bell chimed when she entered. The older man behind the counter looked up from the magazine he'd been reading at the sound. "Evenin', missy."

Amber did not dare speak. She nodded before she grabbed a small shopping basket and began hurrying down the aisle, throwing food inside. Fifteen minutes to get help!

How, with Harris watching through the glass window from where he pumped gas into the car . . .

Amber had to wait as a man ahead of her opened the cooler door. He dropped something on the floor. She moved down and saw a pen on the floor. She started to tap him on the shoulder and point to the writing instrument, but suddenly she stopped, her mind racing a mile a minute.

Her heart was pounding with dread as she prayed that he wouldn't notice that he had dropped the pen. She did not realize she was holding her breath until he removed a bottle of soda from the cooler, then moved away. She grabbed a carton of milk, meat, cheese, a bottle of soda, and the beer.

Amber pushed the pen ever so gently with her foot, easing it along as she moved into the next aisle. When she bent to reach down to a low shelf for a box of cookies, she retrieved the pen.

As she slowly moved down the aisle of baked goods, she pretended to study the different types of bread. She ripped off the top sheet from a pad of coupons mounted on the shelf. She quickly jotted down Lynn's telephone number and wrote: *Please call for help. Life or death.* Hastily she printed her name, then hurried toward the checkout counter. She was brought up short when she spotted Harris standing at the counter, having paid for the gas. He waited for her at the door.

The man behind the counter smiled at her. "That wind is really kicking up out there."

Amber, keenly aware of Harris, stood like a statue. She didn't so much as nod at the other man. She didn't dare. The problem was how to pass the note without Harris noticing.

"That'll be . . ."

Amber barely heard him, her mind on Harris and the note burning a hole in her hand. Hesitating until she had the older man's full attention, she placed the bill in his upraised heavily lined hand. Her eyes pleaded with him as she took the change.

Her heart was hammering with dread when she said, "You gave me back too much money." She had crumpled several bills around the note and placed them in the center of the man's palm. She could read the confusion on his face and guessed that he was about to protest. Quickly she grabbed the bags and dashed out.

Jason was huddled in the backseat. She could see by the fear in his eyes that he'd been terrified the entire time she'd been gone. She smiled weakly and got into the passenger side of the car. Harris was at the wheel. She risked a quick look over her shoulder as they pulled out of the station and saw the older man peering out of the glass door.

"Please," she silently repeated over and over again, not quite believing in the power of suggestion but willing to give it a try. She was so desperate she would be willing to try anything.

Amber hid an unexpected smile as she recalled the times she had chanted that same plea as a child when she wanted to tag along with Brad and Ray. It had worked then. Of course she also combined the pleas by crossing her fingers and toes, plus allowing a pitiful stream of tears to run down her face.

Harris turned off onto a narrow two-lane highway. Amber sat stiff with dismay. There were no road signs, nothing to identify where they were. What now?

"Where are we?" Jason asked from the rear seat.

Harris did not bother answering. He was busy complaining because they hadn't carried the hard liquor he craved.

When they turned off into the parking lot of a motel, the sign read CEDAR WOODS MOTEL with a vacancy sign lit beneath. He eased to a stop in front of the low building with OFFICE painted on the front door. The motel was set back from the road near a thick patch of soaring blue spruce and maples. The area was lovely, with a rustic charm. Unfortunately they were not there to admire the scenery.

"Out!" He motioned to her with the gun. "You stay right where you are, kid. Move a muscle, and I'll hurt your buddy here. Understand?"

"I'm not going anywhere. You just don't hurt Miss Spencer." Jason was scared, but he was also angry.

Amber yearned to tell him not to worry, just try to get loose and run while he could. Trying to wordlessly remind him of their agreement, her eyes filled with tears of frustration. "Don't worry about me."

"Shut up!" Harris grabbed her arm and dragged her across the seat beneath the steering column and out his door. He held the gun in the pocket of his windbreaker pressed close to her side. "Stay close. Let me do the talkin'. You fill out the register. Not one false move," he warned between clenched teeth.

She took him at his word. She hardly breathed as he introduced her as his wife. She cringed internally as he took her hand into his. He booked one room, two double beds. Amber's heart fell when they returned to the car and Jason was still there. She didn't need to wonder why he hadn't made a run for it. Even if he could get loose, she knew . . . he was afraid for her. He was not leaving her alone to face Harris's wrath.

They parked in front of number 26. "Hurry it up!" Harris said to Amber as he held Jason tightly by his arms. "Open the door and turn on all the lights," he directed, yet his hold on the child was brutal. "Now get my bag and the food out of the car. We'll wait here for you, won't we, son?"

"I'm not your son."

Amber shook her head, warning Jason not to draw attention to himself. At his best, Harris was unpredictable.

When Jason moved to help her, Harris tightened his hold on the boy, and she practically screamed, "No! Just do whatever he says. I'm fine."

She was close to losing the tiny thread of control she still possessed over her emotions. Her hands and legs were trembling from fatigue as she brought in the bags. She was ready to burst into tears at the slightest provocation, which wouldn't do either one of them any good.

She forced herself to take slow even breaths in order to calm down and think clearly. She warned herself to stay on guard, ready to manipulate the situation to their advantage as much as possible. They had not done too badly so far. They were both still alive. Even as she told herself this, she knew they had to find a way to get away from this man. He was a walking time bomb.

Both Amber and Jason were too tired to eat the ham and cheese sandwiches she had prepared. Neither protested when Harris tied their wrists to the headboard of one of the beds. At least they were together. Jason was asleep the minute his head hit the pillow.

Amber envied him. She was just as tired, but instead of giving in to her exhaustion, she quietly watched Harris from beneath the fall of her thick lashes. Sprawled in the padded armchair, Harris watched the television while steadily draining one tall beer can after another.

She was determined to stay awake until she was certain that Harris was asleep or too drunk to harm Jason. Amber's head pounded from a tension headache. It had been less than two days, but it felt as if she'd been caged with Harris for weeks. Gradually her eyes were so heavy it was all she could do to keep them open. She shook her aching head in the hopes of keeping herself awake. She mustn't sleep. She had to watch over Jason. Alex and Lynn were counting on her to keep their son out of harms way.

Even though he was drunk, he was a continued threat to Jason. Time and time again she would lift her lashes to encounter Harris's bloodshot eyes on the boy. Jason was curled against her side, safe for the time being. Amber had no idea how she managed it, but she stayed awake until very late, and Harris had passed out in his chair, oblivious to the noise from the television. Only then did she dare close her eyes.

Amber woke early, just before daybreak. She could see through the partially opened drapes that the sky was just beginning to light from the rising sun. The harsh sound of violent retching that came from behind the closed bathroom door must have been what had awakened her. The other bed was empty. Her anxious glance went to Jason. He was also awake.

"How are you?" she whispered.

He shrugged, not vocalizing the question they both feared. Was today the day they would find a way to get away, or was it the day Harris got tired of them and killed one or both of them? Amber had told him about the note she had left with the man in the convenience store and about the phone in the glove compartment.

At first both of them had been hopeful, now they were plagued with doubts. Surely if the authorities had been notified, John McClure and his men would have been there by now.

"How about you? You don't look so good," Jason whispered back.

Amber choked on a laugh. "I bet I smell even worse. What I wouldn't give for a long hot bath and a toothbrush."

"I didn't think I'd ever say this and mean it, but me, too. They aren't coming, are they?"

"Let's not give up hope."

Neither noticed the dark head peering through the window. They were busy listening to the sounds coming from the bathroom. They waited until they heard the toilet flush then the shower being switched on before attempting to loosen the ropes around their wrists and ankles.

"Hurry, Amber."

They were so involved in what they were doing that they both jumped in alarm at the faint sound of glass being cut at the window. A small square was then removed from the window pane just wide enough for a navy leather-sleeved arm to reach inside and unhook the latch.

Shocked into immobility, neither one of them moved as they watched Ray ease his large frame inside, gun in hand. Amber's eyes filled with joy. He was home . . . he was safe! She had no idea how he had found them, but

she was thrilled to see him. When they would have poured
forth their utter relief, he motioned for them to keep
quiet. Amber and Jason gestured toward the bathroom
door, not an easy task with their hands and feet bound.

Backing toward the bed with his eyes on the bathroom
door, he pocketed the gun long enough to use a pocket-
knife to cut through their rope bindings. With the rush
of splashing water in the background, he held each of
them close, thus giving and receiving comfort but only for
an instant.

"He hurt you." He mouthed the words into Amber's
ear with eyes like cold dark steel. His furious gaze lingered
on the bruise on her face and rope burns on her soft skin.

Amber shook her head, terribly afraid. "Nothing serious," she hastily whispered back.

"Did he hurt Jason?"

"No. Please, honey, let's go," she begged, pulling on
his arm.

The drumming peal of water splashing against the porce-
lain tub abruptly ended. Amber and Jason went stiff with
fright, frozen in place and lifting terror-filled eyes to Ray.

He quickly ushered them out the motel door. "Go to
the motel office, and wait for me there. John and his men
are on their way."

"No, you have to come with us," Amber pleaded scared
for him. Surely he did not plan on confronting Harris.
"He's dangerous. He has my gun."

Ray kissed her hard. "Do it," he said, giving her a gentle
shove in the direction of the office. Ray had closed the
door soundlessly in their faces.

Amber wouldn't have moved if Jason had not taken her
hand and tugged her along with him. Amber trembled
with fear as she ran with Jason across the parking lot,
around to the motel's business office. They both had one
thought now. They must hurry and get help for Ray. On
the way wasn't good enough, John McClure should be here
now. Amber had been saying a lot of prayers the last few

days and decided that now didn't seem like a good time to stop.

Ray's feet made no noise on the carpet as he approached the bathroom door, gun in hand. He kicked open the door. Harris jumped at the sound of the portal crashing in against the wall. He dove for the gun on top of his clothes on the floor. Ray was quicker—he kicked it out of reach, putting himself between the door and the gun.

"I didn't hurt them. I didn't touch either one of them," Harris shouted.

"You're a big man with that gun in your hands, aren't you? Attacking kids and hitting women. You want this?" he said gesturing to his gun. "Come on and get it."

Harris's eyes were bloodshot and weary. He backed as far as he could from Ray. "I told you I didn't hurt either one of them!"

Ray didn't move as the rage that had been eating away at him came to the boiling point. He couldn't think of anything he wanted to more than to mash his fist down this bastard's throat. "You touched my woman. I saw the marks you put on her. Is that your thing? You get off like that?"

"It wasn't my fault. She had no business following me."

"What about the kid? How many others have there been? How many have you hurt?"

"None!"

"Did you hurt him?" When he failed to answer, Ray demanded, "Did you touch him?"

"No!"

"You're such a man. Let's see you take me on." Ray's voice was cool, in control—a single muscle jumped in his cheek, the only indication of how deadly serious and enraged Ray was. He pocketed his gun. Ray waited, aching to use his fists on the man.

Harris charged him, giving Ray the excuse he needed. Ray's fist connected with the other man's jaw. Then he delivered a hard punch into the younger man's midsection and sent him flying across the tile floor. Harris was no match for Ray. He didn't even try to defend himself. He crumpled like a rag doll, without so much as a struggle, to Ray's keen disappointment. He was out cold.

By the time sirens filled the early morning air, Ray had Harris tied to a straight-back chair, the motel door open. Amber and Jason came rushing in behind the authorities.

Ray wasn't able to breathe a heartfelt sigh of relief until he could hold Amber against his side. He was not about to let her go. Amber clung to him, needing his strength, his reassuring warmth.

Chapter Twenty-Seven

"Come on, let's get out of here. I'm taking you two home," Ray said. With his hand in the small of Amber's back and the other on Jason's shoulder, he ushered them to his rental car. He was just closing the passenger door when John McClure approached.

"Thanks. I owe you," the other man said, offering Ray his hand.

The two men stared at each other. Ray's temper had cooled enough that he was able to finally raise his hand and clasp John's. The residuals from the urgency, the fear and the rage he'd been holding deep inside, had partly eased after that pitiful confrontation with Harris. For some unknown reason, he couldn't let it go.

John bent down so he could speak to Jason and Amber in the car.

Ray waited quietly not saying a word. When John straightened, Ray said, "I'm taking them home. You can talk to them again later if you need to after they've both seen a doctor and rested."

John nodded. "It will take me a while to finish up here," he said before he moved off.

"Ready?" Ray said, settling behind the wheel, looking from one to the other.

"My car . . ." She shivered, recalling the terror they'd experienced on the long trip out of state.

"They'll see that you get it back. For now they need it for evidence."

"I'm not sure I want it back."

Fatigue was evident in Jason and Amber's faces, and elation that they were truly safe and on their way home shone in their eyes.

Ray concentrated on the road. He tried to ignore the bone-deep rage by assuring himself that she was safe. He took pains not to voice the question uppermost in his mind. He comforted himself with the knowledge that there would be plenty of time later to talk . . . plenty of time.

"After this I swear I won't complain about anything ever again." Jason chatted as the big car sped down the interstate. "Parents, school, my older brothers, girls, nothin'!" He'd been talking for hours, but neither adult shushed him. They considered it therapeutic.

They'd both been through such a terrible ordeal the last few days, Jason even more so than Amber. Ray offered to stop for food, but both Jason and Amber refused. All they wanted was to be home as quickly as possible. When they stopped for gas, Jason went to call his folks. Amber and Ray had a chance to talk privately.

"I've never been happier to see anyone than I was when you stepped inside that window, sweetheart. I had no idea you would be back so soon." Amber's fingers laced with his.

"Can you imagine my surprise when I returned to discover you'd disappeared? That telephone call from the store owner to Lynn probably saved your lives," he said, his voice turbulent with emotion.

Amber was unable to suppress the terror that raced through her system when reminded of their narrow escape.

Lifting her chin so that he could see her clearly, he said tightly, "Forgive me if I'm wrong, but I left under the impression that you would contact John at the first sign of trouble." A muscle jumped in his jaw as if he were gritting his teeth. His eyes were piercingly direct. "If it hadn't been for Lynn, John wouldn't have known you had disappeared along with the ransom money."

"You're angry with me," she acknowledged correctly.

That was putting it mildly. He made an impatient sound in his throat, then said, "Why didn't you keep your promise?"

"I told him about the phone calls and the paint on my walls." She offered no excuse as to why she had purposefully not mentioned any of it during their brief telephone conversations. She wasn't sorry. She had not wanted to upset him, distract him from his work.

"You're lucky to come out of this with only a few bruises," Ray grated out harshly.

"Honey, the important thing is I got there just in time to keep him from hurting Jason." She shuddered. "It's not an experience I care to repeat. He scared me half to death, but it's over now, thank God."

"I can't decide if I'd rather shake some sense into you or take you into my arms and never let you go. You put me through hell!" He slid a hand beneath her hair, caressing the sensitive flesh at her nape. "You're precious to me. I couldn't bear the thought of losing you, baby, especially after waiting so long to really have you." When she started to speak, he shook his head, saying, "Let me finish. Don't misunderstand me. I'm proud of you, Amber. But I can't remember being so scared. Damn it—you gambled on our future happiness. Yeah, I know why you did it. That doesn't mean I'm thrilled by any of this."

"Ray, listen—"

"No! You listen. What did I have to do to keep you safe? Should I have locked you in my town house?" In spite of his rage he took exquisite care as he lifted her wrists to his mouth and kissed the delicate bruised flesh. Ray had faced danger countless times, yet he honestly could not ever remember being so frightened. This incident was right up there with the horror of seeing his best friend die in front of him and not being able to stop it.

"Honey, please don't be angry. I couldn't just sit back and do nothing. I care about Jason. I felt so helpless . . . so responsible." Her eyes filled with tears.

Ray longed to take her into his arms, eliminate her sorrow, but he needed to finish. She had to be made to understand what her actions had nearly cost them both. "This was no innocent crusade, Amber. You were in real danger. Harris had real bullets in that gun. He blamed you for firing him. He demanded money from you, not Jason's parents. You are the one his misguided hatred was directed at. You!" His dark brown eyes glinted like steel. "Do you realize how close you came to dying?"

"Don't, . . ." she whispered as her tears glistened in her beautiful golden eyes.

"Baby, I would have gone after Jason for you—if you'd only waited."

"How was I to know when you would be back?" That was the problem. He was not around when she needed him the most. Amber whispered tiredly, "Ray, please, I know you're upset with me. But I can't take any more right now, especially not your anger."

He reached into his pocket, removed a clean linen hand-kerchief. He used it to wipe her face while his emotions simmered. She was right. He had not been there when she needed him. His absence had nearly cost her her life. He forced himself not to say more. He contained his keen frustration, just barely.

"So now you're not going to talk to me?" she accused unhappily.

"You don't want to know what I'm thinking."

"Just say it!"

"You risked our future on a stupid gesture. What do I have to do? Marry you to keep you out of trouble?"

"Ray!"

"Jason's coming. This will have to wait until we get home."

Amber would have liked to lay her head down and bawl her eyes out, cry until she was empty of all the fear and tension. But of course she could not. Just as she knew she was not calm enough to handle Ray's anger. For Jason's sake she had to gain some measure of control over herself.

Once they were under way, she leaned her head against the reassuring strength of his wide shoulder. She was tired, so tired. Both Amber and Jason slept, giving in to their exhaustion.

It was late afternoon when they reached the small sleepy university town. Jason's parents, Wayne and Ginger Adams, as well as Jason's brothers were all waiting to greet them. Hugs and kisses and tears were exchanged all around. Everyone talked at once. Lynn's tears flowed unchecked. Although Alex was not an openly affectionate man, he hugged his son with tear-filled eyes. He offered his heartfelt thanks to Ray and Amber.

Lynn insisted that they all stay and share supper. Although Amber longed to refuse, she was too tired to offer more than a token resistance, using Lynn's guest room to freshen up.

John McClure arrived just as Ray and Amber were about to leave. Ray, who had not been far from Amber all evening, wordlessly took her hand into his when the questioning started. Jason, on the sofa, was flanked by his parents. Recounting the past few days was more painful than Amber expected. She felt as if she were reliving it all over again. She was dangerously close to tears and trembling with fear by the time John McClure was finished.

With a protective arm around her shoulder, Ray ushered her out. Amber didn't offer even a whimper of protest.

She could have wept with relief when they finally entered the apartment and she was surrounded by the familiar warmth of home.

"Bed?" he asked softly, his eyes on her drooping shoulders.

She shook her head. She tried to smile to ease his troubled gaze but failed. Her spirit was heavy knowing he was angry with her. Unfortunately she was too tired to even discuss it.

Ray sighed, knowing Amber was all that mattered to him. He'd gone a little crazy during the hours he'd feared she was lost to him. Now that they were alone and he could look at her, touch her, know she was safe, the fear squeezing his insides was beginning to slowly diminish along with a little of his rage.

"After being in the cabin for days without being able to wash, I feel so dirty—as if I'll never be clean again." Her fatigue was evident in the sway of her slender frame. She could hardly put one foot in front of the other.

"It's over now, baby." His hands were so tender as he held her close. He brushed his mouth gently against hers. "You're home, and no one will hurt you ever again." He lifted her up into his arms, cradling her easily against his chest. "Just let me take care of you now, angel."

Her sigh was answer enough as she wound her arms around his neck and rested her head on his shoulder. He was here and she was safe. She would not let herself remember how she had felt when she thought she might never ever see him again. It was over. That horrible ordeal was behind them.

Ray shouldered his way into the bathroom, depositing her beside the huge tub. Turning on the taps full force, he dumped a measure of her favorite foaming bath oil into the water before he turned his attention to her. He systematically unbuttoned her blouse, sliding it down her arms, then unfastened her slacks and pushed them down her legs. He kept his own sexual need for her firmly under control.

"Where you goin'?" She looked at him, her hands on the front fastening of her bra.

"Brandy," he said, tightly angry with himself for the way his body was responding to her beauty. She needed his care, his love, not his lust. He let out a sigh of relief when he returned to find her up to her neck in bubbles. He cradled a large brandy snifter in one hand. Ray perched on the edge of the tub, studying her quietly.

Amber was beyond tired, dark bruises showed beneath her golden brown skin. She surprised him when she whispered, "Please, Ray. Don't be mad at me. I'm so glad you're home. I missed you so much, sweetheart." She reached out to caress his deep copper-tone cheek, her fingers lingering on his unshaven stubbled chin. When he didn't respond, she sighed heavily. "Ray?"

Eventually he said, "I think I was more scared than angry. I nearly lost you, my angel." His voice was thick with emotion while his eyes burned from unshed tears. He quickly looked away, refusing to let them fall.

She nodded in understanding. She, too, knew the kind of fear he'd experienced because she often felt it while he was away working. It was not easy to get through, and it didn't go away until she could touch and hold him again.

She continued to caress his firm jawline with soft hands, hoping to reassure him that she was safe. She stroked the deep cleft in his chin before she slowly ran the soft pads of her fingers over the thick mustache framing his full African lips. "You're too far away," she complained, her voice husky with feminine yearning. "Join me."

He knew he needed the reassurance of her soft body in his empty arms just as much as she also seemed to need it. Ray was also impatient with himself for that equally hungry ache deep within that was ravenous to be buried within her moist sheath. Although he refused to give in to it, he could not ignore its existence.

The amber-colored liquid in the glass was clear and sultry like his woman's eyes when she was deeply aroused. His hand quivered when he pressed the glass against her soft mouth. She could hardly keep her eyes open, so heavy was her fatigue. He watched her, making sure she swallowed some of it before he took a generous dose of the liquor.

He knew he had to let go of thoughts of how dangerously

close he had come to losing Amber. It would serve no useful purpose.

Amber took another sip when he held the glass for her, then sleepily watched him roll up his sleeves and kneel down beside the tub. She thought perhaps she should put forth some effort to take care of her own needs, but sighed contentedly when he began soaping her upper body with the bath sponge.

She would have preferred to feel his hands on her bare skin. It had been so long since they had made love. She sighed, taking comfort from his closeness and his quiet strength.

Thankful that Amber was too tired to question the tremor in his normally sure hands, Ray asked, "How soon can you make the arrangements?"

Amber was caught up in the pleasure of him massaging the tightness from her neck and shoulders and failed to understand the significance of the question.

"Hmm?"

"Shouldn't take more than a week, don't you think? We need to contact a minister and order the cake and food for the reception."

Amber's eyes popped open. "What are you talkin' about?"

"I asked you to marry me a few hours ago. You couldn't have forgotten already?"

"Correction. You ordered me to marry you. Honey, I don't need a piece of paper." She caught his hand on her calf, then she met his gaze. "All I need is you."

"If I have any say in the matter, you'll have both. We belong to each other, and I won't rest until the entire world knows it," he said softly. "You're turning into a prune." He motioned for her to stand as he rose himself in order to reach the bathsheet on the heated towel bar.

Amber could not believe what she was hearing. "How can I marry you when the reason behind it has nothing to do with love? I don't need looking after, Ray Coleman.

I need your love. I need to know you have faith in me and that you trust me."

"What the hell does that mean? I offered you my name!"

"Keep your blasted name! I'm interested in your trust! I suppose I should feel honored that you don't want to take a giant step backward and return to the way things were before we became lovers again. Huh?"

"Women! Is it a requirement that you can't have your first lipstick until you learn how to jump to the wrong conclusions?"

"Smart Mouth!"

Ray chuckled, wrapping her in a thick, warm towel and catching her around the waist. "Angel," he whispered against her hair when he realized she was truly upset. He placed a series of kisses along her throat.

"What?" she said impatiently, trying not to melt at his feet in a puddle of unfulfilled longing.

"Amber, what do I have to do to show you how much you mean to me. We made a commitment to each other, remember? I'm not letting you back out of it now. I'm in love with you."

"And I'm in love with you." She pressed her mouth against his neck.

He tilted up her face so he could see her eyes. "So why won't you marry me?"

"Let's talk about this later when I'm not so tired," she whispered, her arms around his neck while she pressed her cheek against his chest. She needed his support just to remain standing.

Amber stared thoughtfully at him, not quite able to meet his penetrating gaze. She knew every line of his roughly chiseled features, from the jut of his strong square chin to the fully drawn masculine mouth framed by the thick mustache. He was capable of giving so much pleasure. There was no question that he knew how to please her sexually. But they could not very well spend their entire life in bed. She needed to know he was safe and would be coming home each and every night as he left for work in the morning.

Ray said no more but he scooped her up in his arms, as if she weighed close to nothing, and carried her into the bedroom. They lay down on the bed together. He covered her with the comforter. She pressed her face into the base of his throat, annoyed that he was still fully dressed.

"One of us is wearing too many clothes," she complained.

"Yeah, and one of us can hardly keep her eyes open," he whispered back, brushing her mouth lightly with his. "Sleep. I'll be right here when you wake."

"Ray . . ."

"Shush, nothing has to be decided tonight."

Amber was sound asleep when Ray eventually undressed, showered, and slipped beneath the covers at her side. He longed to hold her but he did not, knowing she need her rest more than anything else. He discovered that he needed to look at her more than he needed to sleep.

Chapter Twenty-Eight

The sun was high in the sky when Amber woke the next morning. Ray was beside her propped on pillows, coffee mug in his large hand.

"Hi," she said, smiling at him.

"Hi," he said, returning her smile. She looked so pretty with her hair tousled from sleep.

"Can I have some of that?"

"I'll get you a mug."

She stopped him before he could move. "No, I want some of yours."

His eyes met hers, and his pulse quickened. "Don't look at me that way, or you will get more than a sip of coffee." His voice had suddenly deepened, thick with rising desire.

She drank from his cup, licking her lips and drawing his keen gaze to her mouth still slightly swollen and bruised from rough treatment.

"What's the matter?" she said when she saw the way his gaze hardened.

"Nothin' ..." then he amended by saying, "Everything."

She reached out to stroke her hand down his bare chest,

playing with a tight curl before caressing over each flat nipple. She heard his sharp intake of breath.

"Don't . . ." he said, catching her hand and holding it in his own. At her puzzled frown he said, "So much has been left unsaid."

"What is so important that it can't wait until later?" She pouted like a little girl and brought a grin to his wide mouth.

"Our wedding."

"You were serious?"

"Absolutely."

Her look was thoughtful while her voice was so soft when she spoke that he barely heard her. "Why now?"

"It's time."

"What kind of an answer is that? Good grief, Ray, I need an answer. For years you've believed your line of work prevented a permanent arrangement. Now suddenly you've decided you want to get married. What made you change your mind?"

"I haven't changed, but I've finally realized that the two people involved are all that really matters, or rather how they feel about each other. I'm in love with Amber Spencer and have been for a very long time. It's way past time we did something about securing that bond."

It hurt . . . hurt because she was forced to accept that he had finally said what she had longed to hear for so very long. Yet he had said it for all the wrong reasons. He was offering to be her African warrior. That was not what she wanted. She yearned for so much more.

Besides, she hadn't been honest with him about her fears concerning his work. The truth was, he had been right all along. She was not strong enough to disregard the danger he faced as a matter of course. It was wrong of her to continue to pretend it didn't matter. She had to tell him the truth, and she had to do it now. How could she when she loved him so much? She didn't want to lose what they had.

She unconsciously pressed herself against him, her arms

encircling his lean middle as she rubbed her cheek against his muscular chest. Her mind was troubled, afraid.

"Is that a yes?" he whispered as he threaded his fingers into the thickness of her cottony-soft hair.

"I love you so much." She trembled in spite of her best efforts to control her emotions. "We've shared so much together through the years ... the good and bad. This incident with Harris has left both us feeling vulnerable. We mustn't let it cause us to rush into anything. I guess what I'm trying to say is that I don't need you to fight my battles. I don't need a warrior."

"You've got one, Amber. I can't stand back and let anyone hurt you—not ever. If that's your sole reason for turning me down, think of another one because that won't stop me from wanting you to be my wife."

When she tried to move away, he held her fast. His jaw jutted stubbornly. Amber was his life, and he would not even consider letting her go.

Amber closed her eyes, unable to stop herself from trembling as she forced herself to admit, "I've lied to you for years, pretending that the constant danger you face isn't a problem for me. It scares me to death. I nearly panic each and every time you leave on a new assignment. I can't seem to breathe easy until you're back where I can look at you, hold on to you."

Her voice was a mere notch above a whisper when she said, "This last time, the parting was worse than ever before. You've been right all along. I wanted us to become lovers so much that I couldn't tell you about my fears. I couldn't let you guess how much I didn't want you to go back to Lebanon. Our farewell in the airport was a sham. I was petrified of losing you."

Ray had no difficulty understand her feelings, for he had lived them himself as soon as he had learned that Amber had been in danger. "Why the pretense?"

"Our entire relationship had changed. We were so close ... so close. Knowing how we felt about each other made it nearly impossible to say goodbye. I was dying bit by bit as I kissed you good-bye. I cried all the way back to Vermont. Ray, don't you see? I can't promise not to make demands that you can't possibly fulfil. The danger and constant separation just isn't fair to either one of us. It would be even worse if we were married." She tried to hold back a sob but failed.

"Look at me," he demanded softly. When she raised her eyes to his, he persisted, "How much do you love me?"

"With all my heart. But—"

"No . . ." He pressed his lips to hers, giving as well as receiving warm, sweet pleasure. "As long as we love each other, nothing else matters . . . nothing."

When his mouth came back to hers it claimed, possessed, and ravished. Amber clung to him, melting from the hot, hot longing he built inside of her. She pressed her face into the base of his throat, intent on tasting every inch of his warm brown flesh. Her unbelievably soft lips moved over his wide shoulders that flowed down to his hard muscled chest. His skin was hot and sweet, and he trembled with an unmistakable desire when she caressed his nipples each in turn.

"I love you," she murmured an instant before she lovingly washed each small flat nipple with the velvety soft strokes of her tongue.

His heart raced with excitement while his body tightened with a painful urgency. His erection flexed against her soft stomach as she continued her sweet assault on his senses.

"Angel . . ." he moaned thickly. He needed her now, needed to be inside of her wet heat.

Amber paused, raising her head to look at him. "Let me . . . let me make love to you."

There was was no mistaking the love he read in her eyes. His heart hammered with wild expectation. They both knew he had harnessed his male strength and need to dominate. He clearly wanted to make love to her, yet he understood her desire to control their loving. He didn't have a problem with her taking charge of their lovemaking. If it pleased her, it certainly pleasured him.

Determined to control his eager responses to her feminine sexuality, Ray concentrated only on letting her take what she needed when she needed it. He ignored his throbbing sex, which rose thick and insistent against her.

"Ray?"

Instead of reaching for her and not stopping until he was sheathed deep inside of her moist depths, he whispered thickly, "Yes . . . however you want me."

Amber's heart raced. He was hers—all six foot two, one hundred and ninety pounds of dark copper masculinity. Her caressing hands were as soft as silk, dangerously seductive to his inflamed senses. He groaned her name, unable to resist the sweet temptation of her nape. His mouth lingered there, his hands stroking down her spine past her small waist to gently cup and then squeeze her lushly curved behind.

"Ray," she scolded, yet trembled from his touch.

He sighed deeply, forcing his hands to his side.

When her soft lips brushed over his hard stomach, then was followed by the sweet wash of her tongue on his heated flesh, Ray almost came off the bed. He was so painfully aroused that he pulsed against her cheek. He knew what he wanted, what his body demanded was necessary for his continued survival. But his lips were clamped firmly shut, and his hands were balled into fists.

The decisions had to be hers no matter how badly he ached for the sweet hot pleasure only she could give him. He held his breath as she turned her head so she could look at him. His dark eyes smoldered with sparks of desire as his breath came hard and quick, mere pants. It took all his willpower to keep his hands still as he waited.

"Amber . . ." he released the deep moan in spite of his best efforts.

"You want my mouth, baby?" she whispered, then she blushed in spite of herself, but she didn't move away. She was eager to love him as thoroughly as he had loved her time and time again. He had not hesitated to use his teeth and his tongue to give her the utmost enjoyment. There were no limits with him. Her feelings for him were just as powerful, just as unshakable.

Ray bit down on his bottom lip to hold in the gutteral request. It nearly killed him to say, his voice heavy with passion, "I want whatever you want."

"I want to taste you . . . all of you," she confessed an instant before her hot sweet mouth opened and she slowly laved him from the full sensitive peak of his sex down the pulsating shaft to the broad base. She took her time, determined to give him the utmost enjoyment.

Sheer pleasure radiated outward along his nerve endings to the very tips of his toes and fingers. It was so intense that Ray closed his eyes and ground his teeth together. His heaviness below tightened as his manhood prepared to spill his hot seed. "No more," he growled. He grabbed her by the shoulders, forcing her away. He held her locked in his arms, against his heart.

Neither moved for some time. Eventually he said, "Do you have any idea what you did to me . . . how badly I need you." He surprised her when he went on to say, "I almost went out of my mind when I realized that you were with Harris and I couldn't find you."

Amber heard the hard rough edge to his voice. Her soft palms caressed the hard, stubbled lines of his chin. When she kissed his lean brown cheek, she felt the moisture.

She pressed her lips to his. "Don't . . ." Pushing past the barrier of his even white teeth, she kissed him seeking the heady depths of his mouth. It was a soothing kiss. She whispered, "We're together now. Nothing can come between us."

Ray ached deep inside. The need for reassurance lingered in spite of his efforts to dispel it. "Amber . . ." He loved her with every part of his being.

His long-fingered hands caressed her softness, rediscovering and celebrating each lush curve of her slender frame. He cherished the subtle difference in their bodies from the beaded firmness of her enlarged nipples to the damp secrets of her womanhood, down to the smooth soles of her small feet and pink lacquered toenails.

Ray tried to be gentle, worked to be tender, but his unrelenting need for her drove him to lick her nipples until she was moaning from the pleasure. Her breasts were achingly full, highly sensitive to the suction that he carefully applied to each engorged tip. He felt her tremble as he tugged strongly, then sucked harder, driven wild by the sounds she made as she cried out her delight. She curled her silky limbs around one of his hard muscled thighs and rubbed her wet sex against him, bare inches from his throbbing penis.

"You're driving me out of my mind with wanting you." His heart pounded furiously in his chest, his body pulsed with the power of his need.

"Come inside me . . . baby. Now," she demanded. Her small soft hands felt like satin against the unyielding strength of his engorged sex . . . caressing . . . stroking . . . sweetly killing him.

"Shush . . ." he soothed as he thrust his tongue into the sweet depths of her mouth, suckling her tongue. "You're not ready, baby . . . not wet enough," he insisted as he slid down her soft length until he could part the dew-kissed feminine folds with his forging tongue.

His caresses were sizzling hot as he loved her with each slow velvety smooth stroke. Ray closed his eyes as he concentrated on enjoying her feminine essence. He did not quicken the slow, tantalizing strokes until she came apart in his arms and screamed his name as the violently sweet climax claimed her.

Ray couldn't wait an instant more. He had to be inside of her now. He quickly prepared himself then, he repositioned himself until he could plunge heavily into her wet, tight sheath. His whole body quivered. Amber was so wonderfully tight and sizzling hot that Ray quickly lost sight of everything outside of their joined bodies.

"Amber . . ." he groaned as he started moving within her with endlessly strong, demanding strokes. He wanted her all . . . he wouldn't let her hold any of herself back from him. She belonged to him . . . him alone, just as he belonged to her.

Amber's hands laced with his as she followed his lead. They were in perfect harmony as if they were slow dancing—on and on the pleasure went. She matched him stroke for sizzling hot stroke, loving him as completely and deeply as he was loving her.

It had been so long . . . so long since they were together. The danger they had both faced made the coming together an absolute necessity. There was no other way to ease the fear, the stark terror than the sweetness of loving. Ray made love to her, vowing that never again would he let anything separate them—and she clung to him, her slim arms wrapped around him as they gloried in their union.

Amber tossed her head on the pillow, instinctively tightening her body around him, milking him along his swollen length. He hissed from sheer enjoyment while she whimpered, raking her nails along his back. The tightening of her moist heat was his undoing. He could no longer control his long hard thrusts. He lifted her thighs, plunging even deeper, grinding his hips into hers. He was so close to finishing, but not without her.

"Come with me, Amber," he chanted again and again.

The stroke of his thumb over her sensitive pearl caused Amber to scream his name as she climaxed, and Ray's hoarse shout quickly followed as he reached his own powerful completion. They lay trembling in each other arms as gradually their breathing slowed and their bodies cooled.

"My angel," he whispered against her hair as he collapsed beside her, his arms held her close.

"Mmm," she mumbled, snuggling even closer to his side. She was asleep before he could lift the comforter and sheet from were they had fallen on the carpet.

Ray lay for a long time just holding Amber and caressed the smooth length of her back. Haunted by the past few days and nights of fear and helplessness, he knew that he loved her so much it just plain hurt.

When she cried out in her sleep, he stroked her until she was calm and able to sleep deeply.

Ray was tired, but he knew he could not find solace in sleep. He closed the bedroom door quietly behind him. He had disconnected the bedside telephone so she would not be disturbed. He spent much of the day on the telephone, either fielding the FBI questions or assuring Amber's friends and colleagues that she was fine. What she needed most was rest, and he intended to see to it that she got it.

Amber was not certain what had awakened her—the rattle of the wind against the windowpane or the chime of the grandfather clock in the livingroom. The sun was setting as early evening shadows filled the sky. She'd slept the entire day. She quickly showered and dressed before she went looking for Ray. She found him in the living room, staring down into the empty grate, lost in thought.

"Hi." She smiled, joining him on the sofa. "Why didn't you wake me? I slept the day away."

His dark eyes studied her face. "You needed the rest. How do you feel?"

"I'm fine. You look tired. Did you get any sleep?"

"Not much. Can't seem to turn my thoughts off. Hungry? Alex stopped by. Lynn sent a macaroni and cheese casserole and meat loaf. Ginger sent over string bean casserole and chocolate cake."

She smiled but shook her head. "Sounds good but not right now. What's bothering you, my love?"

"Nothing important."

"If it stops you from getting any rest, then it's important." Before he could answer, she rushed on to ask, "You're still angry with me, aren't you? I only did what I had to. I couldn't leave Jason with—"

He pressed his fingertips against her lips. "Enough of that. I'm not angry with you. I understand what you did and why you did it. Angel, what I'm having trouble dealing with right now is my part in all of this. I should have been here when you needed me. Harris would have never gotten near you if I had been home."

"Ray, no!"

He shook his head, his jaw jutted stubbornly. "I let you down. I've stopped blaming everyone else and started facing the truth."

"You were away on assignment, for heaven's sake. You have a job to do. You can't drop everything for me."

"Be honest with me, Amber. Don't you think I heard the bitterness in your voice when you mentioned my job? You hate what I do, don't you?" He watched her positive nod before he went on to say, "Even though the blame lies at my feet, Angel, I want you to know that I believed you were safe when I left. I never dreamed you were in any real danger."

Tears filled her eyes, overflowing the barrier of her lower lashes to escape in a thin trail down her cheeks. "I don't blame you, Ray. Honestly, I don't."

"Stop it! I have had it up to here with pretending," he bit out hotly, gesturing wildly.

"I'm not," she denied hastily.

"Yes, you are!" he ground out.

"Okay, okay—I admit it. The days you're away are the loneliest imaginable, and the nights seem endless." She moved until she could rest her cheek on his chest, over his heart, and curled her arms around his waist. She waited, frightened that she could not make him understand. When his arms tightened around her, she whispered, "Ray, I know how important your job is to you. I've grown to accept it as a part of you. Your work is brilliant because you are brilliant."

"The job is why you won't marry me, isn't it." The room was absolutely quiet as they looked into each other's eyes. His voice was thick with emotion when he went on to ask, "You can't handle the danger and the risk I take, can you?"

"No," she finally admitted unhappily.

"This trip was my last without you. From now on if it's too dangerous for you to come with me, then I don't go."

The revelation didn't bring the relief he expected from her. She was staring at him in utter disbelief.

"Amber, it means we can get married without any complications."

"You can't be serious."

"Absolutely. I'm tired of chasing story after story around the world. I'm ready to stop and take time to enjoy my life. I may want to teach, I definitely want to write, and I also have to make certain that the charities that carry my name reach the children who need it most. I've put that off too long. It means travel, unfortunately."

Her eyes were wide. She couldn't believe she had heard correctly. Leaving his job because of her! How many years would pass before he would begin blaming her? She would be the one who forced him to resign. Was this just another means of protecting her?

When she moved away from him, pacing the living floor, he said, "I take it you aren't thrilled?"

"I don't want you to quit because of me."

He caught her shoulders, forcing her to stop and listen to him. "Wait one damn minute here. What is wrong? Isn't this what you want?"

"Yes . . . no." She shook her head. "I want you to do what is right for you. I should have nothing to do with this decision. Nothing."

He laughed. "You are my life. Your happiness is vital to me."

"Honey, I can handle—"

"Amber!"

"Okay . . . I can't handle it. But I won't let you quit, either."

"You matter to me. I don't want you to be miserable. Why aren't you jumping up and down about this?"

"You can be so mule-headed sometimes, Ray Coleman. You make me sick!"

He chuckled. "Tell me something I don't know.

Angel . . ." he said, cupping her chin in his palm, so she couldn't look away from him. "Talk to me here. Tell me what is going on inside that pretty head of yours."

"I don't want to be the reason you've decided to quit your job. I know what that job means to you. Honey, your decision shouldn't have anything to do with me. Don't you see, someday you will resent me because of it. Oh, honey, I couldn't bear that !" Her eyes pleaded with him to reconsider.

"I'm finished with free-lancing." His voice was firm. Sighing at the unhappiness he saw in her face, he added tenderly, "I promise that if you marry me you'll never, ever regret your decision. I plan to do everything I can to make you happy." As he bent and pressed his lips to her soft pink-tinted ones, he watched a tear spill from thick dark lashes. "Baby . . . don't."

"I'm sorry," she sniffed, feeling as if her heart were breaking. She had been in love with this man since she was fifteen years old. She had spent years yearning to belong only to him. Now that it was so close to happening, she was afraid to move forward. He could be wrong— then what? Time unfortunately could also bring regret and perhaps even deeper heartache.

"Okay . . . okay," he sighed heavily. "Tell me what you want. Just tell me."

Amber couldn't stop crying—she buried her face between his shoulder and neck, sobbing as if her heart were breaking.

He held her, rocking her against his chest. "You've been through so much recently. I shouldn't be pressuring you. It's just that I thought when we became lovers that all we needed to be happy was for us to be together whenever we could manage it. I thought that would be enough. It's not, not nearly enough for either one of us, is it?"

"Ray—"

"No, please let me say this." He stroked her back as he talked. "I've started dreaming about a real home and having a family of our own. I hated being away from you this time, angel. Every minute was like a living hell. I found no satisfaction in the job. It doesn't matter to me anymore. While we were apart, nothing could ease the pain—nothing, that is, but you. You're all that matters to me, angel."

"Oh, Ray," she whispered.

He paused thoughtfully before he went on to say, "The more you talked about wanting us to be together as lovers as well as friends, the more I thought that was what I wanted also. It was only after I returned to Lebanon that I realized that I wanted more, much more than a relationship. Amber, I'm dog tired of waking up alone—tired of being apart from you. I'm sick to death of risking my life. For what? Being the best photojournalist around isn't enough, especially if I don't have you."

He surprised her when he went on to say, "We'll always mourn our baby daughter, but it's time for other babies, Amber. I want us to have a house full and I want for us to watch them grown into fine men and women. I want to someday see our grandkids. Most of all I want you beside me, Amber."

"You won't one day miss the excitement, the danger?" She studied his face through watery eyes.

"I would be lying if I didn't say I was challenged by the work. Angel, I've achieved all I want to achieve. I don't want to dedicate any more of my life to photojournalism. I've made some wise investments. Money will not be a problem."

"Are you really thinking about teaching journalism?"

"Yeah. I enjoyed it when I did it to help out a friend. Who knows? The point is, we don't have to decide now. Whatever it is, you can believe it won't involve putting my neck on the line or leaving my woman alone to accomplish it."

"What about the photography, the showings? What about all those needy children in Africa?"

"You know me too well," he said with a grin. He laced her fingers with his own. "I want to go back to the motherland. I want to try and help. Too many of our black babies are starving to death. I want to concentrate for a time on helping our people, make sure the money goes for helping and not lining someone else's pockets. Yet even though my photographs have brought in a great deal of money to the cause, I believe I can do more. I suspect with my pictures and writings—along with your insight into how best to take care of and educate children—that working together there will be no stopping us. If we take on this project, and I do mean *we*, it will be a mutual decision. I want you to be by my side as my partner, my helpmate, my love."

"Have I told you lately that I love you with all my heart?" She smiled, pressing her lips against his.

He groaned heavily, accepting and returning that sweet kiss. He was grinning when he said, "I'll never get tired of hearing you say it. I love you, angel. I intend to spend the rest of my life making you happy."

Amber clung to him, her soft mouth brushed against the base of his throat. "Now about this wedding. Is next week too soon?"

"Sounds good to me."

Suddenly they were laughing and crying together. The look in his eyes sent her heart soaring, such a wealth of love and devotion. He was all hers for the keeping, while she was his for the taking.

They kissed with all the deep longing and relief in their hearts. They had waited so many years for each other. They had faced so much, lost so much, and felt so much. This was their time.

As they sampled the honeyed depth of each other's mouths, they both knew being together like this had been worth all the uncertainty and all the loneliness they'd had to endure. From this day forward, they belonged together.

Dear Readers:

Your words of encouragement, offers of friendship, and support through your letters are deeply appreciated.

From the release of my first Arabesque novel, FOR ALWAYS, to FOREVER AFTER, my novella, MAMA'S PEARL (part of the anthology A MOTHER'S LOVE), and ALL THE LOVE, your wonderful letters have been viewed as priceless treasures.

Please don't stop now! You may write me at P.O. Box 625, Warren, MI 48090-0625. If you wish a response, please send a self-addressed stamped envelope.

Best wishes,

Bette Ford

ABOUT THE AUTHOR

Bette grew up in Saginaw, Michigan, and graduated from Saginaw High School. She obtained her bachelor's degree from Central State University in Wilberforce, Ohio. Bette began her teaching career in Detroit and completed her Master's degree from Wayne State University. She is currently teaching in the HeadStart program for the Detroit Public Schools. You may write her at P.O. Box 625, Warren, MI 48090-0625. If you wish a response please include a self-addressed stamped envelope.

Look for these upcoming Arabesque titles:

January 1997

ALL THE LOVE by Bette Ford
SENSATION by Shelby Lewis
ONLY YOU by Angela Winters

February 1997

INCOGNITO by Francis Ray
WHITE LIGHTNING by Candice Poarch
LOVE LETTERS, Valentine Collection

March 1997

THE WAY HOME by Angela Benson
LOVE BUILDER by Layle Guisto
NIGHT AND DAY by Doris Johnson

ENJOY THESE SPECIAL
ARABESQUE HOLIDAY ROMANCES

HOLIDAY CHEER   (0-7860-0210-7, $4.99)
by Rochelle Alers, Angela Benson,
and Shirley Hailstock

A MOTHER'S LOVE   (0-7860-0269-7, $4.99)
by Francine Craft, Bette Ford,
and Mildred Riley

SPIRIT OF THE SEASON   (0-7860-0077-5, $4.99)
by Donna Hill, Francis Ray,
and Margie Walker

A VALENTINE KISS   (0-7860-0237-9, $4.99)
by Carla Fredd, Brenda Jackson,
and Felicia Mason

ENJOY THESE ARABESQUE FAVORITES!

FOREVER AFTER   (0-7860-0211-5, $4.99)
by Bette Ford

BODY AND SOUL   (0-7860-0160-7, $4.99)
by Felicia Mason

BETWEEN THE LINES   (0-7860-0267-0, $4.99)
by Angela Benson

SENSUAL AND HEARTWARMING ARABESQUE ROMANCES FEATURE AFRICAN-AMERICAN CHARACTERS!

BEGUILED (0046, $4.99)
by Eboni Snoe

After Raquel agrees to impersonate a missing heiress for just one night, a daring abduction makes her the captive of seductive Nate Bowman. Across the exotic Caribbean seas to the perilous wilds of Central America . . . and into the savage heart of desire, Nate and Raquel play a dangerous game. But soon the masquerade will be over. And will they then lose the one thing that matters most . . . their love?

WHISPERS OF LOVE (0055, $4.99)
by Shirley Hailstock

Robyn Richards had to fake her own death, change her identity, and forever forsake her husband, Grant, after testifying against a crime syndicate. But, five years later, the daughter born after her disappearance is in need of help only Grant can give. Can Robyn maintain her disguise from the ever present threat of the syndicate—and can she keep herself from falling in love all over again?

HAPPILY EVER AFTER (0064, $4.99)
by Rochelle Alers

In a week's time, Lauren Taylor fell madly in love with famed author Cal Samuels and impulsively agreed to be his wife. But when she abruptly left him, it was for reasons she dared not express. Five years later, Cal is back, and the flames of desire are as hot as ever, but, can they start over again and make it work this time?